Fatal Spores
&
Fiery Paths

Also by Kellie Doherty

The Cicatrix Duology

Finding Hekate
Losing Hold

Broken Chronicles

Sunkissed Feathers and Severed Ties
Curling Vines and Crimson Trades
Ink Stains and Ill-Fated Lies

Fatal Spores
&
Fiery Paths

(The Broken Chronicles—Book 4)

Kellie Doherty

Desert Palm Press

Fatal Spores & Fiery Paths
Broken Chronicles – Book 4

By Kellie Doherty

ISBN (trade) 9781954213968
ISBN (epub) 9781954213975

Desert Palm Press
4804 NW Bethany Blvd, Suite I-2, #148
Portland, OR 97229
www.desertpalmpress.com

Editor: Raven's Eye
Cover Design: Rachel George Illustration

Printed in the United States of America
First Edition January 2025

About *Fatal Spores & Fiery Paths* (Broken Chronicles – Book 4)

Zayla was just an infant noxling when her bitterroot offshoot was destroyed by a terrible suncreature. No one from her home survived. And from what she knows of her Nemora history, she shouldn't be alive either. But she is.

There's a constant hum inside her, a shaking that grows more violent and painful each time she harnesses her crafting to do her bidding. Nature is clearly trying to finish the job the suncreature started. Her only hope is to finish walking the path. When she completes this sacred rite of passage, she'll never need to use her crafting again. She has to get to Ratnaa Grove, her final stop, and the quickest way there is through the deadly Cinder Forest. With the help of her sibling Oryn and an alluring musician named Shadre who they met along the way, Zayla fends off bloodthirsty suncreatures and discovers an invasion of evil sun goddess worshippers bent on razing the Groves.

As she struggles to survive, betrayal lurks on every side, and her crafting demands a higher price than even she expected, but the fate of the Nemora Groves, and the world as she knows it, might just lie within her.

Acknowledgements

Hello, my fellow adventurer! Before you officially embark on this grand adventure, make a cup of tea, get cozy underneath a thick blanket, and take a moment to read these words. It's simply an author (me) shouting my thanks to all the wonderful people who helped bring this book to your hands. Dedications are hard to write only because there are just so many people who helped bring this story to life and there aren't enough pages to fit them all. I'll do my best.

First, I'd like to thank my Desert Palm Press folks: Lee Fitzsimmons, for believing in this story of wild nature magic; CK King, for finding some story holes I missed; Rachel George, for always designing a fabulous cover; and for everyone else at DPP who helped along the way.

Second, I couldn't have done this without the support of my family—my mom Deb and my sister Jess. They've always believed in my work. I also have to thank my cats, Raven and Cinder (though they'll never know it or care). They were my constant companions during the many hours of writing, and sources of inspiration as well. (Hello, Cinder Forest and Ravenlock Woods!)

Third, thanks to my writing community—both online and off it. To Molly Gray, Brooke Hartman, Louise Goulet Willis, and Tam Linsey, my critique partners who saw this book when it was nothing more than vibes and fantastical ideas, had no problem telling me when a scene was truly a mess, and made some lovely suggestions on how to make this big story of mine more manageable. To Kerri Stebbins, who helped me carve out many, many Sunday afternoons just for the sole purpose of writing. To my social media community, who constantly cheered me on.

And finally, to all of you, my readers. Thank you for picking up this book and going on this wild nature magic adventure of mine. I honestly couldn't do this—telling stories full of magic and queer characters—if not for you. Thank you so, so much. I hope you enjoy the journey!

Dedication

For all those who have an adventure humming within them.

Chapter One

ZAYLA RESTED AT THE base of a towering mirrorshard mushroom, trying to ignore the male Nemora standing just behind her as she focused on the fungus. The pink bioluminescent glow from the ribbing beneath its cap dappled her bare arms and spread across the morass beneath her, illuminating the surface hyphae radiating outward in a web. This mirrorshard connected to others forty paces away, with a web of pale strands, before joining the underground mycelium network interwoven beneath the wet earth and spreading farther than she could see.

Even now, in the pitch black of night, she didn't need a daygem to light the area. The bioluminescence was enough. Like beacons, the mirrorshards led the way to Myceli Grove, welcoming travelers to the home of the caretakers and growers of all the fungi in the land.

And like beacons, they could lead the sun goddess worshippers straight to Nemora's home. Her worshippers could burn it all down, raze the ground to start anew and burn even brighter. They would ruthlessly kill all who opposed them. A war was coming, and these mirrorshards could lead the enemy right to their doors.

A fresh shiver ran down Zayla's spine, but the humming in her body never stopped. As though she'd bashed her elbow on the corner of a particularly sharp branch, and the resulting tingle vibrated continuously through her. *I only need to use my crafting twice more on this walk,* she promised herself. *Only twice more.*

"We haven't seen a hybrid Nemora in a long time," the man commented from behind her. She'd heard those words many times before. As a hybrid Nemora, a Nemora created from two separate Groves, her existence was rare enough, even without her unique circumstances. The man continued in a low rumbling voice, "Thank you for demonstrating both of your primary Groves."

"Of course." She'd grown a tiny green sprout from a treepod in honor of Dara, the Grove of forests and woods, and for Myceli, she'd grown a small blue mushroom. She'd kept those growths easy, kept her crafting powers gentle, but even then, she could feel the hum grow inside her. She swiveled to face the Myceli Nemora clad in brown robes. "But what you really need me to use is my bitterroot crafting."

The bald Nemora nodded, wrinkled expression growing curious. "We do."

Being a Nemora, her crafting power should've come from one of the seven Groves of the Nemora homelands, then should've been honed by one of their offshoots. Most Nemora came from a single Grove—like Dara—and were intricately connected to a smaller portion of that Grove, centered on one specific type of nature called an offshoot, like the darkwood offshoot. A darkwood Dara Nemora could wield only one type of nature—trees, with their most powerful crafting coming from their offshoot, darkwood.

Zayla was different.

She came from both Dara and Myceli, which meant she could harness both types of nature. She could also wield a third, hybrid crafting. Her poisonous, bitterroot offshoot came from the combination of Dara and Myceli. A hybrid Nemora wasn't unheard of in the homelands, just…rare. And rarer still, with what happened to her offshoot. It was likely why the Nemora seemed so intrigued; he must've heard of her story. *Don't think of that right now. Focus on the mirrorshard.*

"How can you even still connect to that bitterroot crafting?" the Nemora asked. He fiddled with a necklace, a pink gem with a smaller version of the mirrorshard tucked inside.

Zayla canted her head. So, this wasn't just any Myceli Nemora, he was a mirrorshard…perhaps he was even linked to this offshoot. No wonder they'd sent him with her. And no wonder he'd ask a question like that. If Zayla failed and killed these mirrorshards, well…

Perhaps nature wouldn't miss killing him, like it missed killing her.

"I'll try," she said softly, then faced the mirrorshard mushroom once more, swallowing past the lump in her throat.

Her bitterroot offshoot had been destroyed by a suncreature long ago, and all the bitterroot Nemora had died along with it. By all semblance of knowledge, she should be dead too. She'd been told stories, all the Nemora had. How offshoots had to be protected at all costs. As soon as that offshoot was destroyed, the Nemora connected to them died as well. Nemora were as much a part of nature as leaves to a tree. When their offshoot—their most powerful connection with nature—was gone, their crafting lashed back in retribution and killed the Nemora too.

So why not me? Because, I'm a freak, that's why.

A freak that nature hadn't discovered yet. Her unease grew. The more she used her bitterroot, the faster, stronger, and more terrifyingly it lashed back at her.

She stared at the bioluminescent light brightening the web beneath her knees. The Myceli Nemora who lived here didn't know how to turn off the bioluminescence. Not without completely killing the fungus and the mycelium network beneath. She supposed that even that mirrorshard Myceli Nemora behind her, whose crafting was connected to this particular mushroom, couldn't extinguish the light. *Or won't try.* Even now, with the war nearing their Grove. The bioluminescence was natural, a beautiful sight. Who would diminish that?

Someone unnatural, of course. *Someone like me.*

She glanced over her shoulder. "As you know, my crafting isn't stable yet and—"

"Yes, yes," the Nemora cut her off, his tone taking on an impatient edge that frayed Zayla's already taut nerves. "Just do it quickly."

Sighing, Zayla put her hand on the mirrorshard's stem. The Seventh Circle, the leader of this Grove, had told her this could be her real trial for Myceli Grove. As a relatively young Nemora, she was currently walking the path—a tradition where she visited each of the seven homeland Groves and partook in a trial to show off her crafting skills. Normally the trials took place in the center of the Groves, under the watchful gaze of the Seventh Circle who lived there.

But here she'd been hurried along. The Seventh Circle didn't even lower their hood or give her their name, had hardly even looked at her. Their reaction was so unlike the prior Groves she'd visited along her walk; the other leaders had at least been respectful of her. Most of them were happy to show off their homelands to a newcomer. Even Dara's Seventh Circle had watched her craft. Now she understood why the Myceli Seventh Circle had been so unreachable.

They didn't want her to disable the mirrorshards either, but as a leader they knew it had to be done, and Zayla could be the one to do it.

She concentrated on the spotted stem of the mirrorshard, spongy against her fingers. The pale spots on the stem mirrored the pale spots on her skin. A connection. A tell, that she was a Myceli Nemora as well. Half of her at least. The leaf markings intertwined with her spots revealed her Dara connection.

Zayla tore her eyes from the mirrorshard stem and looked behind her, staring at the bald Nemora looming over her. "You'll tell the Seventh Circle that I completed this so I can continue my walk?"

White light sphered out from a daygem in the man's hand. He nodded, his eyes narrowing to slits. "I will. If you do it correctly, the mirrorshards will tell them before I even get back."

The bioluminescent light will be extinguished. Fidgety from the humming within her, Zayla twirled the ring on her finger again and again and again. Her purple ring was nearly lost on her mottled skin, save for the vivid-green, dried mushroom suspended in the sap. The ring was a mark of her true home, a trinket she always carried with her, and twirling it was a meditation of sorts to calm her mind against her body's perpetual vibrations. The movement helped, but only a little. She swallowed hard and turned back around. "All right. I'll...I'll try."

She gripped the spongy stem more firmly, calling on her crafting. Fear bubbled up inside her, churning her stomach. She'd kept her Dara and Myceli crafting small so as to not harness so much of her power, but using her bitterroot offshoot naturally drew more. The more power she used, the faster nature could find her and kill her.

I have to do this. I have to try to protect these people. Zayla took in a deep steadying breath and closed her eyes against the pink light. *Once I finish the path, I can finally move on. Here and one more Grove, then I can finally stop crafting.*

She breathed out and sank into her Nature crafting, stepping into that caged space deep within her mind. At her command, the persistent humming bloomed to life within her. It grew more intense, more demanding, until her teeth chattered, and her bones felt like they were clattering against one another.

She opened her eyes. A dark amber had replaced the mirrorshard's light. Deeper than the bioluminescent pink, the amber had pulled over her vision and brightened in her veins. *Bitterroot,* she thought, intentionally calling on the vibrant hybrid growth that she was most connected to. *Home.* Her crafting gathered like a knot in her palm, pressing into the spongy stem of the mirrorshard. A thin, deep-red root emerged, curling over her hand and fingers, wrapping itself around the stem. The root oozed thick, purple sap, as tiny, vibrant, green fungus sprouted, their domed caps glistening with a glassy sheen, and wound its way upward.

Neutralize the light, she commanded. *Just the bioluminescence.*

The bitterroot dug into the mushroom stem, and the amber glow pulsed in her veins.

The vibrating inside her body intensified until she thought she might break into a thousand pieces. Fear clawed up Zayla's throat. She could feel nature watching her. Judging her. Her crafting wanted to lash back, to shatter her apart with the fury of its tremblings. Her hand clutching the stem trembled, as she fought to hold her power in check.

In a blink, the mirrorshard's bioluminescent glow vanished. One after another, the lights went dark...snuffed out as Zayla's poison spread through the hyphae and mycelium that connected the mushrooms. The beacons, in all their unique and stunning beauty, were gone.

Zayla braced herself, knowing her crafting would lash back at her.

In a burst of agony, thick red bark erupted on the back of her hand, spreading over her fingers, binding them together. Pain lanced through her as the growing bark peeled her nails clean off, leaving only wood splinters in their place. She yanked her hand back from the mirrorshard stem, eyes wide and hand trembling. On her palm, an angry brown sporebruise bloomed on her mottled, purple-green skin.

She watched in horror as the sporebruise spread, bringing with it a wash of fiery pain that flowed toward her elbow like her arm was on fire. A scream clawed up her throat, but she didn't have the breath to let it out. Her heart thudded against her ribs, and a whooshing sound rushed through her ears with each and every beat. The vibrating within her wouldn't stop, so much so she thought she'd vibrate apart.

Stay strong. Every time she called on her crafting, it seemed to get worse. *You can get through it.* Zayla hunched over, waiting for this price of her crafting to pass. Hoping it wouldn't kill her.

One moment of agony.

And then another.

An eternity.

The vice grip on her chest finally loosened. Blinking her crafting away, Zayla breathed in deep, gasping for air. Her arm continued to burn where the angry brown irritation spread up to her shoulder. Thankfully, it had stopped just short of her pale-green tunic's sleeveless trim. The bark that had grown on the back of her hand remained, stiff and unyielding—she wouldn't be able to use that hand for the rest of the night. After a sleep, the bark should flake away.

This is a trial. Get it together. Rubbing her chest with her good hand, she slowed her breathing and peered into the gills of the mirrorshard above her. None of the bioluminescence had survived. The bitterroot tendril stuck to mirrorshard's stem, spreading poisonous spores into the fungus and permanently cutting off that natural light.

Her heart still thundered. If she'd killed the mirrorshard...if she couldn't control her bitterroot spores...surely she'd have to begin the path again. She'd have to call on her crafting many more times. Her powers would lash back even more and would eventually kill her to restore the true order of things. She couldn't let that happen.

The daygem's white light shifted, as the Nemora put a tentative hand on the mirrorshard's stem. He sank into his crafting for a moment before muttering, "The mirrorshards still live."

A shriveled blue mushroom landed in her lap.

"Your token for passing the Myceli Grove trial."

Relief washed over her. She'd passed, gotten her token, and lived. *Only one more Grove.* She tucked the precious token into her travel pack, next to the five others. "Thank you. I'll continue the walk."

A slight rustle and squish of retreating footsteps told her the Nemora had left, his sphere of light ebbing away and leaving her in darkness. She was alone. Sounds of the wild rushed back into her senses—the gentle clicking of insects, wind rustling the sparse vegetation in the morass around her.

A loud croak startled her, and a tiny, white-bodied pip leapt from behind the mirrorshard. For a moment, Zayla had the wild thought it was a suncreature, the corrupted form of natural beasts, but no, the eight-legged pip had brown and green spots dotting its slimy back. It blinked at her with dark-green eyes, then leapt away.

Pushing her good hand into the pocket of her dark trousers, she drew out a small daygem of her own and whispered it to life. White light bubbled out, suffusing the area in a gentle glow. The mirrorshards still looked surprisingly healthy, but the withered trail of her bitterroot was now scarred into its stem.

The vibrating in her body eventually quieted to a gentle hum and she climbed to her feet, ready to resume her journey to the seventh and final Grove of her path. A small bubble of hope filled her. Once she passed that trial, she'd never have to craft again.

Time to go. Shouldering her travel pack, she started walking in the opposite direction the other Nemora had gone. There was no path to lead her away from this section of Myceli Grove, only endless spongy earth spotted with towering mushrooms. Zayla picked her way through, using clumps of tangled hyphae and the occasional stone to make traversing easier.

The daygem's light was just enough to brighten each stem as she passed by. With the safety of darkness around her, she didn't have to worry about the fearsome suncreatures that stalked during the day. *I can't believe I thought that pip was a suncreature.* She laughed at herself, but her thoughts turned to the dangers ahead. Ratnaa Grove was a hard, four-night walk through the Cinder Forest. Going through the barren ashy forest teeming with dangerous suncreatures was a risk, but if she was quick and quiet, she'd make it through. It was either that or a twenty-night walk skirting around the danger.

The watery morass finally gave way to soft dirt, then a pathway of smooth stones made for travelers. Zayla sighed with relief. Walking would be much faster now. The mirrorshards grew smaller, the clusters now only reaching her knees.

A stomping sound—footfalls behind her, running. Confused, Zayla paused to listen. The sounds echoed off the surrounding mushroom stems, making it impossible to know which direction they were coming from. The only thing she knew was that they were getting closer. Zayla pressed her bark-hand to her chest, looking for a place to hide, but her daygem cast everything in shadows.

She took a step, hoping to at least hide behind a small cluster of mushrooms, when something heavy slammed into her.

Chapter Two

THE FORCE OF THE near tackle pushed Zayla off the stone pathway and back into a small clump of knee-high mushrooms, their spongy flesh bending around the pair as Zayla found her footing.

Oryn wrapped their arms around Zayla's middle and hugged her tight, their head brushing underneath her chin. "Noxling!"

"Oryn, it's been ages since I've seen you!" Zayla hugged Oryn, her older sibling, not by blood but by choice. "And don't call me that. You know I hate it." She tried to sound angry, but joy at seeing them wove through her words anyway.

Oryn stretched up and rubbed their palm through Zayla's short hair in a familiar gesture that left a few strands strewn across her cheek. "That's why I do it, sibling."

A laugh bucked in her chest as she pushed Oryn away, full of surprise and delight. Though it had been a few seasons since Zayla had seen her sibling, Oryn looked exactly as she remembered. Where Zayla was tall with light-purple hair, Oryn was petite with sky-blue skin and long, inky black hair that nearly absorbed the daygem's light. Narrow as a twig, Oryn looked like a strong gust of wind could push them over, but Zayla knew better. She'd seen her sibling take down three sun goddess worshippers with ease.

Stepping back, Zayla looked her sibling over, taking in their long sleeves, a high collar that reached beyond their chin, and locks of dark hair hanging over their forehead. As always, Oryn was trying to hide their unique spiral Nemora markings, but Zayla knew, with the war brimming, they wouldn't be able to hide the markings for long.

"Your skin." Concern creased Oryn's face as they took hold of Zayla's bark-covered hand. Their fingers grazed the thick crimson wood as they inspected the damage Zayla's crafting had caused.

"I'll be fine in a night or two." Zayla allowed Oryn to turn her hand this way and that, eyes moving up her hand, wrist, elbow, and shoulder, following the sporebruises that dappled brown on her skin. The familiarity almost made the gentle vibrations within her body cease. Almost, but not quite. "Did you find the rarest library in all the lands?" she asked, trying to change the subject.

Oryn had left before Zayla had even started walking the path two seasons ago, following their passion for rare books to the furthest reaches of the continent.

Oryn grinned. "I did, in a little Nemora village called Fyra. I learned quite a lot during my stay there."

Her sibling always had a yearning for knowledge. They'd even confessed to wanting their own library someday, and Zayla was glad to hear that spark hadn't died down.

"Where's Tyne?" Oryn asked, glancing around.

Heat flooded Zayla's cheeks. Her lover had walked the path with her in the beginning, vowing to be with her every step of the way. Zayla shrugged, trying to look nonchalant, though her heart ached with the memory. "Tyne decided to get…romantically intertwined with another woman in Dara Grove."

"Did they now?" Oryn lifted an eyebrow.

Zayla nodded. "I don't want that kind of relationship, so we decided to part ways."

"Hm." Oryn scowled. "Well, I didn't like them anyway."

Zayla rolled her eyes, recalling how easily Oryn and Tyne had gotten along before Oryn had left. How quickly they changed their mind. Always the protective sibling. "How did you find me?" she asked.

"I knew you were walking the path and thought you'd follow my footsteps, saving Myceli and Ratnaa for last, so I asked them to send word to me once you arrived." Oryn's dark blue lips twitched. "I've been waiting outside Myceli Grove for you."

"How well you know me, sibling." Zayla squeezed Oryn's hand, warmth spreading through her at their words. Oryn had walked the path first, and Zayla had, in fact, followed their footsteps in honor of them. Oryn must've requested a messenger vulnix, a vulpine-like creature with four wings and three tails, who could travel long distances with ease. Zayla searched her memories, recalling a gray and brown vulnix that had darted away the moment she'd entered Myceli Grove. It must've flown straight to Oryn. And even though Zayla was happy to see her sibling, a twist of guilt turned within her.

"Why did you come here, Oryn?" Zayla asked gently. "The sun goddess worshippers are basically at our door. You should be at home, readying and protecting the others. They need all the help they can get."

Their crystal-blue eyes stared at her unflinching. "I am home, Zayla, whenever I'm with you." Oryn's gaze shifted to the darkness in the direction of where Zayla was heading. "You're traveling through the Cinder Forest next, right?"

"I am." She tried to sound strong, but her voice wavered a little. Though she had always planned this route, the Cinder Forest terrified her. Like the Ravenlock Woods to the south, the Cinder Forest was a corrupted place, a battleground for the goddess sisters—Aluriah and Ponuriah—that suffered the consequences of their fury. Lush greenery had once flourished there but now only petrified trees remained. It was a forest locked in the awful place between life and death, filled with dangerous suncreatures who made a habit of ripping intruders to pieces. Not many risked their lives to traverse it.

Zayla would. Every time she used her crafting, the painful effects worsened. If she didn't finish walking the path soon, her crafting would kill her before she had the chance.

Always the shrewd one, Oryn nodded slowly. "I knew you'd want to finish your walk as soon as possible and that would be the fastest way to Ratnaa Grove. You know, as well as I, the dangers in that forest. You need protection." Oryn gave her a wide smile, eyes glinting. "Which means you need me."

Zayla ducked her head. Oryn had always protected her, ever since they were younglings, ever since Zayla's bitterroot offshoot had been destroyed and she was taken under the protection of Oryn's offshoot. Their family raised her like she was their own, so Zayla always called Oryn her sibling and Oryn did the same. Sometimes, it felt like her older sibling had made it their life's calling to protect her, to make sure something as horrible as that never happened again. She smiled, eyes misty with emotion. This portion of her walk *would* be dangerous, and she'd appreciate having her sibling along. "I suppose I do."

Anxiety crept over her shoulders, whispering doubt in her ears. This was Zayla's task, not Oryn's. If something happened to Oryn because of her...she'd never forgive herself, but it wasn't as if she could force Oryn to leave. They were as stubborn as an old unmovable tree.

She rubbed circles into the thick bark on her hand. "I'm worried that if you come with me, you'll get hurt."

"I can take care of anything the Cinder Forest throws at us." Oryn laced their hand with hers. "Let's get started."

"Wait." Zayla pulled away. She leaned down and plucked a handful of small, bright-blue mushrooms from the ground, pocketing them. With the mushrooms, she could access the Myceli side of her crafting, call upon the fungi to protect her if necessary. At Oryn's grin, Zayla shook her head. "Don't get too excited. This is just in case I have to use it."

Oryn nodded, then grabbed Zayla's hand once more. "Always good to be prepared."

Zayla allowed Oryn to lead her down the pathway, through the outskirts of the mirrorshard mushroom fields, the stones lit only by the white light from the daygem in Zayla's hand. Normally the darkness was soothing, but it felt wrong. Her skin itched as if something watched her. The normal mutter and buzz from nocturnal creatures seemed eerily quiet; so much so, the soft footfalls their boots made on the stones seemed to echo.

Oryn stepped in front of her, walking backward and drawing her attention. "You look tired. Have you been having those dreams again?"

"Nightmares, more like," she whispered, recalling the sensation of thick roots wrapping around her, pulling her under water, under mud, into the ground to suffocate. Yes, she'd had one the last time she slept, and the time before that. Her nightmares had started when she was very young, after her home was destroyed. They used to keep her up during the long daylight hours, watching, waiting for something terrible to happen. They had ceased for a while, but lately it seemed she had a nightmare almost every time she fell asleep. "Yes, they've returned."

Oryn sighed and squeezed Zayla's arm in a reassuring way. "I'm not surprised. I'm having nightmares, too. I bet we're all having them these days. The sun goddess worshippers are coming and that'll terrify even the strongest of our kind. You did a good thing by turning off the bioluminescence."

In her heart, Zayla knew Oryn told the truth. Destroying the light would help hide Myceli Grove for a little while, but she couldn't help feeling guilty for ending such a beautiful part of nature.

When Zayla didn't respond, Oryn continued, "It wasn't unnatural, either." As always, Oryn had seen her unease and cut right to it. "Death is as vital a part of nature as life is."

"If that's true, I should be dead already," Zayla muttered, the truth falling from her lips.

Oryn frowned. "But you're not, Zayla, you're still alive, even after all the crafting you've had to do thus far to walk the path. Take confidence in that."

The daygem's light danced across Oryn's features, glinting off a curl of vibrant-blue wood hanging from their ear. Every Nemora carried a piece of their home with them, as was tradition. A trinket, gifted to them when they were created from one of the sacred Nemora trees. Zayla's was her purple ring, that earring was Oryn's trinket.

Noticing that blue wood shook loose a memory inside Zayla, one where her and Oryn were surrounded by that same vibrant cerulean. A full-blooded Dara Nemora, Oryn's home was an offshoot of the primary Dara Grove, a smaller thicket of trees called sobskies, with trunks as blue as the ocean and branches that drooped down like vines. They'd been together among the trees the first time she'd told Oryn her fears of being killed by her crafting, about the strange vibrations in her body, and the intense, terrifying backlash she got regardless of how much she practiced.

"You're young, Zayla," Oryn said, squeezing her hand. "It's normal to have backlash. Every noxling has it. And your bitterroot crafting backlash is probably stronger because your bitterroot is the strongest crafting you can summon. It's your true home after all! But your crafting will settle once you go through the Choosing Ritual. It'll still demand a price, of course, but not one nearly as high."

A breeze blew through the branches around them, clattering them together in a rushed beat that matched Zayla's racing heart. She hadn't told anyone else her fears, and her nerves nearly silenced her.

Oryn's open expression, their eyes wide and caring, made Zayla want to keep talking. Her lip trembled. "It's worse, Oryn, I swear it. Much, much worse than anyone else in my season. Anyone else I've ever met. I don't want to use my crafting." Tears welled in her eyes. "I think it's trying to kill me."

Oryn canted their head, shifting closer to Zayla in the low hollow of roots. "What do you mean, sibling?"

"I-I'm the only one who survived from my bitterroot offshoot. I'm the only one left. I should be dead. I've never heard of any other Nemora surviving after their offshoot was destroyed, and no one else has either. There aren't any other bitterroot offshoots around, so how am I still alive?" A sob clenched her throat tight, but she forced the words out, tears now streaming down her cheeks. "I'm unnatural, Oryn, an abomination of nature. It's why my crafting is always vibrating within me. Because I shouldn't be alive."

Oryn pulled her into a tight hug, arms circling her in comforting warmth.

But Zayla was unable to stop the flow of words spilling from her mouth. "That's why I don't want to use my crafting, sibling. I know it wants to kill me. I know it has to kill me to right the wrong of me surviving that suncreature attack. And I don't want to die."

Her voice cracked, and she broke into uncontrollable sobs.

Oryn held her until the tears dried. They tucked a strand of hair behind her ear and cupped her face in their hands, guiding her gaze into theirs. "I believe you, Zayla, and I'll help you however I can."

Zayla blinked the memories away.

Oryn wasn't the last person she'd told her fears to, but her older sibling was the only person to actually believe her. Other young Nemora had laughed her worries away or told her she was lucky to have survived, that she should be grateful to be alive, literally the last bitterroot Nemora in a world where no bitterroot offshoot thrived. The older Nemora treated her differently—like her survival left her marked. An oddity, something strange. And they were right.

"I feel awful about destroying the mirrorshard's bioluminescence," Zayla admitted quietly. "They were so beautiful."

"I know," Oryn replied just as softly. "But it wasn't for nothing, sibling."

"Soon I'll never have to use my crafting again."

Oryn bumped her hip with their elbow. "Exactly."

Sometime during their conversation, they had followed the path out of the mirrorshard mushroom field. The stone pathway curved sharply to the right, veering away from the Cinder Forest just ahead of them.

"You even did what no one else was willing to do," Oryn said. "And you're one step closer to—"

Zayla stopped, grabbing Oryn's arm.

Silvery moonlight dappled the ground, and the outskirts of the Cinder Forest loomed ahead of them. A canopy of thin, twisted branches arched toward the sky before disappearing into the darkness. A figure stood at the edge, a darker shadow than the forest beyond.

Her heart thumped painfully against her ribs. It could be a wyvern, a massive flying creature that they'd have to sneak past to get into the forest. She'd heard of them this far north. Worse still, it could be a suncreature version. A twisted flying beast corrupted from its natural form into a slavering, vicious hunter that killed for fun rather than food. Fear shivered through Zayla. They'd have to hide from a suncreature so large.

As they crept closer, Oryn pulled three darts from their belt and stepped in front of Zayla. From over their shoulder, Zayla caught the gleam of the dart's slivery metal, the sharp tip, and the gray-brown fletching. As long as their forearm and just as thin, the darts looked weak, but Zayla knew Oryn could throw them with deadly accuracy.

Oryn lifted the darts as they both stepped closer, and the white light of Zayla's daygem finally touched the edges of the strange shadow mass.

Zayla sucked in a breath.

It wasn't a wyvern. It wasn't a suncreature. Yet Zayla's fear tightened as she took in the sight before them.

A dark, stone statue of a Nemora stood with arms outstretched, folds of a cape carved as if frozen mid-movement. A wave of dark rock surged around the woman, rising behind her to a height well above her head; the edges of the wave sharpened to stone blades. Pale-gray ashes littered the surrounding ground, a heavy pile that almost reached the top of the Nemora's boots.

"Those ashes," Zayla murmured. "They must be from a suncreature."

The vile beasts burnt away once killed, turning into ashes just like those surrounding the woman.

Zayla moved past Oryn and crept closer to the statue to get a better look. Her footfalls kicked up some of the ashes, but she hardly noticed. Her whole attention was riveted on the statue. The stone was too detailed—the fine lines beside the woman's eyes, the tightly spiraled hair, the embroidered edges of the cloak were too intricately detailed to be carved. This had once been a living Nemora.

Zayla's breath caught.

This had to be the price of crafting. This woman's final crafting.

Is the woman still alive in there? Zayla clutched her bark-covered hand to her chest, recalling the searing burn when the spores bloomed over her skin. When a Nemora used too much crafting, it took their life as payment. This Hallr Nemora—a mover and breaker of stone—demanded too much of her crafting, so she turned to stone as well. What would it feel like to be completely turned to rock?

Oryn sighed and lowered their throwing darts. They kicked at some of the ashes. The gray powder spiraled for a moment then settled once more. "At least that's one less suncreature we need to worry about. She took care of it for us."

"Took care of it but gave her life." Putting a hand on the statue's cheek, Zayla rubbed her thumb under the woman's eye, cleaning off some of the ash and being careful not to break the delicate, stone eyelashes. She fought to keep her voice steady even as her heart thudded in her chest. "This was recent, otherwise the more fragile features would have broken off."

"This is just a reminder to be careful traversing this place." Oryn made a quick hand gesture toward the statue, a sign of respect that Nemora performed when stumbling upon a crafting backlash as intense as this one. A thanks, of sorts, for giving their life back to nature when nature so strongly demanded it. Zayla hated that gesture.

They both moved away, taking in the sheer height of the rock wave. The stone peaks arched high above the woman's head, and the woman looked upward as well. The suncreature must have been either very tall or flying.

"She was quite the Hallr Nemora," Oryn finally said as they rounded the last of the sharpened points. "Her last act was impressive."

A lilting voice floated toward them from the darkness beyond their sphere of daygem light. "Would've been better if she killed the suncreature—whatever it was—and lived to tell the tale, don't you think?"

Chapter Three

ZAYLA STARTED AT THE woman's voice, jerking a sturdy hooked club she used as a weapon from her belt.

Oryn stepped in front of her to face the direction of the voice, their darts raised, the line of their shoulders tense. "Who goes there?"

A jingling noise came from the darkness, and a silver-skinned woman stepped into the daygem's light. "Oh wyvern shit, I didn't mean to scare you! My name's Shadre. Anoc-suna." The Nemora word for hello slipped easily from her as she lifted her hands in a wave, the loose sleeves of her dark-purple tunic pooling at her elbows. A double-bladed hand axe hung off her belt. She looked Oryn in the eyes, her short height matching theirs. The woman didn't seem afraid of them at all. Instead, she gave them a wide grin.

Oryn remained tense, but Zayla lowered her club. "Anoc-suna."

It was curious to meet someone on the outskirts of the Cinder Forest. Most stayed away. Zayla figured it better to make friends than enemies, especially out here.

"I've just been resting for a bit over there"—the woman, Shadre, jabbed her thumb to her left, somewhere behind the rocks—"and figured I'd come see who was poking around."

"We're not...poking around, just looking. My name's Zayla, and that's Oryn," Zayla replied.

Shadre nodded. "Nice to meet you both."

Zayla eyed this stranger. The daygem's light seemed to glint off this woman as if she were made from metal, and the woman's rust-colored eyes marked her as an Ingo Nemora, the finders and caretakers of ores and minerals—metals. The angled markings on one side of her head, where her silvery hair had been shaved, were confirmation. Long locks hid the other side from view. Black and blue metal jewelry studded and dangled from her ears, a ring curled through her nostril, and her clothing was adorned with metal studs lining the trim. A tambourine hung from her belt next to the axe. The source of the jangling noise.

Zayla had seen plenty of Ingo Nemora, had even visited Ingo Grove for a trial there during her walk. They were always nice to her, but she'd never seen anyone quite like Shadre. A flush crept up Zayla's neck. *She's... stunning.*

The woman glanced over them both, eyes lingering on Zayla's dual markings on her skin and her bark-covered hand, then gestured at the muck on their boots. "Seems like you've been walking a while. It'll be daylight soon. You can rest at my camp, if you'd like." Despite Oryn's raised dart, the woman kept her voice cheerful and light. Nonthreatening.

Something inside Zayla wanted to trust this woman. She could've let them walk right past instead of coming out to greet them, and offering them a place to rest the dangers of the daylight away was a generous act. "We'd appreciate that, thank you."

Shadre turned on her booted heel and walked into the darkness. "This way."

A large section of the rock had been pulled away when the Nemora woman used the stone to protect herself, and the action had formed a kind of shallow cave facing away from the Cinder Forest. A gentle fire flickered inside, casting long shadows on the wall and cooking a spike of meat. Shadre pushed her pack and bedroll to one side, then gestured them in. Oryn left them to do a quick loop around the area, but they hardly needed to. Even Zayla could see that with the cave on one side and the large rock wave on the other, it was a safe spot to hunker down.

"Where are you traveling from?" Zayla asked as she settled down next to the fire. The warmth hit her, chasing the damp chill from the morass away. Her feet ached and the tiredness from travel pulled at the edges of her body. She smothered a yawn before it could escape.

"Just outside Ulin." Shadre turned the spike of roasting meat so it cooked on all sides. The firelight brightened Shadre's angled markings, and Zayla found herself openly staring. Ingo Nemora always had such unique patterns on their skin, which only made this woman more beautiful.

The skinned irill—a creature who lived underground and feasted on roots and tubers—dripped orange blood that sizzled in the fire. The scent of cooked food made Zayla's mouth water. She didn't remember the last time she had eaten...surely not since waking up. *I have to take better care of myself.*

"You?" Shadre asked.

Before Zayla could reply, Oryn came back from their scouting, their gaze flitting between the cave opening, Shadre, and the meat before setting down beside Zayla. They rummaged through their pack and procured a handful of dried fruit, handing half to Zayla. With a long look at the stranger, they stuffed the other half of the fruit into their mouth. *Why's Oryn being so rude?*

A smirk tugged at Shadre's dark lips. "You're smart not to trust me, especially out here." She turned the roasting irill once more before plucking the spike out of the ground and putting it away from the fire to cool. "I'm still going to share my irill if you want it though."

A rush of gratitude flooded Zayla, and she offered half her share of the fruit to Shadre. "I'm currently walking the path; my last stop is Ratnaa."

Shadre perked up, her smirk transforming into a true smile as she accepted the fruit. "Ah, I completed mine not too long ago!" This close, Zayla could tell Shadre was telling the truth. Nemora who hadn't completed their walks had softer, curved markings, but Shadre's Ingo markings were sharper than a sword point. Shadre unhooked her tambourine, the metal making a soft chime. "I'm actually headed to Ratnaa myself, spreading the joy and majesty of music. I'm a wandering musician, you see."

"That sounds like quite the journey." Excitement lifted Zayla's voice, burning some of her tiredness away.

A few wandering musician troupes had come to her and Oryn's home when they were younger. A memory burned bright in her mind of the jovial people, the outlandish theater, and the beautiful music they'd brought with them. It seemed like an exciting life of creativity and movement. Zayla didn't have the creative flair for it. Acting seemed too much like lying. She couldn't do so with a straight face, and any time she played an instrument, it sounded like a dying animal. Still, the life of a wandering healer called to her, something she'd most likely pursue after completing the path, and it always impressed her to meet a creative type. "Do you play other instruments?"

"Oh yes. Best to have a wide range to keep folk interested." Shadre gestured to a flute, a small harp, a tuning fork, and a metal drum that sat atop her pack. All the instruments were made from a strange, blue-black metal.

"I've never seen metal that color before. What is it?" Zayla asked.

"A metal from my home offshoot called duskiron. It's a smaller offshoot of Ingo Grove. Not many Nemora live there, but those who do tend to stay, since the metal is so rare and precious." Shadre raised her hand over the fire to show off numerous duskiron rings. "I was the first to leave, to make my own path, so they made sure I had plenty of trinkets to take with me."

Judging from those instruments and the sheer amount of jewelry on her—all made of duskiron—it seemed Shadre would never be far from her home. A pang hit close to Zayla's heart. Her ring, the sole trinket she had from her offshoot, lay beneath the bark on her hand. She rubbed small circles into the bark, leaving a small wear spot on the wood. The gentle thrum inside her body seemed to heighten in response.

"Well, the metal's quite unique," Zayla finally said.

Shadre canted her head to the side. "You're pretty unique yourself. I've never met a hybrid Nemora before. What offshoot is yours?"

"It's called bitterroot."

"Bitterroot, huh?" Shadre scratched her chin. "I haven't heard of that one."

"Not many travelers have."

Many seasons ago—Zayla didn't know how long—two Nemora from different Groves fell in love. A Dara and a Myecli Nemora walked into a sacred tree together. They wanted nature to gift them a child. Instead of simply extending one of the parents' Groves, nature decided to create something entirely new. Those parents were gifted with the very first bitterroot noxling. Though Zayla didn't remember, she'd been told that the offshoot had been far, far to the south, way off the usual roads and pathways where travelers would venture. Not many people had known about the bitterroot, even when it was lush and thriving, long before Zayla was gifted from a sacred tree for her two mothers. Then, the bitterroot offshoot was destroyed.

She met Shadre's rust-orange gaze, finding only kindness and a hint of curiosity shining within her eyes. "But I guess, now you have," Zayla said lightly.

"Now I have," Shadre repeated. She poked the roasted irill, then slid it off the spike. Ripping the thick legs from its body, she offered two to Zayla and two to Oryn.

Oryn didn't move, even after Zayla gave them a meaningful glance, so Zayla shrugged and took theirs, too.

At that, Shadre smirked and sank her teeth into the thick meat of the irill's body. Pale orange juice ran down her chin that she quickly wiped away. "Where are you two traveling from?"

Zayla opened her mouth to speak but Oryn's voice was like a blunt weapon, "A sobsky offshoot of Dara Grove."

Shock rippled through Zayla at the curt response. The woman had given them space to stay, freshly cooked food, and pleasant conversation. Strangers always gave Oryn pause, but it didn't give them the right to be so snarky.

"Oryn, can I talk to you for a moment outside?" Without waiting for Oryn to answer, Zayla rose, took Oryn by the hand, and pulled her sibling away from the fire. Just outside of hearing range, she spun to them. "Can you relax please?"

Oryn frowned. "You know we can't trust everyone we meet. Especially here. We're right outside the Cinder Forest, sibling. For all we know, she might be a sun goddess worshipper!"

"A sun goddess worshipper who gave us food and a place to stay? That doesn't sound like something they'd do." Zayla hissed, lowering her voice. "Be nice. At least for now. Please!"

Oryn chewed on their lip as if chewing on a response, gaze darting to the forest looming beside them. "Fine, but if she does anything that puts us in danger…"

"Then we can deal with her." Zayla nodded. A soft breeze rattled the dry branches, and Zayla's skin prickled. "Come on."

They went back into the cave and settled down by the fire once more.

Their little side conversation had to be awkward for Shadre, but she took it in stride. She didn't pry any further. "Well, if you're headed to Ratnaa through the Cinder Forest, I'll come with. I know a route that'll circumnavigate the major suncreature lairs."

"Any help to get to Rantaa quicker would be appreciated," Zayla replied. "Thank you."

"Of course! Now eat up, before it gets cold."

They ate in silence, each sinking into their own thoughts. Shadre polished off the irill's body, cracking the bones to suck the marrow out as well. Zayla followed suit with three of the four legs. She tucked the fourth leg between her and Oryn, hoping to save it for them later. Oryn stuck with even more dried fruit from their pack, keeping their eyes on the brightening sky outside. Dawn approached, banishing the deep azure sky away to make way for slashes of pinks and oranges. With a belly full of warm meat, tiredness tugged on Zayla's eyelids, and she couldn't contain her yawning anymore.

Rummaging through her pack, Shadre procured a small duskiron ball. "Let me make this a little more secure." She pushed herself to her feet by the cave opening and held out the orb. The sharp angled markings on Shadre's skin brightened with a golden-brown crafting light. The orb shimmered. Its surface rippled like waves before bursting outward. In a heartbeat, the orb expanded to a web of duskiron metal that covered the cave opening.

Zayla blew out a long breath. The web of metal was a fascinating display of crafting, and it seemed to come so easily to Shadre. More surprising, her crafting didn't even seem to lash back...though to be fair, Zayla didn't quite know what that would look like for an Ingo Nemora.

Oryn stiffened beside Zayla, eyes wide. "You're trapping us!"

"This isn't to keep you in, it's to keep the suncreatures out." Shadre turned back to them, grin slipping at Oryn's expression. The glow in her eyes, and her Ingo markings faded as she let go of her Nature crafting. "I'd rather not stay up and keep guard all day. We're heading into the Cinder Forest, so we'll need all the rest we can get. Is that okay?"

Her question was directed at Oryn, but Zayla answered, "It's fine. Amazing, actually. Your crafting is impressive."

Shadre shrugged. "Most of my kin learn that trick at an early age, so it doesn't take much to do it."

"Lucky." The word blurted out before Zayla could stop it. It was lucky to be able to do something so powerful without fear of one's crafting lashing back. Her cheeks heated, and she dipped her head. Her gaze drifted to the crimson bark that made her hand unusable.

Oryn placed a gentle hand over the bark. "Only a few nights travel to Ratnaa, sibling."

Once she'd finished walking the path, she could finally get some peace.

Shadre settled down next to the fire. "Now if you don't mind, I'm going to get some sleep. You two should, too." Shadre curled away from the fire. Within moments, her breathing steadied into the slow rise and fall of slumber. A talent all in itself.

"She's a strange one," Oryn said dryly.

Zayla turned to her sibling. "At least she understands we're trustworthy, too, falling asleep first like that."

"Too? We hardly know her."

"She seems nice!" Zayla protested.

"You trust people too quickly, sibling." Oryn tightened their hold on Zayla's bark-covered hand, then let go. "Now sleep. You need it more than I do. I'll keep first watch."

Of course they would. Ever alert, her sibling, even with the metal webbing keeping the dangers at bay. Or perhaps, especially with the metal webbing. Zayla shoved the fourth irill leg into Oryn's hands and sighed. "Stop being stubborn and eat this. And wake me soon."

She waited until Oryn finally nodded, then settled into her bedroll. She didn't want to face the nightmares, but Shadre had been right about one thing—they needed all the rest they could get.

It seemed like she'd just fallen asleep when the cracking and crashing of rock startled her awake. Sunlight speared into her eyes as she blinked them open. A large rock thudded down a mere handspan from Zayla's head, sending a spray of pebbles and dust over her. She yelped, covering her face with her arms. A nightmare shook loose in her mind; she was buried alive and suffocating. Fear came flooding back.

Someone tugged on her shoulder, yanking her away just as another rock tumbled down where her head had just been. "Zayla, we need to move," Oryn commanded. "Right now!"

Chapter Four

SHARDS OF DEBRIS RAINED down as Zayla struggled to her feet, frantically trying to orient herself in the cave. Dust clogged the air, and she tried to cough it free from her nose and lungs. A rumbling sound like a rockslide vibrated the stone beneath her feet.

Shadre's back was pressed hard against her metal webbing. She seemed to be staring at the back of the shallow cave. Brown blood dribbled down to her eyes from a cut on her forehead. "Didn't think they'd break in from the other side," she shouted over the rumbling.

Zayla spun. A large hole in the cave wall had opened to the gray petrified trees of Cinder Forest beyond. That was not an escape route. A glowing red eye shifted into view, large enough to completely cover the hole. The eye blinked and pulled away, replaced by a set of sharp, white claws as long as Zayla's forearm. With impressive force, the suncreature tore at the cave wall. A bright-blue bundle bounced along the stone floor. *My mushrooms!* The creature's claws raked the stone, slicing the mushrooms into useless bits.

"No," Zayla breathed. One source of her crafting, gone.

Fear swept through her, hot and fast. She stepped back until she too pressed into Shadre's metal webbing. Zayla's Nature crafting surged, answering her fear, wanting to protect her.

She didn't give in. Grabbing the hooked club tucked inside her belt with both hands, her fingers wrapped around the sturdy dark handle and raised the weapon to strike. Only then did she realize the crimson bark had fallen off, revealing fresh purple-green skin. *The price for my crafting paid.*

Oryn grabbed their throwing darts from their belt and stepped in front of Zayla, shoulders tense and footing steady. "It looks like it's alone. We can take it."

"We don't need to take it," Shadre said. "We just need to wait a moment."

The suncreature's violent tearing sent rocks flying. Another stone slammed into the ground next to Zayla's boot.

"Wait?" Zayla yelped, flattening herself against the webbing. She was starting to doubt this woman's ability to make rational decisions.

More rocks crumbled inward. The hole was now wide enough for Zayla to walk through without ducking, but the huge suncreature couldn't reach them. Its white-scaled arm groped around uselessly. Its low rumbling growl shook the loosened debris. Obviously annoyed it couldn't get to its prey, the suncreature yanked its arm free and started to pace. The sound of its claws crunching over the ground made her cringe as the familiar humming wound through her back and neck. She twitched, her club jerking forward.

"Wait," Shadre said again, quietly, mistaking Zayla's twitch for intentional movement.

"Wait for what, exactly?" Zayla whispered.

A thunderous crash rumbled through the cave. Stones and shards of rock flew toward them. She covered her face with an arm and squeezed her eyes closed. Surprisingly, none of the rocks hit her.

"For that," Shadre whispered.

Zayla could hear the laughter in the woman's voice and her eyes popped open.

Oryn stood tensed between Zayla and the beast. Two enormous crimson eyes glared at them. A white-scaled reptilian snout parted to reveal pointed teeth, like a grin of anticipation. The creature shoved itself forward again, only a few paces away from its next meal. Its horns brushed the broken ceiling and debris rained down around its massive head and shoulders.

Sickening heat radiated from the creature. Zayla tore her eyes from the terrifying creature to see Shadre's lips turn up in a smile, her eyes glinting with mischief.

The woman is enjoying this. She enjoys the danger.

As if immune to fear, Shadre reached out and patted the annoyed suncreature on its snout, narrowly missing a snap of its razor teeth. Then she spun on her booted heel.

She's actually turning her back on the beast. Idiotic, or terribly brave.

Zayla's breath caught at the woman's boldness either way. With a brief flash of golden-brown Nature crafting, the duskiron webbing sucked into itself and formed a shiny metal ball in Shadre's palm once more. Zayla hissed, "What are you sunsick, tempting fate like that?"

"Sunsick, no." Tossing the ball from hand to hand, Shadre winked at Zayla, then grabbed her pack and strolled nonchalantly out of the cave.

The beast let out a deafening roar, and a wash of fiery light poured from its maw, nearly blinding Zayla. The humming in her body amplified, as if it drew power from that horrible sound, and vibrated through her with a new intensity, shaking her teeth and rattling her bones.

Silent fear sliced through her as she stumbled backward, tripping over her feet in her haste. The suncreature roared again, trying to back out of the cave, but its horns curved too far upward. It couldn't back out.

Somehow, Shadre had known. Known the creature would be stuck.

Still off balance, Zayla quickly found their belongings and turned away from the cave. In a heartbeat, Oryn was by her side, keeping her upright with a firm grip. They followed Shadre a few hundred paces away. Oryn turned to Zayla and pulled her into a hug. "I'm glad you're okay," they murmured.

Zayla wrapped her shaking arms around Oryn. "You, too, sibling."

"I'm only a little banged up." They lifted their arm, letting the sleeve fall away. Several shards of stone had embedded themselves deep into Oryn's blue skin. Brown blood oozed over the inflamed and swollen flesh.

"Oryn!" Zayla dug in her pack, pulling out a small jar of poultice and a roll of clean cloth.

"Ever prepared, noxling," Oryn teased, though they gave Zayla a grateful smile. Ever since their shared youth, Oryn was always the one to get hurt, and Zayla was always the one to fix the wounds.

Rolling her eyes, Zayla went to work tending to Oryn's cuts, while Shadre stood nearby, patient and silent. Zayla gently plucked the shards of rock from their skin, then slathered a yellow-green poultice onto the numerous cuts.

Oryn patiently endured, calm under Zayla's practiced hands.

"Thank you, Zayla." Oryn's smile settled Zayla, calming her racing heart and quieting the hum within her body. She felt peace, for a moment, before fear and uncertainty ebbed back in, like light melting away the darkness.

She lowered her voice so Shadre couldn't hear. "I can't believe Shadre pet a suncreature."

Oryn gave her a meaningful, wide-eyed look and nodded.

Shadre stayed quiet while Zayla tended Oryn's wounds until the moment Zayla tied the last knot in the bandages. "You don't need to whisper. The creature can't get to us, but we should head out. Come on."

Tightening her bag, Shadre repositioned her instruments like she had not a care in the world. After flashing Zayla a dazzling grin, Shadre circled back to the cave and disappeared beyond the rock. Zayla and Oryn followed.

Shadre's shoulders shook with laughter as she pointed to the large, scaled body of the suncreature who'd attacked them. Its claws scrabbled uselessly against the stone, the angle wrong to break the rock; its thick torso twisted as it tried to wriggle its way out. Zayla held her breath, but even though slivers of rock fell away, the stone held. Its long tail whipped back and forth in anger.

"You're laughing?" Oryn said in a low voice, staring at Shadre like she'd grown an extra head. "We could've been killed!"

"You were fine." Shadre chuckled. "Suncreatures are scary, but also wildly dumb sometimes. When they panic, they get confused. It won't be able to get out of that for a while. If ever."

The suncreature roared, quaking the ground. It twisted and curled and yanked and shoved…and couldn't get itself free.

"Why?" Zayla tilted her head at the creature. With each frantic movement, the scales rippled over glowing, crimson skin, like water glinting over stone. Almost mesmerizing, if also terrifying. Even now, out of immediate danger, Zayla's heart kicked into a frantic beat.

Shadre stepped into Zayla's personal space and tapped the side of Zayla's head with a knuckle. "Horns." She smiled and held Zayla's gaze for a moment, then another. The mischievous glint died away, and Zayla thought she saw concern swirling behind the woman's rust-orange eyes. Then, Shadre winked and moved away. "It won't hold forever. Let's get going. There's a trail of sorts not far from here."

With Shadre leading, the trio made their way into the Cinder Forest.

The night before, the forest had loomed over them like a creature stalking and waiting to pounce. In the daylight, the forest looked almost…docile. Silent, save for their boots crunching over the stony ground.

And enchanting.

Unlike the Ravenlock Woods in the south, where a single touch could literally turn the graying and blackened trees to ashes, it seemed like the trees in the Cinder Forest had been transformed into something different. They looked gray and black and dead like their siblings to the south, but here and there, where the outside bark had been pulled away, the trunks glimmered like precious stones.

Zayla wanted to stop for a closer look, but Shadre kept their pace at a fast clip. Zayla lengthened her stride, unwilling to brave the light of the day too far from her companions. Perhaps Shadre and Oryn hadn't noticed the glimmering. The sun beat down onto Zayla's shoulders, sweat immediately beading on her skin. She felt too exposed, walking in the sunshine when she should be sleeping, but if that's what it took to get to Ratnaa Grove and complete her walk, then she'd push through the anxious feeling. She twirled her ring around her finger again and again and again, grateful she could reach it once more.

Farther inside the forest, the charred bark had been completely stripped away, simply decomposed to ash that swirled around their boots. Entirely bare tree trunks and branches glimmered and glinted in the sunlight. Blue-green, deep orange, shiny white, glazed brown…so many colors.

She'd never seen anything like it, and it took her breath away. Something—an urge, a curiosity, another force entirely, she didn't know— drew her hand toward a particularly large trunk as wide as a carriage. She reached out, wondering what the blue and green surface felt like…

"Don't!" Shadre's voice cracked like a whip in the quiet surroundings.

Although Zayla heard the warning, heard the urgency in the woman's voice, it sounded far away…like it had traveled through water. The warning couldn't be for her. Surely not. Even if she wanted to, she couldn't tear her eyes from the glimmering tree.

Cold. Hard as rock, as if this had never been a tree to begin with. The blue-green trunk glimmered under her palm, slick as glass, but when she looked closer, she could still see the grains of wood.

"Amazing," Zayla breathed.

"Watch out!" Shadre yelled.

A scuffle broke loose behind her—around her—but it didn't matter. The only thing that mattered was the tree. *So beautiful.* It took her breath away. In fact, she didn't need to breathe at all, did she? A faraway worry niggled the back of her mind.

Someone grabbed her shoulder and yanked her around, breaking her contact with the glimmering tree. Oryn shook her roughly, breathing hard, blue cheeks pale, eyes wide. "Zayla!" they said. "Are you all right?"

Zayla sucked in a deep breath like a gasp, choking like her lungs couldn't get enough air, like she'd been held underwater for a long, long time. "Oryn?" her voice felt rough, scratchy. She blinked at the shocked, scared expression on her sibling's face. "What happened?"

A flash of movement caught her peripheral vision. A bone-white serpent as long as her forearm emerged from the layer of ash on the ground. Its eyes glowed like embers. A suncreature! As she drew back, the creature reared into the air, jaws open. Leathery wings unfolded. Before she could register what was happening, the thing flew straight for her face.

Zayla lifted her club, but it was like her shaking hands were trapped in mud.

The creature hissed, the metal tip of Oryn's dart diving straight through its side. The serpent writhed, then fell limp. In the blink of an eye, it began disintegrating into cinders and ash that fell free of Oryn's dart.

Oryn pulled Zayla away from the tree, back onto the barely discernible path, where Shadre stood holding her hand axe. "There's more! Come on."

For the first time since being mesmerized by the glimmering trees, Zayla finally took a decent look around. Gemstone-like trees. Ashy ground. And...and... Zayla's mouth dropped open.

Glaring sunlight bounced off the bone-white scales of dozens and dozens of serpentine suncreatures. Some curled around the branches, others slithered through the ash. All of them had strange star shapes on their backs. She heard more still, shifting behind her. Burning cinder eyes stared back at her everywhere she turned. The serpentine creatures hissed, low and threatening, as they slithered toward them.

The star shape suddenly made sense. These were corrupted versions of starbacks, territorial serpentine creatures whose bite could paralyze a person in a few nights if they didn't get treatment. A suncreature version amplified the original creature's natural abilities, which meant these creatures could probably paralyze in moments. Maybe instantaneously.

Zayla's heart thudded, her body going numb with fear. There were so, so many, surrounding her and Oryn and Shadre. Everywhere she looked, crimson eyes stared back. Suddenly her idea of traversing the forest seemed like a very bad one. *Not even one night in and we've already been attacked twice.* She gripped her club, hands trembling. Oryn pressed against her side. They couldn't retrace their steps, not with the enormous suncreature they'd trapped in the cave behind them. They had to keep going, but first, they had to survive these starbacks.

Chapter Five

ORYN MOVED IN FRONT, darts at the ready. Her sibling was always calm, even now, the still eye within a tornado's wrath. Zayla lifted her club and wished she could wrap some of that unending calm around herself to slow her racing pulse and steady her thoughts.

Shadre glanced back at them, a wild glint in her eye. "Didn't realize the starbacks pushed this far south. Oryn's right, we should probably consider getting out of here."

Even as she spoke, two large starback suncreatures—the length of Zayla's outstretched arm—launched into the air, unfurling wide, leathery wings. One aimed for Shadre's face, the other angled toward her legs. Before Zayla could yell a warning, Shadre moved with a dancer's grace, slicing her hand axe through the air as if it was an extension of herself. Both suncreatures fell, cleaved in half before Zayla could utter a word. The suncreatures burned away into ash. The others pulled back, hissing angrily.

"Move." Shadre's sharp word made Zayla start. "Now! If we get out of their territory, they'll leave us alone."

Zayla ran, darting past the starback suncreatures writhing toward them. Oryn and Shadre followed close behind. The horrible hissing followed.

"By your left boot!" Oryn shouted at her.

Zayla swung her arm down, her gaze following as an afterthought. Her club thudded against a suncreature's open jaws. The impact wasn't as hard as she intended. Her body was still sluggish from whatever the gemstone tree did to her, but the impact did stun the creature and, thankfully, Zayla pulled away.

Two more suncreatures launched from the ashes, flapping their leathery wings in front of her. Startled, she stopped. Her crafting sang in response. The warmth bloomed from her feet, spreading up her body to the very tips of her fingers. *There's no life in this forest. Does my crafting even work in here?* The thought sliced through her mind, stabbing her with panic. Her crafting was never her first pick, but here in the Cinder Forest, she didn't even want to try. Swinging her club once more, she struck across the creature's wide, flat face. The impact sent the creature spinning away.

The second starback suncreature glanced at its writhing brethren, then cut its burning crimson gaze back to Zayla. The creature hissed. Multiple fangs extended from its gaping maw as it dove toward her.

A dart flew over Zayla's shoulder in a burst of wind and sank deep into the creature's eye. The sudden collision spun it off course and into a pile of ashes.

Oryn appeared beside her, giving her a little shove. "Keep running, Zayla. And don't look back."

Zayla kept pace with her sibling but couldn't follow all of Oryn's advice. Craning her neck, she glanced over her shoulder.

Hundreds of crimson eyes followed them, white scales glinting in the sunshine. They flew deftly around the gemstone-like trees, darting between the branches with eerie grace. They slithered through the ashes, the crimson glow beneath their scales like red vines reaching for her.

Her breath seized, cold vines of panic choking her.

Like a sunsick fool, she tripped and stumbled to her knees. Pain scraped her palms as she caught herself.

The horde of suncreatures grew closer. To Zayla's ears, a wave of their hissing crested into a roar. From the corner of her eye, she saw Shadre running toward her, but her focus remained on the suncreatures pursuing them.

"Zayla!" The Ingo Nemora woman threw something that glinted dark, blue-black at the oncoming horde. Her eyes burned golden-brown with her Nemora crafting, the sharp angled markings on the back of her outstretched hand brightened to match, and the tiny ball of metal expanded outward like a bomb. Impossibly long spears shot from the device, in every direction, impaling multiple suncreatures. The rest scattered. "Keep running!"

Someone yanked her to her feet and hauled her along. "Come on," her sibling said.

The trio ran, yet the hissing followed. Zayla's lungs ached. Her legs burned. Her body hummed with strange, echoing vibrations. A stitch twinged red-hot in her side. Her crafting sang inside her, answering her fear, longing to be free, but here, in the depths of the Cinder Forest, where everything was dead and ashes, could she even call on nature to do her bidding? Were there even any trees or mushrooms alive to command? She didn't know, and she was too afraid to try.

Zayla heard a few more thuds and angry hisses, but she didn't look back. She couldn't bear to see those crimson eyes again. The glittering gemstone trunks gave way to burnt, gray, ashy trees.

Finally, the hissing ebbed into silence.

Shadre jogged up beside her and Oryn. "We can stop running now."

Zayla slowed. "Are we outside their—their territory?" she panted, rubbing her aching sides as she tried to calm her breathing.

Shadre flashed her a tired grin, huffing a little, though her rust-orange eyes were wide and wild. "Must be. They're not behind us anymore."

Zayla didn't want to look back and get caught in the sea of crimson eyes staring at her, hunting her. She clenched her jaw and took the risk. All she could see were gray, dead trees and ashy ground. No white scales, no leathery wings, no fangs. No crimson eyes. The suncreatures had stopped their relentless pursuit. She let herself sag under the flood of relief.

When she glanced at Shadre's soft profile, her relief faded. The woman had said she'd been through these woods, could get them safely through. This last encounter hadn't been at all safe. Had Shadre lied? Suspicion hooked its ugly claws into Zayla's heart. *Why?*

"I thought you knew a better way through the Cinder Forest." Oryn's voice dripped with venom. They didn't even sound winded. Or maybe their anger had pushed their exhaustion aside. "Yet you led us directly into those suncreatures. Zayla could've gotten hurt." A pause, as if her sibling waited for Shadre to respond, but the woman remained silent. "We all could've gotten hurt," Oryn pressed.

"I didn't know they had pushed that far south," Shadre said again. "We wouldn't have been attacked had we not stopped in their territory. Since you were planning on traveling through the woods, I assumed you already knew about the tahmtrees and their lure of glittering gems." Her gaze flicked to Zayla, whose cheeks burned. Her pause had almost gotten them killed. Shadre sighed. "Obviously I was wrong."

"Tahmtrees?" Oryn glanced at Zayla, who shook her head. The curious gemstone trees didn't sound familiar at all.

As part of the Dara Nemora, her and Oryn's education would've—should've—gone over these strange trees. Was it because their teachers didn't want to travel into the deadly forests? Did even they know what this forest held? The thought sent a ripple of guilt through her. She'd brought her sibling along with her into this dangerous territory. She should've done more research. She should've read about the dangers.

Shadre arched an eyebrow at Oryn, like she couldn't believe a Dara Nemora didn't know of these unique woods. "Some people call them trance trees," she offered. When that didn't help, she explained, "It was said that, after the intensity of the battle between the goddess sisters, Ponuriah's powers altered this place, forever. The ashes from the dead and the wide variety of minerals from Ratnaa Grove sank into this decaying wood. Combined with Ponuriah's unique, ancient crafting, it petrified the trees...turning them into something else entirely."

Bile rose in Zayla's throat. It all circled back to Ponuriah, the fiery deity said to harness the sun and the heat of all fire itself. One who told her followers to burn the world to start anew. Those same followers who wanted to capture the Nemora homelands and who were in their lands, right now. Suddenly the gemstone trees didn't seem so captivating anymore. "Why did I fall under their...trance when no one else did?" Zayla asked.

"You wouldn't be the first, nor the last." Shadre said. "Their strange beauty captivates people, lures folk to investigate. I've heard not many people can resist it." Shadre eyed Oryn. "Did you not feel the pull?"

Oryn frowned. "Not even the slightest. You don't either, I assume?"

"I did," Shadre admitted. Then she shrugged. "But I knew enough not to touch shiny things in the middle of the Cinder Forest."

The words held no anger or accusation, but Zayla's cheeks burned hotter still. "Why did the tree make it hard for me to breathe?"

Shadre's eyes went wide. "Wyvern shit, you actually touched it? I can't believe you were able to run."

"What did it do to me?" Zayla pressed.

"Tahmtrees are poisoned. Some sort of film or sheen on the inner wood. It paralyzes people." Shadre looked at Zayla, awe clear in her expression. "I can't believe you touched it. I've heard it can actually kill people."

Oryn made a strangled noise. "Why didn't you warn us ahead of time before we entered the Cinder Forest?"

"I guess I should have." Shadre ran a hand through her hair. "Look, I didn't think. I...I *should* have told you. I'm sorry."

Oryn scowled and turned away.

But the genuine apology loosened the hooks of suspicion from Zayla's heart. Something inside her unwound, and she breathed a little easier. "Let's just keep going. How many nights will it take to get through the forest with your aid?"

"Three at most, less if we walk through the day and night," Shadre replied. "But I wouldn't suggest that, for obvious reasons. Better to set up camp and sleep in shifts than to walk tired through these woods in the daylight."

Zayla nodded, suppressing a shudder. She'd rather not walk in the woods ever again, but at least Shadre's route was a full night's walk less than she'd been planning.

The trio walked deeper and deeper into the Cinder Forest, following some unseen trail Shadre seemed to know by heart. Thankfully, they didn't run into any more suncreatures. They pressed onward, even as night pulled over the sky and stars glinted overhead.

Oryn slowed their pace, so Zayla did as well. Once Shadre had pulled far enough ahead, Oryn muttered, "I still don't trust her."

The conversation by the cave came back to Zayla—Oryn's immediate accusation that Shadre was a sun goddess worshipper in disguise—but it still didn't seem to fit what Zayla had observed of Shadre, thus far. "She could've just let us die back there. If she was a worshipper, why not let the suncreatures take us? We could've been a sacrifice to her goddess."

The sun goddess worshippers often traveled with the suncreatures, letting the terrifying beasts be the first to attack before coming in themselves to deliver the fatal blow to anyone the creatures left. Any sane person who saw the telltale crimson eyes knew it was best to hide or run, rather than face the beasts and the second wave of worshippers that might be behind them.

Oryn mulled over her words in silence. "But she led us directly into a suncreature's territory when she told us she had a safe way through."

"Didn't you hear her? She hadn't realized the starbacks expanded their territory," Zayla replied, parroting Shadre's words. Something inside her believed Shadre, something deep that she couldn't shake. "It just...it feels like she's telling the truth, sibling."

"She might've been telling the truth about that, but she could have another motive for helping us." Suspicion threaded through their words. "I don't like it, being with her. Not in here. We're already surrounded by dangers, Zayla. I don't want to be traveling with one."

"She's not proven to be a danger, Oryn." Zayla squeezed her sibling's arm for reassurance. "Not everyone we come across will be the same as Lurri."

Guilt twisted inside her as the name slipped through her lips.

Just saying his name seemed to spark something in Oryn. They stopped walking. Crystal-blue eyes stared into the distance, sinking deep into a memory neither of them wanted to talk about.

Lurri. The Ratnaa Nemora had walked into Oryn's sobsky offshoot one night and sauntered right into Oryn's young heart. Zayla remembered his brilliant crimson skin traced with opalescent markings that matched his eyes, and a voice smooth as fine mulled wine. Oryn was impressionable and open-hearted. Trusting. The man and Oryn connected almost instantly and had been a pair for two seasons. Long enough to become part of the sobsky offshoot community. Long enough to make an even younger Zayla feel jealous that the man was stealing her sibling.

The vile man stole his way into Oryn's heart, then shattered it.

One early morning, just before dawn, Lurri led a trio of sun goddess worshippers into the sobsky offshoot. Oryn was still asleep when Lurri and the others came to kill them. The man had tried to remove Oryn as a threat before Oryn could come into their power with the type of crafting they alone could harness.

The betrayal sliced Oryn deeper than the gemstone blade Lurri used to cut Oryn's throat. Zayla had woken to a tornado. Violent gusts shook the sobsky trunks, whipping the vines like maddened tentacles. She'd run outside just in time to see Oryn yell and lift their hands. Golden-brown light poured from their eyes and burned from the unique markings on their skin. Zayla had never seen crafting light that bright. Oryn's howling wind screamed through their community, lifting Lurri and the sun goddess worshippers high into the air. The sickening cracks of their bodies thudding to the ground had faded from her nightmares, but the sight of Oryn fainting, blood gushing from a deep gash on their neck, was burned deep into her memory.

The elders in sobsky blamed Oryn for inviting danger into their offshoot. They blamed Oryn even more for killing the would-be assassins, so there was no one left to interrogate. Oryn had been forced to hide their unique Nemora markings ever since, just in case more assassins came hunting.

Zayla cupped Oryn's neck, pushing past the tall collar they wore, to settle her palm over one of the curved markings on her sibling's skin and pull them from the memory. Oryn's markings weren't like the numerous kinds of leaves that Dara Nemora proudly wore, but rather like gusts of wind. Oryn was a Gale Nemora, one of the rarest and most powerful Nemora alive, and Zayla tried her best to guide her sibling back to the present.

"You promised me you wouldn't bring up his name, Zayla." A muscle twitched in Oryn's jaw, the only tell that they were truly angry.

"Sometimes we have to bring up the past in order to not make the same mistakes in the future," Zayla murmured, though the words felt like a dagger twisting in her gut. She hated how the mention of Lurri's name made her sibling feel, even now, even after death, and hated herself more for tearing open the old wound.

"Why are you two lingering so far back?" Shadre's voice carried toward them from ahead. "We should stick together."

Oryn glanced that direction before turning their liquid gaze back to Zayla. "I know not everyone will be like Lurri, but we still must be careful."

Zayla called to Shadre, "Be right there." She reached for Oryn's hand. "We will be careful. If Shadre gives us any sign of worry, we'll leave."

Oryn pulled away. "She's already given us all the signs we need, Zayla," they whispered. "You're just too trusting to see them."

Without waiting for a response, Oryn turned away and walked a few paces ahead, leaving Zayla behind to wonder just how much damage she'd done bringing up the memory of Lurri. Her gaze slipped past her sibling to Shadre, leading them through another sparse thicket of spindly gray trees.

She hoped the damage was worth it.

Chapter Six

MOONLIGHT FILTERED THROUGH THE spindly dead branches, giving Zayla enough light to see Shadre's Ingo markings glimmering on the silvery skin on the side of her neck as the metal crafter led the way between the petrified trees. The sharp angled markings trailed down her neck, slipped under the straps of her sleeveless tunic, and emerged to wind down the backs of her arms. A clinking sound followed the woman wherever she went, the metallic tink-tink of her instruments rattling with each step. The noise, however soft, was a relief against the stark silence in the surrounding forest.

Oryn's words about this Ingo Nemora woman stuck like a thorn under Zayla's skin. Could Shadre be dangerous? Could she be a sun goddess worshipper? Zayla's bond with her sibling far outweighed whatever slight trust she put in their new companion, yet here she was letting Shadre lead them through the Cinder Forest. If Shadre really was a sun goddess worshipper, she could be guiding them deeper into the forest, into some kind of trap, instead of to Ratnaa Grove. The cult could torture them for information on their homelands, use them as slaves and force Zayla to grow food for them, or even simply kill them. She didn't want to think about what would happen if her sibling were captured. What would the sun goddess worshippers do with a Gale Nemora?

And yet, striking out on their own might be just as foolish. In a forest such as this, perhaps...and Zayla hated to think this way...but perhaps keeping an eye on a potential threat was a good idea.

Shadre kept a relentless pace throughout the night, winding around the trees and keeping her eyes on the ground as if there was a clear-as-day path. She glanced over her shoulder, every once in a while, catching Zayla's and Oryn's eyes, checking in on them, but never saying a word. A few times she'd hold up her hand to stop them. Something far away would shake the ground and make trees groan. Zayla thought she saw a few pinpricks of crimson light, eyes in the distance. After a moment or two of breathless silence, Shadre would nod and continue walking.

Oryn remained a few steps ahead of Zayla, not looking back at all. Anger radiated off her sibling's tense posture, churning guilt in Zayla's stomach. *I should have never brought up Lurri.* But as the night progressed, their stance softened. Movement always helped clear their mind, and Zayla could see that physically happening now.

Zayla wished she could let her worries wash away as easily, yet her sibling's worry had become her own. She looked from side to side, between the trees, stiffening at every shadow.

A sharp crack of a tree branch breaking nearby stole her gaze. Zayla held her breath. Her heart thudded like a drum as the darkness burned away a few hundred paces to the left of them. All three of them slipped behind trees to hide. The ground trembled beneath Zayla's boots.

A large shadowy mass suddenly launched into the air. With each beat of its wings, crimson light glowed, banishing the darkness away. A suncreature soared up, maneuvering its sleek, feathered body through the sky by a dip and curl of its long flowing tail. The creature scanned the treetops, circled around, then flew away from them. Its hulking, glowing mass grew smaller with each beat of Zayla's heart.

Shadre patted both of their shoulders, and after a meaningful look and a finger pressed to her lips, kept walking.

Dawn blushed pink after the long hike through seemingly endless barren lands. Shadre finally stopped beside another small corpse of the dead, gray saplings. The ashy ground sloped downward, forming a bowl surrounded by a wall of branches that hid them from view.

"We can rest here," Shadre said in a hushed tone. She pushed into the desiccated thicket and put her pack down with obvious care not to jangle her instruments too loudly. "We'll eat. Sleep in shifts. Move again as soon as everyone's rested enough."

Zayla followed, glad to finally take her weight off her aching feet. They ate a nearly silent meal of dried fruit and spiced jerky, none of them seeming to want to break the eerie stillness.

Oryn pulled out a bundle of darts from their bag. The sharp pointed tips reached past their fingertips, while the fletched ends stretched past their wrist. They slid the darts into a custom holster on their belt to replace the ones they'd thrown during the escape.

"That's a unique type of weapon to wield, Oryn," Shadre murmured.

Oryn glanced around as if expecting a suncreature to suddenly appear.

Shadre shrugged, her gaze scanning the sky lightening between the spindled trees. "Haven't seen any suncreatures in a while, so I think it's safe to talk a little." She motioned at her instruments. "I can't stand the quiet, so I usually play, but here..." she trailed off.

Oryn nodded, then carefully put the remaining bundle of darts back into their bag, not meeting Shadre's eyes. "I like darts. It's the only weapon that I can use effectively."

Shadre leaned back on her palms, tilting her head so her silvery hair flowed over her shoulder. "I think that's the most you've said to me the whole trip."

Zayla suppressed the laugh that bucked in her chest. Shadre was right, but Oryn wouldn't appreciate the remark or her laughter.

To her surprise, Oryn's lips twitched into a wry grin. "I only just met you two nights ago. We've been walking through a dangerous forest. Haven't had much time for idle chatter."

"True!" This time, Shadre did laugh, a quiet chuckle. "Well, in any case, I'm impressed by how efficient your darts were against the starback suncreatures. You did well!"

Oryn gave a nonchalant shrug, but Zayla knew her sibling had practiced for seasons to throw their darts by hand without resorting to their wind crafting. When combined with Oryn's unique abilities, those darts became even more deadly.

After a beat of silence, Oryn offered, "I...haven't seen metal crafting used exactly like yours. That was impressive as well."

"Yes!" Zayla couldn't help but jump in. "That tiny ball exploding into spikes. How exciting."

"It was nothing," Shadre replied, though Zayla noticed a darker gray tinge to her silvery ears. "A useful trick I learned back home."

Under Shadre's curious gaze, guilt wormed through Zayla again. The entire incident had been her fault, and the trance tree had prevented her from doing anything useful. She never wanted to be that powerless again.

"I noticed neither of you used your crafting," Shadre said lightly. "Either on the starbacks or on the reptilian suncreature in the cave. Do you not have much to give?"

Zayla blinked a few times at the bluntness of this woman before her. Heat burned across the back of her neck. Asking about someone else's crafting...well, it wasn't something one usually did in polite company. "That's a bold question," Zayla replied, trying to shrug off the sting.

All crafting—whether it was Nemora Nature crafting, Divus Blood crafting, Vagari Animal crafting, or Elu Moon crafting—was innate, but varied person to person. Some folks were simply more powerful than others. And all crafting demanded a price—like the bark that had immobilized Zayla's hand. Like the Hallr Nemora woman who had turned into stone. Some people could pay the price easier than others.

Zayla never really felt like she had much power at all, but then, she'd never really tried to access her full crafting abilities. Not when it lashed back so violently each time she tried.

"Well, yeah," Shadre replied with a shrug. "But we're going to be traveling together for a while, a few more nights at least. I need to know what I'm working with." She looked at Oryn. "You're from a sobsky offshoot, right? I've heard Dara Nemora can grow entire trees to spear through their attackers. If you can't, that's fine. I just need to know. And also—" Shadre raked her intense rust-colored gaze down Zayla's bare arms where lighter purple spots intertwined with darker leaves stood out against her mottled green-purple skin. "—since you're a hybrid Nemora, what can you do? Can you grow us a...I dunno, a giant tree-mushroom we could climb to see farther ahead?"

Of course Zayla couldn't. And she knew Oryn wouldn't use their crafting, not at the risk of revealing what they could do, but a small part of her didn't want to admit her weakness to someone so formidable. The woman had faced down at least a hundred suncreatures without so much as a blink. She tossed her Nature crafting around like it didn't backlash at all. Stacked up against Shadre, Zayla felt more useless than ever.

"As a hybrid Nemora, I can access both Dara and Myceli Groves to grow trees and mushrooms...and I can also access my smaller hybrid offshoot, bitterroot. The mushrooms I took from Myceli Grove got buried under the rock from that reptilian suncreature attack...but honestly, I don't even know if our crafting will work in here. I don't think there's even dirt under all this ash," she replied softly. To prove her point, she scooped up a handful of lifeless, desiccated ash and sifted it through her fingers. "Even if we had the seeds, I doubt we could grow trees here where everything's dead or corrupted."

She could sense Oryn getting uncomfortable beside her by the subtle shift of their weight. Zayla rested a gentle hand on their knee, and the tension eased. For being the most powerful crafter around, they certainly got awkward when the subject of crafting arose. It made Zayla's chest ache. They had to hide their markings under layers and layers of clothing. They couldn't use their powers like everyone else. They couldn't even talk about their crafting anymore, not when the elders of the sobsky offshoot had scolded Oryn so badly after the encounter with Lurri. And they'd only just met Shadre. Trust came slowly after that betrayal, and sometimes not at all.

"But I've seen Dara Nemora pull wood from their weaponry. Why can't you do that with your club?" Shadre pushed.

"It's treated, so I can't use it for my crafting," Zayla lied past the growing lump in her throat. She didn't like where this conversation was headed. She technically could use her club as a source, but...she wouldn't.

Not unless she desperately needed to, but she couldn't just say her crafting was going to kill her if she used it. Not out loud. Not to Shadre, regardless of the grain of trust they were building. So, she barreled onward. "It had to withstand mold since I recently walked through Myceli Grove. Damp air and such."

"Treated, hm?" A grin softened Shadre's features. "I once got involved with this sailor a few seasons back. Out on Imogen Sea, the only wood she had was her ship and it was treated to withstand the saltwater. Like your club. Her offshoot gifted her with this thick wooden spear. She could wield that thing like a bolt of lightning. That spear—and that woman—saved my ass more than once."

"I can't see you needing to be saved by anyone," Zayla said honestly.

Shadre grinned. "I wish you could've told Gyre that! She'd laugh until her ribs cracked." The woman caught her gaze, held it with an intensity that left Zayla breathless.

The thought of Shadre snuggling up with another woman, sailing on the high seas, made Zayla's chest tighten. *I like her.* The realization came unbidden in Zayla's mind. She quickly squelched the momentary giddiness. Now wasn't the time, and Shadre wasn't the woman. Not when Oryn distrusted her still.

"To answer your original question, even if I had the means…I just don't like using my crafting. It backlashes too often for me to be comfortable with it." Zayla's whisper filled the gentle silence that had fallen between them. "And Oryn has their darts, so they don't really need to use theirs either."

"Fair enough." Shadre shrugged as if the statement didn't faze her. She eyed the rising sun. "We should try to get some sleep."

"You first, sibling. You have to be well-rested to protect me," Zayla teased, giving Oryn a small grin.

Oryn gave a long-suffering sigh, but Zayla didn't miss the dimple forming in Oryn's cheek as they turned away. She patted her sibling on the shoulder, then left them to settle in.

"We both don't need to be awake, you know." Shadre scooted closer so they could talk quietly. Zayla's heart kicked up a beat. "I'll keep an eye out."

Zayla shook her head, willing her racing heart to slow. Why did this woman's nearness affect her like this? "I need to stay awake. Just in case. It's what Oryn would do for me."

"They seem very protective of you," Shadre said after a moment. "That's good. It's good to have someone watching your back."

"Oryn always has." Zayla hugged her knees to her chin.

"Is that why you call each other siblings?" Shadre asked. "Or are you actually blood family?"

Zayla shook her head. "Oryn isn't blood family, though they might as well be after all the adventures we've had together. They've been looking after me since I was young."

Dawn's pink and yellow light slanted through the trees and settled on the gentle curves of Shadre's cheek. This close, Zayla noticed the tiny glint of a duskiron stud over her eyebrow. She wanted to know more about this powerful, enigmatic woman. "Have you always traveled alone?"

A hint of sadness crossed Shadre's eyes. "Mostly. I had a brief stint with the Knights. I got the chance to travel with one of their brigades, but their life wasn't for me."

"There's no shame in that. Not everyone is cut out to be a Moon Knight." The Knights were trained warriors, skilled in battle and hardened by the blood they spilled. They knew how to kill. Some even relished it. Zayla's people didn't. Her thoughts, as they so often did these nights, turned back to the coming war. Her troubled, distracted gaze fell to Oryn's sleeping form and the gentle rise and fall of their breath. The battle would force her sibling to join soon enough—to use their powerful crafting to aid in the war—and Zayla couldn't bear the idea of it. Her gut tightened with anxiety. "At least the Knights are in the front line, keeping everyone safe."

Bitterness flooded Zayla's mouth. They weren't keeping everyone safe, not really. There weren't enough Knights to guard the Nemora homelands, so it was up to the Nemora to guard themselves. That was why she had to kill the mirrorshards' natural bioluminescent light. Some Nemora joined the Knights out of necessity, but most of the people who lived in the Groves were peaceful—gentle caretakers of the lands itself, not fighters. Not bloodletters.

"Some people say the Moon Knights are losing," Shadre muttered.

Zayla snapped her gaze back to Shadre. "What?"

Shadre sighed. "The worshippers are already on the mainland and moving fast through the southeastern coast, traversing the Ravenlock Woods. I've heard a lot of people were killed already, and even more injured."

Zayla's skin prickled. "As soon as I finish walking the path, I plan to become a healer to help our people, mend those who are injured in the fight against the sun goddess worshippers and those who failed to hide from their wrath."

Myceli Grove was forced to hide, and Zayla knew from walking the path, other Groves chose to meld into the protective shadows as well. It wasn't fair that this war forced her gentle people into battle. The longer she thought on it, the stronger the never-ending hum inside her body became. Deeper, like the low growl of a pyrewolf and just as angry. She might not be able to fight, but she could take care of those left behind.

"That's a noble profession. I think we're going to need all the healers we can get." Shadre glanced around before continuing in a whispered tone, as if worried the suncreatures would hear. "I heard they already burned through Rok and Juu, and they were headed to Laidly Grove next. Some folks I met even said they already hit Northtown."

"Northtown!" Zayla went numb. Rok and Juu were southern cities that sparkled like the many riches they boasted. Laidly Grove was a stunning freshwater lake, home to the Laidly Nemora, a kind of standoffish group Zayla had the honor to meet during her walk.

But Northtown was in a northern territory. This territory. Her palms grew sweaty. Northtown was close to the Cinder Forest. Close to Myceli Grove. It seemed she had dimmed the mirrorshard mushrooms just in time... if she hadn't, the sun goddess worshippers would've followed them straight to the Myceli Nemora.

Shadre shivered, though the air was warm. "I know the Moon Knights will do their best to hold them off and defend our homelands but..."

They both sank into a restless quiet, not needing to say more. Shadre watched the now bright sky, fingering her lute in silence. Zayla toyed anxiously with the long strands of fabric hanging from her tunic, as her thoughts lingered on the war. If the sun goddess worshippers had taken Northtown, that meant they were close to Ratnaa Grove as well. The final Grove in her walk. She desperately wanted to get there to finish walking the path, but they could be walking right into the midst of a battle.

Will Ratnaa even be there when we arrive?

Chapter Seven

UNKNOWN SPORES FILLED ZAYLA'S lungs, pushing out all air as crimson eyes watched roots yank her beneath the ground. Flames crackled everywhere Zayla looked.

More than once, Oryn shook her awake from the nightmares. Finally, she stayed awake with the acrid scent of ash filling her nose and mouth.

The strange vibrations within her body grew more intense, as if they too wanted her to be alert. She stared at the dead branches and deep-blue sky above her, willing the awful sensation to end. She couldn't stand the constant hum. Just as no other Nemora survived when their offshoot perished, no other Nemora felt the odd vibrations. Every time the hum increased, she felt even more of a freak, at odds with her people. More alone.

Her primary Groves, Dara and Myceli, branded her a pariah when she attempted to return to them. Apparently, hybrids like her weren't welcome there. Gritting her teeth, she ignored the sensation the best she could. Though it felt like her bones would shake right out of her skin.

Finally, she'd had enough and rose. Even with the sun descending toward the horizon, her skin burned. Beads of sweat trickled down her brow. Her body ached from last night's hard trek, but she knew they'd have to walk even farther tonight.

When she adjusted her tunic, she discovered it no longer sat right on her body. The nox all young Nemora went through had changed her form during sleep, shifting her body toward male rather than female. The curve of her breasts no longer held the tunic as it should. Instead, her broad shoulders felt like they might tear through the fabric. She ran her fingers over her sharp chin and down her muscular chest, not even needing to check under her pants to know her genitals had changed as well. The uncomfortable press of the lump between her legs told her as much.

"Of course, this would happen here," she murmured, tucking her now baggy tunic into her belt, so it fit better over her flat chest. Her throat tightened with a wave of disappointment she always felt when the nox shifted her form to male. She hated this part of the nox, presenting as male, even if it was only a few nights before she'd return to her desired form once more. For other Nemora, the fluidity of genders was a blessing, an opportunity, a chance to figure out who they truly wanted to become at the end of their walk. Zayla, on the other hand, had chosen her form a long time ago. The nox just didn't listen.

"Pay it no mind, sibling. You're as radiant as ever." Oryn offered her a flask of clean water.

She ignored her sibling's outstretched hand and grumbled, "I just want this part to be over and done with."

"I know." Oryn set down the flask. "But Shadre and I know you're female. You don't need to feel uncomfortable around us."

Oryn was right—no one else was in the Cinder Forest with them, so no one could unwittingly misgender her, but Zayla didn't want to appear male, at all. She didn't even want to be nonbinary like her sibling... though nonbinary wouldn't feel nearly as uncomfortable as male.

"Damn nox." Shadre gave Zayla a pitying, albeit understanding, smile. She climbed up to the rim of the bowl they'd camped in, ash kicking up in clouds behind her. "You look like you need a moment. Let me check the perimeter."

Zayla was grateful for the privacy and the chance to pull herself together. Her hands tightened into white-knuckled fists on her lap. The first time she'd transitioned to male she'd burst into tears. Now, it just made her angry. "I just hate being seen as male."

Gentleness infused Oryn's voice. "Use the gender-clarifying flower I gave you; it might make you feel more...yourself?"

"Yeah, good idea." Digging into a pouch inside her bag, Zayla found the wooden pin Oryn had given her when she first experienced the nox. The carved flower petals looked more like a swirling cloud of vibrant, yellow-white smoke.

She pinned the flower to the breast of her tunic and breathed a little easier. The pin was a sign to others that, though she was young, she knew she was female and wanted to be known as such. Male Nemora going through the nox wore a single wooden leaf carved from purple-black wood, and nonbinary Nemora wore a white-blue circle of wooden roots. It was an easy way to know the pronouns the young Nemora wanted, and that simple definition lifted the weight from Zayla's shoulders. Even though no one was around, it just felt better to have her true identity clearly displayed on her person.

She closed her bag and lifted the flask from the hard ground. The warm water sluiced down her parched throat. After taking a long gulp, she handed it back to Oryn. "Thanks for reminding me."

Oryn ruffled Zayla's hair. "We're almost to Ratnaa Grove, sibling. Soon, you won't have to worry about the nox, ever again."

Zayla started to nod, but something unbidden intruded into her thoughts. Worry immediately churned her stomach. She filled Oryn in about what Shadre had said during the night watch, watching her sibling go paler with each word. She could almost hear Oryn's thoughts mirroring her own. *What if everyone's dead. What if—* An awful realization crossed Zayla's mind, one too horrible to say out loud, but this was Oryn. This was her sibling. She could tell them anything. "What if the Seventh Circle isn't around to give me my final token?"

A look of worry flitted through Oryn's eyes.

"If the Seventh Circle isn't around, we'll have a lot bigger problems to worry about, Zayla," Oryn replied quietly. "People are dying. We're in a war with the sun goddess worshippers."

"I know people are dying. And I know how selfish it is to think about my walk, but be honest, what can I really do about the war?" Guilt made her bones go cold and sharpened her tone. "My crafting is trying to kill me, Oryn. I can't do anything helpful until I go through my Choosing. You know that better than anyone."

Oryn shook their head. "I know you think—"

Zayla's voice pitched as anxiety clawed up her throat. "What if the sun goddess worshippers destroyed the sacred tree? I need that tree for the Choosing. I can't stand another moment of my crafting or another moment living within the nox. I have to choose."

Each of the seven Groves had a sacred tree, ones that had been around since before the Great Rift. Ancient Nymphs cared for and cultivated these trees that had survived the goddess sisters' wrath. The image of Myceli Grove's massive tree bloomed in Zayla's memory. Dark branches had reached like arms toward the sky, fingertips unfurling with multicolored leaves. After walking the path, the Nemora went through a Choosing Ritual within one of the seven Groves.

"Even if the sun goddess worshippers burned everything else in Ratnaa to the ground, it's unlikely they'd burn that tree. Their Nemora need the sacred trees as much as we all do." Oryn's tone was even and measured as they twined their fingers with Zayla's. "But suppose they did; they need to keep at least one sacred tree alive in order to survive, to keep having noxlings, to keep going through their Choosing, to keep nature itself in balance. One tree has to survive. You'll be able to complete your walk, I promise. In fact, Ingo Grove isn't that far south."

"Would they let me?" Doubt had Zayla pulling away and twirling the purple-amber ring on her finger. "Even though that's not the final stop of my walk?"

"It would be unconventional," Shadre's voice came from above them as she stood between two petrified trees.

Zayla started. She hadn't even heard the woman's approach. Her ears burned with embarrassment. Her confession to Oryn seemed even more selfish now.

The sun had dipped lower still, casting her in deep, yellow-pink light. Shadre put a hand on the duskiron flute at her hip. "But we Ingo are unconventional folk, I'm sure they could make an exception during a time of war. Besides, you're already unconventional."

Zayla stared at the woman. "How?"

"Well one, you're a hybrid, which already makes you unique, and two you're not ending your walk at Myceli or Dara. It would make the most sense for a Dara-Myceli Nemora to end in one of those Groves, right?" Shadre shrugged and gave her a half smile. "I mean, I ended in Ingo."

The words hit Zayla like spiked barbs, and tears pricked the backs of her eyes. Of course she'd want to complete her walk at Myceli or Dara.

But she couldn't.

Neither Grove would accept being her final stop. Since she was a hybrid, not full-blooded in either Grove, they thought she was tainted somehow. She pressed her fists against her eyes, refusing to think about it. The thick male knuckles felt unfamiliar and wrong, another reminder of how nothing about her walk was how it should be.

"Oh." Zayla hadn't heard Shadre slide down the bank before gentle hands touched hers, urging them back down to her lap.

Zayla opened her eyes to see Shadre at eye level with her.

"I'm sorry, I didn't mean to bring up a sore subject when you're already having a tough go at it. You can end your walk wherever you want."

"I will." Zayla swallowed hard to stop the tears. She didn't want to get into it with Shadre. *Not now, not tonight.* Not after the nox had already made her so uncomfortable in every way possible. She pushed herself to her feet and dusted the ash from her clothes. "Let's just go. The faster we get to Ratnaa Grove, the sooner we can see what we're dealing with."

Shadre led the way out of the hole, picking through the deeper ash piles in the darkened forest so their footsteps were muffled. Even though suncreatures normally slept through the night, the back of Zayla's neck prickled. The hum shifted restlessly within her. She eyed the bare trees. Thumbing their darts as they walked, even Oryn seemed to be on edge. Shadre paused every so often, lifting her hand to tell the siblings to stop. After a few moments of listening, she'd continue.

Zayla's vibrations coalesced just behind her breastbone at the same moment a roar thundered through the air. A second one answered. The sound seemed to come from everywhere, all at once. Terrified, she hunched down. Oryn squatted beside her.

Shadre put a finger to her lips and pointed ahead of them. She didn't look terribly shocked or scared, as if she had expected the horrifying sound. Bravery or recklessness, Zayla still couldn't tell which side the woman fell on.

Zayla's breath caught. In the twilight, she saw two large felines with forked tails stalking ahead of them. The creatures had to be longer than a four-person carriage. Sleek, white fur covered rippling muscles as the creatures sank low to the ground, their pointed ears flattened on their heads and their lips pulled back to reveal white fangs dripping crimson saliva. It took a few heartbeats to realize the feline suncreatures weren't stalking them, but tracked something Zayla couldn't see. A low rumbling rose from the suncreatures' throats.

Oryn tensed beside her, breathlessly silent.

Zayla's heartbeat felt like a pyerwolf thrashing against a cage inside her chest. Surely, the creatures could hear it. One of the suncreatures' ears flicked, and Zalya's palms slickened around the handle of her club. She didn't dare even breathe.

One moment.

Another.

An eternity.

A sudden pounce, long white claws extended, and a cacophony of hissing and growling and grunting ripped through the air. The other suncreature followed, and braying noises ricochetted through the dead trees. Finally, the mournful moan of death settled upon their prey. The forest fell silent, except for the snapping and crunching of bones.

Features calm as ever, Shadre motioned for them to follow her.

"Are you sunsick?" Oryn hissed.

The musician kept walking without paying them any attention.

Walking seemed like a crazy idea when suncreatures were so close, but staying also seemed ill-advised. The hunters seemed busy with their kill.

Now...or possibly never. Zayla rose first, pulling Oryn up and tiptoeing over to Shadre, then they all crept away from the twin suncreatures. Once the growling and bone snapping faded behind them, Zayla turned to Shadre. "Did you know those suncreatures were there before they growled?"

"Yup. They've been nearby since we started our hike tonight."

Oryn paled. "What? Why didn't you tell us?"

"They were pretty far away from us and upwind. They kept to the ground like we've been doing. Why do you think we haven't seen any other suncreatures nearby?" Shadre asked with a smirk. "Those two were clearing the path to Ratnaa, so I let them lead."

Oryn shook their head, muttering curses under their breath.

Shadre is reckless. Still, Zayla couldn't help but appreciate the unique approach to keeping them all safe. It had worked, as far as she was concerned. And worked well.

They continued their relentless trek through the dead forest. The woods got darker and darker as the sun set. Zayla's feet began to throb, and her shoulders ached from the weight of her pack. The vibrations within her made the aches feel even more pronounced. She twirled her ring, trying to distract herself, but something tugged on her mind. She followed the thread before it slipped away. She'd always tried to ignore the sensation or distract herself from the tingles beneath her skin, but they'd never been this centralized. This strong.

Maybe I should pay attention.

Maybe this time...maybe just this once, she should listen. Here in the Cinder Forest, surrounded by dead trees and graying grounds instead of vibrant natural life, might be the perfect time and place to open herself up to the curious feeling that had plagued her body ever since she could remember.

She let go of her ring, and focused on the strange, pulsing tremors ever present inside her. The feeling spread outward like spores. They settled in her left shoulder, down her left arm, into her hand and fingers, tugging toward the twin suncreatures they were skirting. Were the vibrations a way to detect nearby suncreatures?

Another concentration of vibrations stayed within her chest just behind her breastbone, as if hooked there, pulling her forward. Was there a suncreature ahead of them? There was nothing on the horizon, just an endless span of dead trees and ashy ground as far as the eye could see in the dark.

But she hadn't noticed the two feline-like suncreatures until they'd roared. *Shadre knew, though.*

Zayla picked up her pace. "Shadre, are there any more suncreatures ahead of us?"

Shadre cocked an eyebrow. "No. I wouldn't be leading us this way if there were suncreatures waiting for us ahead."

"You let those other suncreatures lead the way!" Oryn exclaimed.

Zayla smacked Oryn's arm. "It turned out to be helpful."

"It was crazy!"

"It was both." Shadre shrugged. "I get that, but I don't see any ahead of us. And normally they're sleeping now anyway, since it's nighttime. Speaking of which…" She pulled a daygem from her pack and activated the shard of crystal with a muttered word. Dim, white light banished some of the darkness away. "I figure we can use some light." She hooked the gem onto her pack as her eyes flicked to the empty sky overhead. "Just not too much."

Without waiting for a response, Shadre pulled ahead again.

Oryn shifted things around in their pack for a moment, pulled out two more daygems, and handed one to Zayla. One let out a soft pink light, the other a quiet purple. Standard daygems were pure white; creating other colors used up too much of an Elu's crafting abilities. Colors were rare. Expensive, even. Zayla looked at her sibling, who quietly explained, "These were gifts."

True dark soon settled on the Cinder Forest. Zayla couldn't even see the trees on the horizon, yet Shadre kept up her confident stride. She even pulled out her duskiron flute. Her beautiful soulful song wound through the trees, mingling with the soft breeze.

Though the notes were lovely, the song shivered down Zayla's spine. What if the music woke a suncreature? She picked up her pace. "Maybe you should stop playing? I'm worried a suncreature will hear."

A long, measured look speared right through Zayla, but Shadre tucked the flute away. "I wouldn't want to make you worry," she murmured with a small grin.

Zayla's skin prickled from the intense stare. She tore her gaze from Shadre's and motioned to the forest ahead of them. "How do you know where to go?"

Lifting the daygem, Shadre pointed to a nearby tree trunk. "See that?"

The tree looked no different than all the rest. Zayla shook her head. "I don't know what I'm supposed to be noticing."

"Look there." Shadre reached up and lifted Zayla's chin with a soft touch of a finger. The gentle nudge sent sparks through Zayla's body. She swallowed hard and tried not to make much of the simple gesture. She still saw only graying bark.

"I…I still don't see it. Whatever it is."

"Here." Shadre moved closer behind Zayla, stepping onto a boulder to align their heights, then wrapping an arm around Zayla's shoulders. Tilting Zayla's chin a little more, Shadre pointed with her other hand. The musician was so close, Zayla could feel the heat from her body. She noticed a soft scent of musk mixed with…something else…something earthy. And as much as she tried to ignore how it made her feel, as much as she willed it not to be so, Zayla's heart kicked up a notch. Her cheeks seared.

Focus on what the woman is showing you, not how she's making you feel. Zayla blinked a few times, then focused on the gray trunks.

Shadre moved the daygem a little, shifting the light until something glinted.

"What is that?" Zayla murmured.

Shadre chuckled. "A trail!"

The pieces clicked into place, and Zayla turned to find Shadre grinning, eyes crinkling at the sides. "That's how you know your way through the forest." Zayla smiled back.

"I left some duskiron pins jammed into the tree trunks when I came through here last. Immovable. Hard to see." Shadre's arm lingered on Zayla's shoulders like a comfortable pet lounging on its person. Zayla thought she saw a hint of darker gray on Shadre's silvery cheeks, but mischief simmered behind Shadre's eyes. "But for me, hard to miss."

Shadre winked, then unwound herself from Zayla and continued walking.

The woman's hips swayed in a mesmerizing rhythm, the moving grace of a dancer…or a predator. She had a confidence that sent another hard kick in Zayla's belly. *Not the place. Not the woman.* It had been a while since she'd been intimate with anyone, but not here. Not in the Cinder Forest. Not with a woman Oryn mistrusted. Not Shadre, even though it seemed from the curious glances and playful winks like she might feel the attraction as well.

Oryn stepped in close and knocked their shoulder with Zayla's arm. "Come on, sibling."

They both started after Shadre, matching her stride as they moved into a small ash-covered clearing. They'd nearly reached the center when the hum inside Zayla's body increased. It shifted to her right side, down her arm and her hand, to the very tips of her fingers, before zinging back up to her chest, and settling against her heart. Suddenly, she knew.

Something was coming toward them. Something fast.

She grabbed Oryn's arm and yelled for Shadre, "Shadre, wait! Something is—"

An enormous roar shook the ground, and fear sliced right to Zayla's core. Shadre jerked around and looked up, her eyes widening.

A massive suncreature flew out of the darkness and smashed into the ground, separating Zayla and Oryn from Shadre with its looming, hulking body. Light from the daygems barely reached the creature's snout in the air high above them, until the suncreature lowered its head and blinked two large crimson eyes at them. Its broken horns caught the light, and Zayla's heart nearly stopped.

The scaled suncreature from the cave had found them.

Oryn pushed ahead of Zayla, protecting her with their body, arms wide. They already had two darts out. Always ready no matter what.

Zayla harnessed her fear and nervous energy into action. Unhooking her club, she gripped it tight. This time, she wouldn't freeze. This time, she'd be helpful. This time, she'd be ready too.

Chapter Eight

HER HANDS SHOOK, GRIPPING her club as she stared up at the scaled suncreature. Her thoughts tumbled. Suncreatures usually slept the night away. The beasts were more powerful during the daylight. *Why is it out right now? Why is it still hunting us?* Her gaze skipped past the creature, frantically searching for a place to hide in the clearing. The empty ashy ground surrounding them offered little cover. The sparse tree line seemed ages away, and those dead trees would easily break under this creature's wrath.

The suncreature bellowed. A deeper roar immediately answered, and a high-pitched shriek came soon after.

To Zayla's horror, two more scaled, horned suncreatures landed beside the first, shaking the ground so much that she almost lost her balance. Similar in shape, though varying in size, the two new suncreatures snorted at one another before turning their gazes to Zayla and Oryn.

The first one—the largest—huffed a wave of acrid air onto Zayla, its breath so hot it felt like it singed her hair, then shifted its gaze behind it toward Shadre. The squat suncreature stared at Zayla, while the taller one, with a scar across its snout, locked eyes with Oryn.

Picking their prey, it seemed.

"Hide, Zayla," Oryn muttered, glaring daggers at the massive creatures towering above them. "I'll take out the suncreatures."

Oryn's sphere of pink light suddenly dimmed to nothing. They had extinguished their daygem, probably trying to hide in the darkness. *Good idea.* Zayla deactivated her purple daygem and let the darkness swallow her. *Let's hope these creatures can't see well in the dark.*

But there was nowhere to hide. Moonlight bathed the clearing in a gentle silvery glow, and she felt more exposed than ever in the once calming light. Zayla tightened her hands around her weapon. Her body was bigger and stronger in her masculine form, but she doubted she could defeat a suncreature. Her club looked like a mere twig against the scaled beast's massive hide. *If I'm useless this time, we could die.* The thought shivered down her spine.

On the other side of the clearing, Shadre yelled, sending Oryn into action. They flung their darts—one at their suncreature and one at Zayla's, trying to pull the attentions of both. Bursts of crimson blood hit the ground with a sizzle as each dart met its mark.

Letting out a ground-shaking roar, the squat suncreature slashed at Zayla with its long claws.

She leapt backward, using her club to protect her face. The impact shook her whole body. Shards splintered off the dense weapon as the suncreature's claws sliced wood right off her club. Her arm ached from the impact, but she maintained her grip. Thank every root and spore her club was made with the hardest darkwood around, or it would've shattered.

Another dart spun out of the darkness and landed with a sickening thunk into the creature's corded neck. It didn't seem to notice—or maybe didn't even care—and continued to stalk toward Zayla.

Fear pierced Zayla's body just like the dart had pierced the suncreature's scales. The strange hum echoed within her, and her crafting swelled, aching to answer the call. She almost reached for it, but a thought flashed into her mind. Suncreatures sometimes liked to play with their food before eating it. If she could hide, keep her distance but keep its attention, she might be able to distract it long enough for Shadre or Oryn to kill it. To do that, she had to move. She couldn't let her crafting immobilize her like it had her hand. Pushing her crafting down, she stumbled back, back, back away from the suncreature. *Hide,* Oryn had said. *Hide.* Every bone in her body told her to move, to run, to get away.

Spinning, she angled for the sparse trees far behind her, the only hiding place she could see and a far cry from perfect. She ran hard, still clutching her club. The spindly trees grew closer. She had to be sure the creature was still following her, so she glanced back.

In the moonlight, she could just see the squat beast. Crimson-yellow light poured out between its scales, creating a strange, shifting, fiery outline. The suncreature lowered itself, then surged toward her.

"No!" Oryn's strangled cry came from somewhere to her left.

Claws barely grazed Zayla's leg, sending a curve of bright-white pain through her and forcing her to her knee. The ground thudded as the other set of claws sank into the dirt beside her, sending a choking cloud of ash into the air.

Move. Do something, right now!

Choking on ash and blinking back tears, she swung her club down on the claws next to her, using every ounce of power in her body to smash the hardened wood directly onto the suncreature's claws. The impact sent a shuddering ache through her arms. In a sharp crack, the claw broke under her masculine strength.

But her club broke in half. Only the shattered handle remained in her shaking hands.

The suncreature yowled in pain.

She held onto that club handle for dear life, knowing it was the only living thing she had in this dead forest, the only living wood she could pull from to use her crafting if she desperately needed to. In this fight, and beyond.

The suncreature yanked its foot back, shaking it like it was trying to shake off the pain.

Pushing past the agony in her leg, Zayla took the moment of distraction to dart behind the widest dead tree she could see, one barely as wide as her. She pressed a thick palm on the slice on her leg, thankful that her now-male hands were wide enough to cover more of the wound. It oozed, but she gritted her teeth against the pain. Mercifully the cut wasn't deep, just long. Glancing around, she tried to spot the others, to find Oryn in the darkness. She could only see the terrifying fiery silhouettes of the suncreatures moving between the spindly trees. *Let Oryn and Shadre be okay.*

In the cover of darkness, she snuck away from her first tree and pressed herself against another. Her wide shoulders stuck out beyond the thin trunk, so she shifted to the side and prayed to every root and spore that the creature couldn't see her. Massive footsteps shook the ground. Her heart thundered, and her hands grew slick around her broken club. She tried to slow her breathing, but panic tightened around her chest and forced her to take short, quick gasps of air.

Fiery light flashed to her far left and far right between the trees. The suncreatures were hunting them. Zayla's skin prickled. The darkness was always so comforting, a protective shadow to hide in. Now, it felt just as terrifying as the daylight. *Why are these creatures hunting us now, at night? Could revenge have pushed them to do this?* Zayla didn't even know if the suncreatures could feel revenge...but it certainly seemed like they could right now.

A sudden crack and what sounded like the soft clatter of broken branches to her right startled her. She pressed her lips together to keep from yelping. A pair of large crimson eyes emerged from the clouds of churned up ash. They blinked almost lazily as the suncreature came closer and closer, looking this way and that.

A wave of hot, bitter air washed over Zayla. She froze. *Please, let it be blind in the dark.*

The suncreature's glowing crimson eyes locked onto hers.

No! They *could* see in the dark. Zayla activated her daygem, hoping the light would blind the creature since it was so close to her. Purple light sphered outward, illuminating a long snout and curled horns. Wide crimson eyes squinted in the sudden burst of light.

Zayla darted right, nearly stumbling from the flare of pain in her leg. She tried to circle around her tree, to put it between her and the suncreature. With a powerful swipe of its claws, it shattered the petrified wood. Zayla scampered left, frantically searching for a place to hide, but the remaining trees around her were useless. Some were only as wide as her wrist.

She ran.

And the suncreature followed.

Its claws got her again, raking a long gash on her arm. The force of the graze sent her crashing to her knees. Blood spilled down to her elbow and her hand went numb before beginning a slow aching throb that she knew would be agony later.

Panic caught in her throat, squeezed her lungs tight. *Think.* Shadre and Oryn were too far away to help. Running wasn't an option. Her club was a shattered handle, the splintered wood next to nothing against the thick, scaled hide of the beast. *What can I do?*

The suncreature circled her, playing with her like a pyrewolf pup with its prey.

At least she'd managed that much. At least she'd kept its eyes on her while Oryn and Shadre took out the other two. *I hope they killed the other two.*

An angry roar in the distance told her they were at least still fighting. Still alive.

A bloodcurdling scream turned Zayla's body to ice.

She watched the suncreature's movement, facing the beast down, trembling as her purple light caught the poofs of ash that spiraled up from each of its heavy footfalls. The others weren't coming to save her. Maybe they even needed saving themselves. She had to do something. Anything.

There was only one option left. It scared her even more than this suncreature did.

Zayla opened the tight cage she kept around her crafting and let her powers free. *I have to.* Her vision fogged over with amber light as her Nature crafting took hold. Because she was a hybrid Nemora, she had to pick which one she wanted to harness—Dara, Myceli, or bitterroot. She only had a piece of shattered, living wood at her disposal. She had only Dara.

A forest grew in her mind's eye; a canopy of bright-red spindly flowers; thick, crimson-purple trunks; and dark roots jutting deep in the soil. She'd visited one of her mothers' offshoots on her walk, a byriuu forest. The deep-purple leaf markings on her skin flared.

Responding to the crafting light, the suncreature rose up as if to lunge at her, opening its wings to their full, terrifying span.

Zayla remained focused. *I need a weapon*. Thick, crimson roots emerged from her broken club and sharpened into spear points. The hum swelled, as if anchoring her to the ground, keeping her steady. She met the suncreature mid-lunge, jabbing the side of its neck.

The suncreature shrieked and veered sideways. Blood sizzled on the ground. The beast landed with a loud thump and swung around, lashing out with its spiked tail.

A shield! Zayla willed the weapon to change again. The roots spiraled around and around.

The blow skidded harmlessly off her heavy, circular shield. The force had knocked her arm aside and sent the vibrations within her body into chaos, echoing the slam again and again. The sensation felt deeper than the warnings, more intense. This rampage was more terrifying, as if the ricochet of the energy inside her might make her explode.

She held onto her shield, readying her crafting for another onslaught. She had to save herself. Had to help the others…if she could.

The suncreature twisted its head to the side, opening its massive jaws. Long, white teeth and a glowing crimson maw filled Zayla's vision.

She yelped, transforming the roots of her shield into a bulky staff just in time and twirling it in a counterattack. The suncreature bit down, sinking the staff into the soft flesh of the upper and lower jaws. Two sharp teeth sank into Zayla's sides and she screamed at the stabbing pain, but the staff kept the bite from snapping her in two.

A roar boiled up out of the suncreature's throat and a waft of hot, pungent air blasted Zayla free. She landed hard on her back. Her skin burned and her ears rang. Her staff snapped in two, falling to the ground, and the suncreature reared back. It snapped its jaws a few times, huffing and snorting.

With no time to think, Zayla leapt to her feet and grabbed both pieces of her staff. The hum inside her body demanded her attention, threatening to shake her apart. Her teeth clattered in her skull. The world even seemed to wobble around her. Something was wrong. She could feel the sensation deep within her soul. She knew if she kept going—

My crafting is going to kill me.

Something thumped into her side, throwing her into the air. The suncreature's tail.

She landed several paces away with a hard crack to her head. The world darkened around the edges. Her power snapped away, concentration lost in the tumble. She grew weaker, faint, as blood poured from her wounds.

Thick bark erupted across her right shoulder, encasing her entire wounded arm down to her fingers in heavy crimson and freezing her joints. It was as if her whole arm was carved out of wood. *No!* Zayla panted and tried to stay conscious. Right now, at the most awful of moments, her Nature crafting lashed back at her. She had called on Dara—on the Grove of trees—and she would be consumed by them.

Her cheek seared where bark grew from it and completely covered one eye, making her partially blind. Panic surged. She clawed, uselessly, at the bark on her face with the fingers of her good hand. Her crafting demanded a toll of her body, and she could do nothing but pay. *Stop. Please stop.*

The transformation continued. Her hip, her leg, her torso. The bark squeezed so hard, she could barely breathe. She recalled the Hallr Nemora at the edge of the Cinder Forest, stone face forever frozen in determination.

My crafting is killing me. The realization thundered through her. Her heart thudded. Blood rushed through her ears. She writhed as splinters pushed through her lungs, like her bones were made of roots that wanted to burst from her flesh and sink into the ground.

She lay on her back, unable to move. Unable to think. Barely able to breathe. Waves of agony echoed inside her body.

The backlash finally slowed and settled into an oppressive weight that pinned her to the ground. Nature crafting forgave enough to keep her alive and aware. The vibrations within her finally settled, too, now a steady hum in her forehead, her chest, her toes.

The scaled suncreature loomed over her, its wings flared in triumph.

Its giant crimson eyes crinkled in the corners, as if it grinned at her.

All for nothing. The thought speared through her quicker than any blade. A sob escaped Zayla's lips.

Chapter Nine

ZAYLA REFUSED TO CLOSE her one good eye against the panic clawing at her. She wanted to be like Oryn, like her sibling. Calm like the eye of a storm.

But as the suncreature bore down on her where she lay helpless on the ground, fear sank deep into her bones. The predator finally had its prey. Crimson eyes locked onto hers. The unnatural beast opened its jaws horrifyingly wide. Its long fangs dripped with glowing, crimson saliva.

I'm going to die here.

A glint caught her peripheral vision. Tiny balls of metal tore into the suncreature's cheek and jaw like shrapnel, ripping the flesh before exploding in rapid succession. The creature shrieked and took several ground-shaking steps backward. A sickening stream of crimson-yellow blood leaked from its mouth.

"Oryn?" Zayla gasped. The bark on her cheek cracked as she craned her neck to see not Oryn running toward her, but Shadre.

The area brightened with white light as the woman skidded to a stop between the massive suncreature and Zayla. Silvery hair flung to one side and revealed the keen, needlelike markings along Shadre's neck. Dark, burnished copper, her Nature crafting was clear for anyone to see. Her pack was gone, along with all her instruments. Her clothes were ripped, and fresh blood oozed from a gash in her side. She must've defeated her suncreature and, instead of fleeing to safety, had come back.

She's protecting me.

A surge of gratitude rushed through Zayla, followed quickly by a tickle of fear. Where was Oryn? She tried to move but the red bark sheath made it nearly impossible. Groaning in pain, she looked for her sibling. "Where's Oryn?"

Shadre had pulled out her hand axe. "Taking care of their suncreature. I don't know how many darts they have left, but they seem to be effective."

Darts? Why isn't Oryn using their powers? Her sibling must still be trying to hide their unique crafting from Shadre. Oryn's distrust ran deep, and for good reason, but these massive suncreatures warranted the risk.

Out of the darkness, beyond the daygem's glow, massive claws swiped at Shadre with terrifying speed. Zayla gasped, but Shadre ducked, letting the attack sail above her head. Holding her breath, Zayla watched the woman's Ingo markings burn brighter. Her hand axe glowed to match. She threw her weapon toward the suncreature. The axe hurtled through the air, growing thinner, bigger, and sharper with each rotation until a blade as large as a splitting maul neared its mark.

The suncreature shifted, blocking the blow against the hard scales on its shoulder. The weapon spun away into the darkness. As if laughing at them, the suncreature snorted. Blood still dripped from its wounded mouth.

"This one's tough." Shadre glanced at Zayla, the glow from her Nature crafting burning in her eyes. She breathed hard, exertion clear in the tight lines of her face. Blood trickled from her nose. "Can you move?"

Bracing her good arm on the ground, Zayla tried to sit up. White-hot pain rippled through her sides where the suncreature had bitten her. After a few agonizing moments, she was upright, legs still straight out before her. She stared at the red bark encasing her left leg, barely able to focus beyond the haze of pain. Some small part of her mind realized she was whimpering, as she tried to bring her good foot underneath her to stand.

"Okay, then." Shadre drew up to her full height, rolling her shoulders back. "Just keep at it and try to get away while I keep our friend busy."

The woman was short, but to Zayla, she seemed to stand taller than any mountain. Staring down a suncreature like that. Fearless, just like Oryn. Shadre seemed entirely unfazed that she had just lost her primary weapon. She pulled out a palm-sized duskiron hand drum Zayla hadn't noticed before. The instrument seemed to melt in Shadre's hand then reform into a lethal hand scythe with a blade as thin as paper.

"Come on, buddy," she said to the suncreature, "let's dance."

Shadre launched herself at the suncreature's side, narrowly avoiding its claws while slashing with her hand scythe. She carved a section of scales off its ribcage and kept moving past it.

The suncreature roared and spun toward Shadre, angling away from Zayla to hunt its new meal.

Zayla needed to move, immediately, while Shadre had it distracted. In a feat of strength only her now-male body could provide, she pushed past the screaming pain and shoved herself to her feet. One bark-covered hip and its leg jutted out at an awkward angle. Her arm hung uselessly at her side, but she remained upright, fighting the dizzying sway of the ground beneath her.

I need to keep moving. Squinting with her uncovered eye into the darkness, she saw a thick tree stump about fifty paces away. *If I can get behind that, maybe I'll be safe.* She took a deep breath and limped forward. Her good leg nearly buckled from pain, but she gritted her teeth and kept moving.

A large mass caught the edge of her daygem's light. She gasped and nearly lost her precarious balance as she braced for an attack.

Her daygem's purple light settled on a familiar scaled form with broken horns. A large duskiron spear jutted from its head. The creature's scales curled and bent inward as she watched it turn to ashes from the inside out. Zayla looked toward Shadre in awe. How much of her energy had she used up to kill this thing? It was a marvel that Shadre was still standing.

The light of Shadre's daygem darted around as the woman kept the other suncreature busy. She slashed in rapid succession at the creature's chest, sending scales flying. Crimson-yellow embers of blood splattered in the air. The beast slashed back, but Shadre miraculously parried its claws with her hand scythe. The suncreature spun and its spiked tail ripped across Shadre.

She crumbled. The suncreature lifted razor-sharp claws to strike a killing blow—

"No!" Zayla shouted. Her leg threatened to give out, but she caught herself before she fell. "Come get me, you sunsick thing."

The suncreature halted its attack and swung its massive snout away from the groaning woman on the ground. It cocked its head toward Zayla, as if surprised its first meal wasn't dead already. The beast roared its anger, spread its wings, and launched into the air, then dove right at Zayla.

There was nothing she could do. She had no weapon. She had no strength for crafting. She couldn't even move to get out of the way. Her body felt heavy, like she was entirely carved out of wood. The world grew fuzzy at the edges and started a slow spin around her.

"Zayla!" Oryn's yell sliced through the air.

A burst of howling wind screamed through the darkness, snatching the suncreature into its spiral. Another gust slammed the creature into the ground hard enough to leave a crater. The creature gave a terrible moan.

Zayla caught a glimpse of Shadre's shocked expression before Oryn skidded to a stop in front of her, blocking Shadre from view.

After one quick glance at Zayla, Oryn set their shoulders and faced down the suncreature.

Dread and awe churned in Zayla's stomach at what her sibling was about to do.

The creature had gotten to its feet and crawled out of the crater. It shook its wings, snarling at Oryn.

Oryn stepped a few paces forward with lifted hands. Their spiraled markings shone so bright it hurt to look at them.

The air around them answered.

Wind whipped around Oryn. The gust picked up ash, turning pure white as it spun. When Oryn pushed their hands toward the suncreature, the wind followed suit, spiraling into a terrible gale before capturing the suncreature in its whirling midst and lifting it off the ground again. The wind twisted and howled. The screaming wind muffled whatever sounds of pain the suncreature bellowed. The intense force tore the beast's wings off its body and continued spinning until the suncreature's limbs ripped free as well. Glowing blood gushed outward, making the ashy wind look like a tornado of fire.

Oryn lowered their hands, and the wind immediately died. An eerie silence filled the air, broken only by the thumps from bloody chunks of the scaled suncreature falling to the ground and quickly burning away to dark-gray ash.

Turning away from the gore, Oryn blinked their crafting away and returned to Zayla. Blood dripped from a fresh wound on Oryn's forehead that looked scarily deep. Their clothes were a shambled mess, torn and bloodied and not covering their markings at all. Thank every root and spore, only her and Shadre witnessed their fury.

Their fierce expression immediately gentled with a hand under Zayla's arm, holding her upright. "Are you okay?"

"Yes. Thank you, Oryn," Zayla managed. With the suncreature gone, her fear left only exhaustion in its wake. Tiredness seeped deep into her bones. "But Shadre—"

"The hells was that, Oryn?" Shadre stumbled over, clutching her side and gaping at Oryn. "You're a Gale Nemora and didn't think to tell me?"

Chapter Ten

THE WHOLE OF THE Cinder Forest looming around them held its breath along with Zayla. She had to know how Shadre would react to Oryn. Would she accept them as they were? Her gaze flicked between the pair.

Shock painted Shadre's features, as if she was insulted that Oryn hadn't revealed their crafting right from the start.

Oryn merely pressed their lips together, staring back as if made from stone.

"So?" Shadre snapped. She pressed a piece of spare cloth over the wound on her side, but it seemed like her disbelief—no, maybe even anger—Zayla couldn't quite tell—made Shadre forget about her injuries. Her outrage didn't stop the blood from immediately staining the cloth. "What do you have to say for yourself? You're a Gale Nemora!"

"I know what I am," Oryn replied, slow and soft. Their calm belied the power held within. They pressed a hand to their wounded forehead, blood oozing between their fingers. "But I don't talk about it."

"Don't talk about it?" Shadre's voice pitched with each word. "You're one of the most powerful Nemora to ever exist! Hells, you shouldn't even exist. My fathers told me bedtime stories about your kind. There hasn't been one of you since right after the Great Rift!"

There hadn't been a Gale Nemora since directly after the war between the goddess sisters. The natural world was decimated in the battle, scarred from the fires and unbalanced by the goddesses' wrath. Nature created powerful beings to help knit the world back together again.

Nodding, Oryn ticked them off one by one. "Gale to help the wind currents settle, Inferno to calm the raging fires, Firma to rebuild the ground, and Aqua to infuse the land and air with water and help things grow."

Zayla had heard the stories again and again, and still it shocked her that her found-family sibling had inherited the powers of one of those powerful beings.

"Those beings died off," Shadre whispered.

"Yes, but nature decided the winds are needed again." Oryn shrugged. "So here I am."

"Why are you hiding yourself instead of out there fighting?" Shadre scoffed. "We're losing, but you can kick those sun goddess worshippers' asses. You killed that suncreature in an instant." She pinned Oryn with her gaze. "Why not tell everyone? Give them some hope. Your very existence could turn the tides of war."

"It's...complicated." Oryn's eyes slid off Shadre and took in the darkness around them, always watching for the next attack. Though after that display of power, Zayla doubted any more suncreatures would come around soon.

"Complicated?" Shadre narrowed her eyes.

"My sibling was attacked." Zayla jumped in, feeling the need to complete the story when Oryn pressed their lips together once more. She knew Oryn would never bring it up. "When we were younger. Sun goddess worshippers snuck into their sobsky offshoot and tried to kill Oryn because of their unique crafting abilities. The elders demanded that Oryn keep a low profile, to hide who they really were for their own protection."

"Protection? It sure looked like you're capable of taking care of yourself, and probably the sobsky community too." Shadre stepped back and swayed a little with the movement. The blood from her side wounds had soaked through the cloth she held and now ran down one leg of her pants.

Oryn opened their mouth to respond, but Zayla said, "Look, I know this is fascinating, but you both need to sit down. I have to check your injuries."

"No." Oryn immediately put a hand on Zayla's arm. "We have to keep moving."

"What?" Zayla breathed. "I can hardly move, let alone walk, and Shadre looks like she's going to fall over."

"No, I'm not." Shadre stumbled over to retrieve her axe, visibly annoyed. "I'm perfectly fine."

"We have to leave this area," Oryn insisted.

The healer side of Zayla went into overdrive. "Moving when we're this injured isn't a good idea," she argued. "You both look like you need stitches, and so do I, probably." She glanced down at the crimson wood that covered her arm, abdomen, and leg. She didn't see any fresh blood dripping from her body like on the other two. Her body still ached, though, a steady throbbing beneath the wood. "Or at least time to rest."

Oryn held her gaze, worry swirling in their blue eyes. Her sibling licked their lips before muttering, "There were four that day the assassins attacked, Zayla, not three. I missed one. And now that I used my crafting so visibly, they'll have an easier time tracking me."

Howling wind. Three bodies crunching into the ground. Oryn bleeding out. Zayla blinked the memories away. "The elders...no, someone would've noticed."

"They didn't. One of them got away, and they've been actively hunting me ever since. That's why the elders wanted me to keep quiet, to hide my markings, to never use my crafting. That's why I left the sobsky offshoot to travel. Not to find rare books, but to keep moving so I'd be harder to track. I've been hunted every single moment since that attack. Including now."

"What?" Shock rippled through Zayla. "You never...why didn't you tell me?"

"If you knew, you might try to protect me, and I didn't want you to get hurt." Their eyes met Zayla's. For the first time, she saw fear. Not for their life, but for Zayla's. "And if there are any hunters nearby, I just put up a beacon for them to find me. So we have to move."

Shadre scowled. "How many people are after you?"

"The hunting parties used to be small—maybe two or three—but they got smarter. Now there are at least ten at a time." Oryn sighed and shook their head. "Just turn off the daygems, okay? We have to go. Right now."

Zayla turned off her daygem. Darkness consumed the trio. When Oryn looped their arm through hers and pulled her along, she did her best to keep up. Fiery pain shot up her side. She gasped and leaned on Oryn.

Shadre came up beside them, grunting. "But how could hunters possibly get here so quickly? We're in the middle of the Cinder Forest. I haven't seen anyone else in here, and I certainly haven't noticed anyone following us."

"I don't know," Oryn replied, voice thick with worry. "They always manage to find me."

A spike of panic spun Zayla's thoughts. She didn't know how injured her sibling was and didn't know how much of their crafting they'd used to kill the suncreature. All Zayla knew was that she'd be no help at all, and Shadre wouldn't either. They had to keep moving.

They stumbled through the darkness, using only the moonlight to see. The world was shades of gray and dripping with shadows. Zayla hoped, this time, it would hide them from whoever hunted Oryn. *People are hunting my sibling.* A vine lashed around her heart and squeezed.

They hadn't gone very far before Shadre's usually quick wit dimmed to groans, and Oryn breathed heavily. Zayla wrapped her arm under Shadre's shoulder and helped her limp along.

"Come on," Zayla whispered, her strides shortened by her stiffened leg. "A little farther."

While it seemed like the other two were fading, Zayla felt stronger. It took her a moment to realize the pain from her injuries had long since faded. Even the humming constantly inside her body had dulled. She decided not to overthink and be grateful for the reprieve as she helped support Shadre's ever-increasing weight. They reached a stony outcropping jutting from the ground. A small hole opened up beside the rock, and the moonlight revealed a cave beneath the stones.

A hiding spot. Thank every root and spore she'd spotted it.

Zayla didn't know how far they'd walked, slow as they all were, but it had to be far enough. "I think we left whatever it was behind," she whispered, gesturing to the hole. "Let's just rest here for a moment."

Shadre slipped into the cave first, searching for dangers. After a moment, she peeked out. "It's safe."

Oryn slipped into the cave, Zayla following close behind. Moonlight filtered through the opening, casting pale white light onto the rocks. The cave was surprisingly large, a wide, low area with unnaturally smooth stone walls. At the back of the cave, a small pile of burnt wood told her someone had camped there. A Hallr Nemora could move stone as easily as breathing. Zayla wondered if the petrified woman they had seen on the outskirts of the Cinder Forest had created this space.

Shadre and Oryn slumped against the wall on one side of the cave. Both were pale beneath their markings, eyes closed and breath heaving. *I have to help them.* The thought spurred Zayla on. Cursing her useless bark-covered arm, she fumbled with some supplies from her pack: clean cloth, a jar of sticky green poultice made from herbs and plantlife, some twine, and a bone needle. *How will I ever do this with one hand and nearly blind?* She didn't know, but she had to try. *But who should I tend to first?*

She needed more light but didn't want to alert anyone or anything nearby to their presence. She stuffed their packs into the small cave opening, closing them in, then activated a daygem. Pure, bright-white light filled the space. Both Oryn and Shadre winced, but Zayla felt something inside her unwind. It felt good to see again.

Then it was awful.

Shadre and Oryn looked worse than she'd thought. Blood stained half of Oryn's face and dripped from their jaw onto their shoulder. Fresh blood welled past Shadre's arms and crossed over her side. Head wounds were dangerous, but if the cuts to Shadre's side were deep enough it might already be too late. Zayla limped toward her, but the woman waved her away.

"These are just scratches," Shadre muttered, closing her eyes and leaning her head back against the stone. "Tend to Oryn; that head wound looks horrible."

"Don't be ridiculous. You're bleeding too much for them to be 'just scratches.'" Zayla had been training to be a healer for most of her life; she knew bad wounds when she saw them. Sitting in front of Shadre, Zayla angled her wooden leg so it wouldn't get in the way and used her wooden arm as a prop. It felt awkward, but at least it worked. Kind of. "Let me see."

The musician's purple tunic stuck to her skin, the normally bright-yellow trim now a dark brown. When Shadre lifted the torn fabric to just below her breasts, Zayla was immediately caught off guard at how well-toned Shadre's stomach was. Defined lines ran from rib cage to hip bones. The sight was terribly distracting, even covered in blood. Her cheeks burned, and she pressed her lips together, focusing on the three long, deep gashes on Shadre's side. The flesh around the edges was jagged, and blood flowed freely from each, creating bright trails over the darkened crust.

"I need to stitch these up." She realized too late that she wouldn't be able to thread the needle with her bark-covered hand. "Oryn, can you—"

"Here," Oryn interrupted, passing an already threaded needle toward her.

"Thanks." Zayla gave Shadre an apologetic look. "You'll need to hold the wound together while I stitch. And...it will hurt."

"Wait." Shadre unhooked a flask from her belt and took a long, deep swig. "It'll hurt less now."

Zayla set to work as Shadre pinched her wounds shut. The stitching process was as awkward and slow as Zayla feared. Trying to distract Shadre from the pain, she asked, "What kind of alcohol was that?"

"Mead." Shadre sucked in a breath between clenched teeth as the needle bit into her flesh. "Made from some hooded blazeflower I found on my travels mixed with shadowberries from up north. It's really quite goo—ouch!"

"Sorry, sorry," Zayla said. She moved the stitches a little farther from the edges of the wound. It was so terribly hard to judge distance with only one good eye. "Got too close there."

"I'd say." Shadre blew out a breath, then started coughing. Brown blood splattered onto the stone next to her.

Alarm rushed through Zayla, but Shadre quickly shook her head.

"It's fine," she said, hoarsely. "Really. That's just backlash from my crafting. Metal attacks my bloodstream, makes me nauseous. I'll cough up blood for a little while. Nothing I can't handle."

So Shadre really had used a lot of her crafting. *She protected me and suffered backlash for it. Now it's my turn to help her.* Zayla turned back to her stitching with more focus than ever.

"Thanks for saving me, by the way, distracting the suncreature like you did," Shadre said.

"You saved me first," Zayla replied.

"True, but you were mostly holding your own." Shadre took another swig from her flask. "I'll admit, I'm kind of hurt that you lied to me about not being able to use your club as a part of your Nature crafting...but I'm glad you had it."

Now Zayla's cheeks really did burn, both from the compliment and from being caught in her lie. "Like I said, I don't like using my crafting."

"Because it backlashes since you're still going through the nox." Shadre nodded, then sighed. "Your crafting is really intense. I don't remember mine being that violent. And to have it happen when you're in the middle of a fight with a suncreature! Such bad luck."

"It's not bad luck," Zayla murmured. She had the curious urge to tell this woman the truth. Shadre had saved her life, after all, had risked her own skin to protect Zayla. Had stood over her facing the suncreature. No one, aside from Oryn, had ever done that for her. And, just like when she decided to follow the urge to see what the vibrations within her body finally meant, she followed this urge as well.

"My offshoot was destroyed when I was an infant noxling," she whispered. "There was nothing left. I think my crafting lashes back so much because I should've died when all the other Nemora did, when my mothers did, when my entire offshoot did. Every other offshoot that was destroyed, whether by sun goddess worshipper attack, or suncreatures, or natural means, meant that all those Nemora perished as well. It's...abnormal...that I'm alive. It's why I wasn't really welcomed to end my walk at Dara or Myceli. I'm unnatural in their eyes. And I think my crafting wants to kill me to restore the balance."

The silence that followed her words felt so, so heavy. She hadn't said her thoughts out loud to anyone, save for Oryn, in many seasons. No one believed her. They thought she'd gone mad with her offshoot gone, so she stopped mentioning it. She lowered her head, not daring to meet Shadre's gaze while she finished stitching the wounds closed. When she grabbed the jar of green poultice, a gentle hand stopped her.

"That's amazing that you survived…and awful." Shadre's voice was surprisingly low and gentle. "Crafting must be terrifying. I'm sorry."

Her throat tightened. *Is Shadre mocking me?* When Zayla lifted her gaze, she only saw sadness in Shadre's expression. Not humor. Not disbelief. Not even wariness. Just sorrow. Zayla wanted to say thank you. She wanted to throw her arms around this woman and hold her tight. She wanted a good many things, but she couldn't properly hug Shadre with only one good arm, and she didn't trust her voice not to crack when expressing her gratitude.

So, she dabbed poultice over the stitched-up wounds. The fresh, herby scent filled the air around them.

"What is that stuff?" Shadre sniffed.

"A poultice made from pyrewolf claw ferns, starblossoms, and bulrock root," Zayla explained. "It'll help pull any toxins from the wounds. You'll have to change the wrap tomorrow, then keep the area clean and dry after that."

Since Zayla couldn't tie the bandage one-handed, Shadre took the cloth and covered her own wounds, then secured it with strips of longer cloth Zayla supplied. Lowering her ripped tunic, Shadre leaned back against the cave wall. "Thank you, Zayla. A healer and a badass fighter. Not a bad combo."

Shaking her head at the compliment, Zayla turned her attention to her sibling. Thank goodness the pair had sat close to one another, Zayla only had to shuffle over a little to get to Oryn's side and assess the damage. Her sibling had sagged against the cave wall with their eyes closed, breathing steady but shallow, fingers still held firmly over the gash in their head. They looked exhausted and vulnerable. Zayla couldn't remember a time when she'd seen Oryn like this.

When Zayla gently pried Oryn's fingers from their forehead, she discovered that the wound had crusted over a little on its own. Relief washed over her like a warm bath. She started to clean the wound. "You were lucky, Oryn," she murmured.

"Oh yes, I feel lucky," her sibling replied with a sarcastic bite, though their lips turned up at the corners.

Spreading a thick layer of the green poultice over the cloth, she pressed it against the gash. Oryn's crystal eyes flew open, darkening from the pain.

"Sorry, head wounds always bleed a lot, but this one isn't bad." Zayla cupped Oryn's cheek with her hand. They sagged once more, and worry flashed through Zayla, hot and bright. "Are you okay?"

"Fine, sibling. Just tired. I haven't used my crafting in a little while, and you could say I'm...winded."

Zayla chuckled at the terrible pun, then sobered.

"I shouldn't have come with you into the Cinder Forest, Zayla," they murmured. "I'm just bringing danger along when there's already enough around with the suncreatures."

"I'm glad you're here, Oryn, and I'm glad you told us about them," Zayla replied just as quietly. She squeezed their hand in a reassuring way. "We can keep watch and even help you if they try to attack us. You know how good of a fighter Shadre is."

Shadre chuckled, then coughed a bit more. "Yeah. I can take 'em."

Something in Oryn's gaze shifted, darkened. They seemed...sadder, and their gaze flickered down to their lap.

"Thank you, but I wouldn't want you two trying. I've had to kill a good many of the hunters just to keep myself safe. Even then, sometimes I wasn't fast enough," Oryn admitted. Each word seemed to carry so much weight, and their shoulders sank.

"What do you mean?" Zayla's breath caught. *What's happened to Oryn while I've been on walk?*

"Wherever I went for safety, the hunters would find me. They'd burn the area down, so I couldn't return," Oryn admitted, their lip trembling. "I tried to kill the hunters before they attacked. I tried to save the people who helped me from the inferno...but I couldn't save them all."

"Wyvern shit, Oryn, you've been through it," Shadre muttered, then coughed in a way that sounded like pebbles rattling inside a can.

Zayla's heart broke for her sibling, at the weight she knew they carried. She'd been worried that Oryn would have to fight at the frontlines during this war against the sun goddess worshippers. She hadn't known Oryn had been fighting this whole time. "I'm so sorry, sibling."

Oryn lifted their gaze with a sudden intake of breath. "No, I'm sorry. I was so worried about you, Zayla. I'm sorry I couldn't get to you sooner during that suncreature fight."

Zayla squeezed Oryn's hand again. "You came to my aid just in time."

"No, I didn't," Oryn said roughly. They looked past Zayla, a curious mix of emotions flitting through their eyes before finally landing on something Zayla could only describe as respect. "Thank you, Shadre. For taking care of Zayla when I couldn't. You have no idea how much that means to me."

"She was holding her own just fine, Oryn, but that's what groups do—they look after one another." Shadre waved the compliment away, though a curious expression swirled through her eyes. Shadre jabbed a finger at Oryn. "And you. You're not half bad, either." The smile in Shadre's voice caused a little glow in Zayla's belly. Finally, they were, kind of, getting along. "But it *would've* been good to know there are hunters..."

Zayla scooted back to rest on the other side of the cave wall. Oryn started saying how they needed to eat and drink and rest, but their voice sounded strangely far away. The strength Zayla had found earlier was quickly ebbing. Sleep now tugged at the edges of her mind. She needed to rest.

Her eyelids fluttered closed. Exhaustion from the day's walk, the intense battle, and the backlash of her crafting finally took hold. Before she could do anything to stop it, her consciousness slipped away like liquid through open fingers.

Chapter Eleven

THE SOFTEST BED OF moss comforted Zayla. No, not moss. The spongy material beneath her felt velvety, like a mushroom cap. She lolled her head to the side and opened her eyes. All she could see was gray sky and massive, flat-headed, dark-purple mushrooms on the horizon. Veincap fungus.

Just touching the veincap mushrooms made most people sick, but veincap fungus was her mother's offshoot of Myceli Grove, which meant Zayla was half veincap. These deadly mushrooms couldn't hurt her. Her current bed felt comfortable, familiar.

Yet something was off. Wrong. *How am I in a mushroom field?* The last thing she remembered was blood dripping down Oryn's face. The slashes on Shadre's side. A small cave. And people had been hunting Oryn...

I'm dreaming.

"I need to wake up," she murmured past sluggish lips.

As if in response to the sound, thick strings of white mycelia burst from the veincap mushroom beneath her, wrapping around her arms, legs, and chest. She gasped, struggling. More strands burst from the mushrooms around her and caught around her head and neck. Needle-sharp tips pierced her skin, diving beneath her flesh. A cold sensation flooded her, like ice running through her veins.

Not just a dream. A nightmare.

"No, no, no." Zayla's chest seized, and she struggled against the mycelia. "You can't keep me here!"

She tried to rip the strands away, but they only tightened their hold. More strands slithered onto her wrists and fingers. It felt as if all the mushrooms had grabbed onto her. Every single one of them had made a connection. The white mycelia pulled tight. The ones inside her froze. She couldn't move. Couldn't even speak.

I have to wake up. Please. Please let me wake up.

Multicolored specks of light rose from the fungi, filling the air. No, not light. Spores. Giant spores multiplied again and again and again. The cloud grew thick, so thick it pressed in all around her like smoke. A deep, earthy scent filled her nose, her mouth, her throat, before finally shoving into her lungs, suffocating her. It felt like her whole body, mind, and spirit were made of glowing mushroom spores.

Please. Wake up!

Zayla jolted awake with a gasp. Her eyes flew open. She jerked upright, immediately taking in her surroundings. Pure sunlight filtered in from the rocks partially covering the entrance. A rough, tan blanket lay pooled in her lap.

Oryn and Shadre startled at Zayla's sudden movement, looking up where they sat close to one another, obviously mid-conversation. Open flasks and several slices of bread sat between them.

"Sibling, you're awake!" Oryn exclaimed, though the words were quiet. Setting down a slice of half-eaten bread, Oryn stood and crossed the cave toward her.

Zayla blinked a few times. She expected to see a fight, to see Oryn and Shadre struggling with mycelium, just like she had been. She expected the nightmare to have bled into the real world. "I...I had a nightmare."

"Oh, Zayla, I'm sorry." Oryn scooted closer and put a hand on Zayla's cheek. "We were wondering when you were going to wake up, sibling." Their voice lowered still. "I was starting to get worried."

"Worried?" Zayla tilted her head. "Why? I was only asleep for a moment."

"A moment?" Shadre chuckled then shared a knowing glance with Oryn. "More like a night and half."

"What?" Shock jolted her. The dream had felt so quick.

"We didn't want to wake you after everything you did for us. Your crafting took so much out of you," Oryn explained while Shadre nodded. "We slept in shifts; I just woke up a little while ago."

Zayla pressed a hand into her hair, eyeing her companions. Color had come back into Shadre's silvery cheeks, and a fresh bandage covered Oryn's head wound. They both looked well-rested. They had even changed their clothes. Shadre wore a sleeveless, yellow tunic that clung to her curves and dark slacks tucked into thick boots. Oryn was buttoned up in a high-collared, long sleeved, gray jacket.

Oryn drank deeply from flask of water, then nudged the other flask to Zayla in a clear indication she should drink—which she did. The water felt like a cool spring against her parched throat. She really had been asleep for over a night.

"This was a great hiding spot, Zayla, especially after we moved the packs inside and I covered the opening with some rocks, so it looked a little more natural." Shadre gave her a grin. "But you did good."

The compliment warmed her like a hot drink, banishing some of the chill from the dream. "Thanks."

Zayla yawned, then rubbed her eyes with her thick fingers, still not used to the more masculine feel of them.

Wait. *My eyes.* It took her a moment to realize she could see out of both of them. She'd been so concerned for her sibling and Shadre she hadn't noticed that the bark covering her eye had crumbled away, and the wood covering her bare, muscular torso had as well. A quick lift of the blanket revealed two things—her pants were gone, and her leg was free of the crimson bark. Fresh skin covered her leg from hip to ankle—soft and slightly lighter purple than before. Most of her arm had been freed as well. Only her forearm remained covered in a thin layer of bark. She could use both hands again.

The gashes on her leg and her torso had healed. Shocked and confused, she ran a trembling hand down her muscular chest—idly wondering where her shirt had gone. She gently pressed on the area she knew that suncreature had torn open. No pain. No aching. No caked blood. Not even a scar remained. This had never happened before.

She gently touched the bark on her forearm. This wound had been deeper than all the rest. Perhaps it needed more time to heal?

She lifted her wide-eyed gaze to her sibling's.

Oryn's grin widened. "That's also why we didn't want to wake you. Your bark started to glow, and we didn't want to stop...whatever process was happening."

"More like beneath the bark. We could see glowing along the edges wherever it touched your skin," Shadre explained.

Zayla struggled to find words. While she was grateful most of her wounds had healed—in just a night and a half no less—this was just another sign she was odd, abnormal. She blew out a breath. "It's...this is not natural. Healing takes time and energy and...and stitches! I've never heard of a Nemora healing themselves like this. Only a Divus can heal people so fast. Blood crafting heals...not Nature."

"It's amazing, Zayla." Shadre rested a hand on Zayla's bare arm. Respect, and something else Zayla couldn't quite place, shimmered behind her eyes. "Not abnormal. Not strange. Amazing. You're amazing!"

Amazing. The word sank deep into Zayla's being. This strong, brave, stunning woman had called her amazing. She tucked the feeling away. Shadre's warm palm stayed on Zayla's arm, and the air between her and Zayla tightened.

"Actually..." Oryn began slowly, as if trying to recall a memory deep among many. "I've read about one or two Myceli Nemora healing themselves that fast in prior generations, kind of like mushrooms do."

Blinking suddenly, as if remembering Oryn was there, Shadre finally removed her hand. Zayla's skin still tingled with giddy awareness.

Turning her attention to her sibling, Zayla arched an eyebrow. "Why have I never heard about it then? I'm the Myceli Nemora here…or I'm half Myceli at least. Of all Nemora, I should've been one to learn about it during my studies."

"You didn't come with me when I visited the Athenaeum of the Ancients to learn the history of the Gale Nemora. I got to read all kinds of remarkable tomes there when I was a noxling," Oryn replied with a shrug, looking at Zayla with newfound curiosity. "What you can do is rare, Zayla, really rare."

"Oh." That was the only thing Zayla could think to say, still digesting the information. A rare power. Not an abnormal one, not a strange one…a rare, amazing power. Shadre's words warmed her to the very core, and Oryn's words only intensified the sensation.

The warmth was short-lived as breeze filtered in through the rocks covering the cave entrance, raising goosebumps on her bare skin. She rubbed her chest, trying to cover the silence. "So…um…where's my shirt?"

"It was ripped by the crimson bark. So were your pants." Oryn pointed to a pile of bloodied clothing, and Zayla recognized her dark pants poking out. Oryn rummaged through Zayla's bag. "Do you have any spare clothes?"

"Of course I do," Zayla replied, just as Oryn pulled out a simple green, sleeveless tunic and flowing cream-colored pants. A more masculine style since the nox demanded it. "Where's my—"

As if reading her mind, Oryn set her flower pin atop her new clothes, the one marking her as a female Nemora.

"Thanks, sibling." Zayla squeezed Oryn's hand.

"I'll give you some privacy." Shadre shifted some rocks away from the entrance of the cave. Light poured fully into the cave, brightening the space, pooling on the white walls and highlighting the way Shadre's silvery cheeks had flushed a dark brown. Shadre wiggled out, shoved the rocks back into place, then was gone.

"I think she likes you," Oryn commented, poking Zayla's side and grinning.

"Be quiet," Zayla hissed, a flush rising to her cheeks. She hadn't missed the friendly interactions between Shadre and Oryn, the simple acts of kindness they seemed to be showing each other. "You two seem to be getting along better."

"We've been talking," Oryn replied with a wry smirk. "She's certainly not my type, but she's also not as bad as I first assumed."

"Not as bad," Zayla repeated, matching her sibling's enigmatic smile. If Oryn approved of Shadre, and if they ever got out of the Cinder Forest...Zayla didn't let herself finish the thought, though she couldn't stop the giddy sensation inside her body. It had been a while since she'd felt this attracted to someone...and it certainly seemed like Shadre had felt the same pull. Even Oryn had noticed. Zayla pulled the pile of clothes toward her. "You give me some privacy, too, sibling."

Oryn's quiet chuckle filled the space as they turned around and busied themselves with putting the packs together, getting ready to resume the rest of their journey.

After a quick change into some fresh clothes that actually fit the sharp, angled planes of her masculine body, Zayla squeezed outside the cave, with Oryn following. Shadre sat on a boulder, getting her own gear together.

Zayla munched on a thick slab of bread covered with cheese and dried fish. Sunlight beat down on her bare arms. A bead of sweat trickled down her spine. The sun had already reached its apex, so now was technically the most dangerous time to be out. After some discussion, Oryn and Zayla decided that didn't matter much anymore. For some reason, the flying suncreatures had attacked at night, instead of during the day. If the three of them walked day and night, sleeping only in short bursts, they'd reach Ratnaa faster, and hopefully, stay ahead of any hunters.

Oryn stepped up beside her, plucking a bit of cheese off Zayla's bread to pop into their mouth. "I'll be right back. Ablution break before we head out." They wandered off, heading behind a nearby outcropping for some privacy.

After tightening the straps on her pack, Shadre gave Zayla a curious, lingering look.

Zayla met Shadre's inscrutable gaze, crunching on the last bite of her meal. "What is it?"

"Just musing on how different you look as a man," Shadre replied.

A boldness took over Zayla, making her arch her eyebrow. "Like what you see?"

Shadre made a face like she just bit into something sour. "Not really my style. You?"

"I prefer partners who are nonbinary or women." Zayla hoped Shadre didn't notice how her voice caught on the last word. While she was attracted to those two genders, she preferred women most. She'd never given men a second glance. "None of them had badass spears, though."

Shadre smirked. "I'm sure they were just as interesting as my pirate fling."

"Pirate?" Zayla cocked her head, loving how the smirk played on Shadre's lips. "You said she was a sailor."

"Did I? Must've been a slip of the tongue." Shadre winked. She kept Zayla's gaze a moment longer—just long enough for a burn to start on the back of Zayla's neck—then lifted her voice. "Oryn, you done yet?"

Oryn appeared around the rock, tightening their jacket. "Keep your voice down, Shadre. I'm glad to only just have met you a few nights ago. If I had to travel with you any earlier—or any other place besides the Cinder Forest—the hunters would've found me immediately."

Zayla's jovial attitude fell away. She glanced between the petrified trees, searching for any movement. "Have you noticed any sign of them in the time I was asleep?"

Oryn shook their head. "Not at all since we've entered the Cinder Forest."

"Maybe they use nature to track you, but they can't in here, since the forest is petrified?" Zayla offered, hope lifting her voice. That would be one of the few benefits to traveling through such a dangerous space.

"I haven't been able to figure out how they hunt me." Oryn rubbed the back of their neck. "But we need to keep moving. We have to get to Ratnaa so you can complete your walk."

Always thinking of others, her sibling. Zayla squeezed Oryn's shoulder, then turned to Shadre. "Can you guide the way from here?"

"I should be able to sense my pins from here." Shadre's brows furrowed as she concentrated on the duskiron pins that formed a path to Ratnaa. Shadre's eyes flicked to the right, as if anchoring to something, but when she started walking, her path angled to the left. "It's this way," she said.

The trio walked in silence for a little while, passing thick gray trees with spindly branches and rock spires that jutted into the sky like teeth. Every snap of a branch and swirl of ashes made Zayla suck in a breath. Behind every petrified tree and gray pile of stone, she expected an attack by suncreatures, worshippers, or even hunters.

But it was just the wind pulling dead branches from the trees and creating ash motes. The wind, and nothing else.

Oryn gave Shadre a sideways glance. "So…"

Shadre intertwined her fingers behind her head, looking skyward. "So. You were talking about your responsibilities."

It was a statement, not a question, as if they had spoken on this topic before. Well, Zayla *had* interrupted a conversation between them with her sudden waking. Not wanting to do it again, she remained quiet and kept a sharp eye around them while the pair chatted.

"Yes. This responsibility." Oryn said. They lifted their hands then clenched them. "Nature gifted me with this massive power, so I'll serve my people the best I can but…"

"But sometimes you'd rather be in a quiet cabin full of rare books, a crackling fire, and all the time in the world to read," Shadre replied.

Oryn's perfect night. Oryn must have spoken about this before for Shadre to be that specific. *I wonder what Shadre's perfect night would look like.*

When Oryn nodded, Shadre continued, "Well, what I was going to say before we were so rudely interrupted by someone startling awake—" She caught Zayla's gaze and winked again. The heat crept to Zayla's cheeks. "Is that you should be whoever you want to be."

Zayla smiled. It was nice to see Shadre being this way with Oryn. Encouraging. Hopeful. It made her admire the woman even more.

Oryn rolled their shoulders, as if working out a kink. "I can't, though. I have to save our people. I have to end the war. It's why I was created."

"Then after." Shadre knocked Oryn on the hip playfully. "After you save our people and after you end the war. Make that cozy cottage be your reward."

"Perhaps, it would be nice to have something to look forward to," Oryn replied.

They walked, and walked, and walked some more—passing by pale boulders and spindly trees over an endless horizon of ash—until night fell and dawn blushed pink on the horizon once more. They kept a steady pace, pausing only to drink water or nibble on some bread, but it seemed like all of them had energy to spare…or wanted to make up time. Every time Zayla caught Shadre's gaze, the musician would give her a playful, flirting smirk, and Zayla couldn't help but return the gesture. The only noise came from the soft footfalls of their boots as they traversed the ashy landscape. Even Oryn had relaxed; the tight line of their shoulders had eased.

"All right. We have about a night's travel left to Ratnaa Grove." Shadre turned to face them both. Her expression grew serious. "Listen, before we walk any more, I have something I need to tell you."

"What is—" Oryn's words were cut short by an arrow sunk deep into their leg. They doubled over in pain.

Gasping, Zayla's eyes widened. "Oryn!"

She was torn between rushing forward to help and locating the archer. Movement snagged her attention. A figure partially hidden behind a dead tree to their left had notched another arrow and taken aim. Straight at Oryn's heart.

Chapter Twelve

ZAYLA DIDN'T TAKE TIME to think. Her gaze followed the path of the arrow flying toward Oryn. Stepping in front of Oryn to block them with her body, she raised her bark-covered arm like a shield. The arrow sank into the crimson wood of her forearm. Splinters burst outward from the impact. The force made Zayla's arm collide with her chest, shoving air out of her lungs. The arrow's shaft quivered, the tip embedded into the bark, but there was no sharp jab of pain, even when Zayla grasped it with her other hand and yanked it free.

Oryn's shocked expression mirrored her own.

Before Zayla could react further, another figure rose up from the ashes. A third appeared from behind a rocky outcropping, just behind them. Slowly, more figures came into view. They were surrounded. Zayla counted at least ten dressed in loose layers of gray and crimson.

"Hunters," Oryn hissed through gritted teeth.

Chaos erupted in the Cinder Forest as all the hunters lunged at once. They moved in some horrible, choreographed dance.

Shifting to a defensive stance, Zayla stayed with Oryn while Shadre dashed out to meet the closest hunter. Her double-bladed hand axe melted and reformed into a short, metal polearm tipped with a thin, serrated blade. She sliced the hunter's legs, and dark blue blood splattered on the ground. An Elu, a Moon crafter. Without hesitation, Shadre thrust her blade into the hunter's neck.

Zayla's skin prickled. An Elu crafter could create a shield as easily as breathing; why hadn't that hunter? Shadre was fast, but not that fast.

Beside Zayla, Oryn lifted their hands, swirled markings burning with golden-brown light from their Nature crafting. Wind howled through the trees in reply. The wind buffeted the hunters back, keeping them at bay. Oryn flicked one of their darts, impaling a hunter in the forehead. Most of the other hunters bent lower and clawed at the wind, trying to reach Oryn. Two hunters stooped and clutched their stomachs. Their eyes bulged moments before they exploded in whirlwinds of flesh and brown blood, as if tornadoes had formed within their bodies. Oryn clenched their hands, and a third attacker stumbled, grasping his throat like he couldn't breathe.

Zayla knew that hunter would never breathe again.

A shift of movement caught her attention. The archer was readying another arrow. Zayla's crafting hummed within her, and she reached for it.

She had to. Oryn's life was in danger. A golden film immediately pulled over her vision, and her crafting thrummed, the strange vibrations echoing the power. She gripped the broken splinter that used to be her club. It was the only piece of living, untreated wood she had. She remembered the way the wood splintered off her arm when the arrow pierced the bark on her forearm, and focused her will on the broken fragment of her club.

Splinter and fly. The eyes.

Zayla's wood shot out and burrowed into the archer's face.

The hunter screamed, dropping her bow and tearing at her face with her hands.

Shadre's sharp yell of pain pulled Zayla's attention. Three hunters surrounded Shadre, clothes and hair whipping around in the wind. Shadre swung her polearm with deadly precision, but her side bled with a fresh injury. Two female hunters lunged for her with hooked scythes, another looped around to Shadre's back, unknown to her. He drew back his scythe, aiming for her spine. A kill slice.

Zayla's chest seized. "No!"

"No," Oryn shouted at the same moment and slammed the whirlwinds of flesh and blood into the hunter. The force shoved the man into a tree, impaling him on a limb.

Zayla watched Shadre parry one scythe and used the blunt end of the polearm to smack the weapon out of the hunter's hand. With an expert swing, she sliced the hunter's neck open, then turned to the second one.

Another hunter darted in from the right, heading for Oryn.

Zayla sprinted toward the woman.

The woman's crimson metal rapier glinted as she swung.

Zayla lifted the shard of wood just in time to stop the blade from reaching her face. The wood held firm, but the force from the blow shook Zayla's arm. Only the strength she gained from her masculine form kept her upright.

The woman sneered, her dark eyes glittering with malice. "You think a piece of flimsy wood will stop me?"

Zayla clenched her jaw. "Yes."

Impale. A tree branch grew in her mind's eye. The bark on her forearm suddenly jutted outward in a point and speared through the woman's throat.

As orange blood gushed from the wound, the hunter's eyes widened, and the sneer slipped from her lips. She gave a guttural moan, then dropped to the ground. Dead.

Yes! A vicious sense of pride ripped through Zayla, but an undercurrent of worry made her stomach flop. This hunter was a Vagari, an Animal crafter. They used their companions to attack. Where was the beast?

"Zayla!" Oryn shouted behind her, and Zayla spun. Somehow two hunters had grabbed her sibling and wrenched their arms out to the side. Oryn needed their hands to direct their wind.

But instead of sinking a blade through Oryn's chest or slitting their throat, the twin hunters wrapped something shiny onto both of Oryn's wrists and backed off.

The glow of Oryn's Nature crafting immediately vanished. The wind died down.

One of the hunters whistled, and the remaining three moved back a good twenty or thirty paces, picking their way through the dead bodies until they were out of range.

Zayla raced to Oryn's side, heart thudding against her chest. "Are you okay?"

Shadre backed up to them, keeping her eyes on the remaining hunters. "What happened?"

Oryn ignored them both, trying frantically to remove the wristbands. The crimson metal seemed to be fused onto Oryn's skin.

"What are these?" Oryn asked, their voice higher than usual. "What have you done to me?"

The hunters didn't move. One of them even grinned. It seemed like they were...waiting for something.

Oryn shook their head, back straightening. They lifted their hands, a wrinkle forming between their eyes as they concentrated.

Zayla expected wind to billow, ash to fill the air. She expected to see the hunters flying toward the sky, weapons ripped from their hands.

Oryn's eyes remained a clear, crystalized blue.

"Oh no," Shadre muttered, color draining from her silvery skin.

Had this been the hunters' plan all along? To get those cuffs onto Oryn? It explained why the hunters didn't use their crafting—to force Shadre and Zayla away from Oryn and allow a few hunters to slip by. Somehow the cuffs stopped Oryn from accessing their crafting.

Two flimsy pieces of metal had stopped one of the most powerful Nemora alive.

Another thought sank through Zayla cleanly as a knife. If the sun goddess worshippers who were attacking her homelands had these, everyone on the continent would be craftless. Defenseless.

Zayla breathed hard. *I have to protect my sibling. Now, more than ever.* The thought burned through her. Her crafting pulsed, flowing down her arms, into the bark covering her arm, over the broken club gripped tight in her fist. *I'll do whatever it takes to drive these hunters away.*

Before she could do more, a shock of pain vibrated through her head. The last thing she saw before darkness overtook her was Oryn's panicked expression.

Chapter Thirteen

A POUNDING IN ZAYLA'S head woke her. Her body felt heavy, weighted down, like she was waking up from a thousand season slumber. Swaying slightly, the pressure under her legs and back told her she was being carried by someone. Darkness pressed in all around her, but not a comforting black like the protective shadows of night. It felt more like she was being smothered. She cracked her eyes open but found only more darkness. Something covered her face, blinding her and pressing against her lips too, sealing them shut. Rough scratchy fabric had been wrapped tight around her ankles and wrists. A throbbing sensation at the back of her head pounded the memory into her thoughts. She'd been hit by the hunters. Hunters that were after Oryn.

Zayla's gut twisted. *What happened to Oryn? How did those cuffs take away their crafting? What are the hunters doing to Oryn right now?* She laced her shaking fingers together, needing something—anything—to do. She wished she could talk to Oryn, her heart ached with that need. *I have to do something.* When Zayla tried to move, all she managed was a shudder. Even though she'd just woken up, she felt exhausted. All her energy had drained away.

The grip under her shoulder and legs tightened. The swaying continued as the person who was holding her walked at a brisk pace. Her cheek was pressed against a fabric-covered chest, a heartbeat thumped frantically beneath her ear, and an earthy, nutty scent filled her nose. Her skin prickled in response. *Shadre? Thank every root and spore it's her.*

"Look, I don't think this is a good idea anymore." Shadre's voice vibrated against Zayla's cheek, briefly masking the frantic heartbeat. "Hells, I made a mistake."

What was she talking about?

"A mistake, she says!" Another voice seemed to echo Zayla's own confusion in a low, rumbling tone. The voice sounded close, like they were walking next to Shadre. "He's a Gale Nemora!"

"They," Shadre corrected softly.

Zayla held her breath. They were talking about her sibling. What was going on here?

"Him, they, it. Whatever." Annoyance filtered through the person's sour tone. "Fine, *they're* a Gale Nemora. *They're* the best thing you could've delivered, Shadre."

Confusion pulled through Zayla's mind. Shadre was talking to the hunters. They knew her name. Was Shadre... working with them? With a dagger's edge, that thought frayed Zayla's nerves. Shadre couldn't be working with the hunters, not after everything they'd been through, not after everything they'd done for one another. It couldn't be possible.

But how well do you actually know Shadre? A cruel voice that sounded kind of like Oryn's curled through her mind. *You've only just met her a few nights ago.*

Zayla's gut writhed. Shadre was a fearless woman who'd faced down suncreatures, who patted one on the sunsick snout, who had saved both her and Oryn's lives multiple times. Zayla might not know a lot about Shadre's background, but she felt like she knew *Shadre.* Knew her attitudes and actions. Knew her as a person. They'd grown close. Shadre would never betray a friend, especially like this.

Would she?

Laughter came from above her—Shadre and the hunter chuckling together. Talking idly, as if they'd spoken before. Had a history. It seemed like Shadre had led Oryn and Zayla directly to these people and, judging by their conversation, had formed an actual plan to do so.

Have I been wrong about Shadre all this time?

A sickening sensation wormed its way through her. Oryn's first thought, their first instinct to distrust Shadre, their attempts to keep her at arm's length, the warnings Zayla so easily dismissed...

Oryn was right.

Tears formed behind Zayla's eyes. Guilt twisted through her like a knife. She'd trusted someone she shouldn't have—and nurtured feelings for someone she shouldn't have. Worse still, she'd gotten her sibling captured. The very thing Oryn had been running from, fighting against, killing for, had come to pass. All because of Zayla's careless heart.

"Technically I *didn't* deliver the Gale Nemora to you," Shadre scoffed. "I went the other way. The damned hunters found us and sent word to you."

Shadre's companion isn't a hunter. The realization sent a chill through Zayla's body. The hunters wouldn't have left Oryn's side. Zayla remembered Oryn's story of how long and how hard the hunters had been tracking them. Surely the hunters were still around. So who was Shadre talking to?

The other voice chuckled. "Well, good thing we have ins with them as well, then, eh?"

After a moment of internal debate, Zayla decided to remain still and listen. She didn't know where Shadre's loyalties lay, but it was obvious she was in league with people who were after Oryn. She stayed as relaxed and limp as possible, listening to the conversation unfold around her.

"You have ins with everyone, Chip," Shadre's voice sounded light, but the frantic heartbeat beneath Zayla's ear hadn't slowed, despite what felt like an easy walking pace. "I don't like that they're here, you know, following us. My side still hurts from where one of their sunsick fighters slashed it open."

"Aw, you're doing just fine," the rumbling voice—Chip—said.

Something clapped close to Zayla's head. She was jostled as Shadre stumbled.

Shadre's arms tightened to keep Zayla steady. "Hells, Chip! What was that about? You nearly made me drop her."

"Let me carry him," Chip replied.

"Her, not him, Chip." Shadre huffed. "Come on, don't you see the flower on her tunic?"

"Fine, let me carry her," Chip pressed.

"No," Shadre almost growled. Her fingers dug into Zayla's shoulder. "I'll take her. You'll have your hands full with the Gale Nemora anyway. They're already putting up a fight."

And as hard as she tried not to, Zayla stiffened, and Shadre's arms tensed in response.

The world swayed more rapidly as Shadre picked up the pace, presumably to leave her present company behind. Breath fanned by Zayla's cheek. "Keep still, Zayla, it's better if they think you're unconscious. At least for now."

Unease roiled through Zayla's stomach. She didn't know where Shadre was taking her, but at least they were moving away from Chip. *She must be taking me someplace safe.* Zayla forced her hands to relax on her chest, her shoulders to slump, but nothing could stop the incessant pulse rushing through her ears.

"Good," Shadre whispered. The softness in Shadre's voice made bile rise in Zayla's throat. Even if she was taking Zayla to a safer location, the woman was working with people who were trying to hunt Oryn. She knew their names! It would take a lot of talking to explain that away.

Shadre fell silent, and honestly, Zayla was glad for it.

The air grew colder. Her skin prickled with goosebumps. The acrid scent of ash vanished, replaced by a mineral-like, earthy scent that reminded Zayla of a swamp. Shadre's footfalls made more sound here—

wherever they were. Instead of being padded by layers of ash, each footfall made a distinct crunching noise. Zayla wished she could take in her surroundings, if only to know how to escape later.

Shadre's gait lengthened and seemed to tilt downward.

Zayla began to count the woman's steps, both to see how far down they traveled and to give herself something to do. This mess was all her fault. She had to get Oryn out, with or without Shadre's help.

At twenty paces, Shadre turned left. Another fifty, she turned right. Straight for at least a hundred. Two hundred. Three hundred. Still heading downward. Shadre's heartbeat slowed the deeper they went. The gentle hum inside Zayla's body grew stronger, pulled to her left, then her right, then spread throughout her body. *Great.* Multiple suncreatures were nearby. As if she didn't have enough to deal with.

Shadre came to an abrupt halt. "We're here. I have to leave your blindfold on for now, but I'll get the other bindings off."

Where was here? Zayla couldn't ask past the rough cloth covering her mouth.

Shadre lowered her, sitting upright on the hard ground. Sharp rocks poked Zayla's clothing and jabbed her skin.

"There's a wall." Gentle fingers cupped the back of her head, twisting into her hair and guiding her back so she wouldn't smack into the surface behind her. Shadre's hand slipped away, allowing Zayla to lean back. "I'm going to take off your mouth gag now, and remove the ropes," Shadre said.

Soft fingers gently pulled the cloth off her lips, leaving the blindfold in place. Next, the bindings around Zayla's wrists and ankles loosened. Not enough to fall off, but enough that Zayla could easily slip free of them. She went to pull off her blindfold, but fingers caught her hand.

"Hold on," Shadre whispered, letting go.

Zayla waited. Surely this was part of Shadre's plan to explain her actions. They seemed far enough away from the hunters and Chip.

Footfalls crunched away from her. Something metallic clicked. "Okay. You can remove your blindfold now."

Zayla yanked the blindfold away, blinking at the sudden rush of flickering light. She wanted to ask where they were, how long she'd been out, where they took Oryn, what the plan was now that they were away from the others. The words died on her lips as she took in her surroundings.

She sat in a small, semi-circular room that glittered like a million multicolored stars. Smooth, solid gemstone surrounded her. The floor was a brilliant blue, the walls vibrant green. A crimson ceiling topped it all.

Pink-orange crystals held flaming torches that cast flickering light into the space. Shattered pieces of precious stones poked into her palms as she pushed herself to her feet. The whole place was made up of giant gemstones. The vivid colors were only broken up by veins of black rock and dirt—and the duskiron bars Shadre stood behind, looking at her with resignation in her eyes.

Zayla was numb. The woman wasn't trying to take her away from Chip and the others. She wasn't trying to bring Zayla someplace safe to talk things through. *Shadre imprisoned me.*

Shock pushed all other emotions away and forced Zayla to move closer to the bars. "How could you?"

Chapter Fourteen

ZAYLA WRAPPED HER HANDS around the bars of her cell, the duskiron cold against her thick, masculine fingers. A gemstone tunnel expanded beyond Shadre, tilting up into darkness. They'd come down that way, Zayla was sure of it. She held her breath, waiting for Shadre's reply.

"I mean…you did want me to take you to Ratnaa Grove," Shadre finally replied with a shrug.

"Don't be quippy," Zayla snapped, completely over the woman's nonchalant attitude. Her shock at her surroundings had worn off, replaced by a cold fury for the woman standing before her. Anger sharpened her next words. "You betrayed me. Betrayed us! You're working with the other side. With the hunters."

"Not the hunters," Shadre replied with a shake of her head. She pressed a hand to the bandages that wrapped around her side. "I didn't even know about them, remember?"

A sickening kind of vengeance pulsed through Zayla at the sight of Shadre's bandages. The hunters had slashed her, wounded her. *If only they'd done more.* "Then who are you working with? Certainly not me or Oryn."

A curious expression flitted across Shadre's features, disappointment or maybe sadness. When she finally spoke, her voice was soft. "Family."

Before Zayla could ask about what the hells kind of family would kidnap innocent people, footsteps crunched down the tunnel. A short, squat man with mottled pink and yellow skin stretched tight over a bald head sidled up beside Shadre. He had to be a reptilian Vagari with that kind of skin.

Shadre's expression hardened. She had said these people were her family…but he didn't look anything like her. A found family then, not by blood. Zayla knew how strong those bonds could be.

Worry prickled the back of Zayla's neck. Since the man was a Vagari, that meant he had a companion animal. She glanced around, but didn't see any creatures…though to be fair, reptilian creatures could easily blend in with their surroundings. It could be looking right at her, and she wouldn't even notice.

"Oryn?" The familiar rumbling voice snapped Zayla's attention back to the Vagari. *Chip.* Shorter then Shadre, Chip wore simple layers of gray and black-scaled armor. Many pouches lined his belt. Twisting his fingers down a thick, black beard, he looked at Shadre. "That the Gale Nemora's name, eh?"

Oh no. Zayla's eyes widened. She'd unknowingly given these strangers her sibling's name, but if Shadre was working with them, why hadn't she told them earlier?

Shadre pressed her lips into a thin line then turned to look at Chip, her expression slipping into a smug grin. "See?"

The man gave a slow nod in return.

Zayla didn't know what that interaction meant, but given everything that had transpired, it couldn't be good.

"Where is Oryn?" Zayla pressed closer to the bars, trying to see past her captors. The gemstone walls expanded farther, curving to the right and left, like the cave was a giant dome. If she craned her neck, she thought she saw another set of bars beside her, though the crystal wall blocked most of her view.

"They're not in here," Shadre replied.

"You think we'd put you in the same cell as the companion you're traveling with?" Chip chuckled. "Fat chance."

Zayla glared at him.

"Shadre here told us to keep you alive. She said you have valuable information." Chip narrowed his large oval eyes at her. "You already gave us their name, so that's a good start."

Zayla squared her shoulders and lifted her chin. She wouldn't give him any more information about her sibling.

Chip arched a dark, oily eyebrow. "Tell me everything about the Gale Nemora."

"Fat chance," Zayla retorted.

Shadre smirked.

Chip folded his muscular arms, the uncanny pink-yellow skin stretching across his forearms. "Sit with your smugness, then," he sneered. "We'll see how long that lasts." His gaze raked across her neck and arms, where the leaf-and-dot markings decorated her mottled skin. "Our boss might have some other uses for you anyway. Come on, Shadre, let's go talk to the Gale—no, to *Oryn*."

He clapped Shadre on the side and trundled up the gemstone tunnel. Shadre followed close behind, not even bothering to look at Zayla on the way out.

Zayla huffed, pulling against the bars to test their strength. Even with her masculine form, the bars didn't budge. She had to get out, had to help Oryn. And slap Shadre if given the chance. *But how can I escape?* She didn't have her pack, just the clothes on her back and the ropes from her bindings. They'd even taken her untreated wood, which meant accessing her Dara crafting was out of the question. She highly doubted any mushrooms grew among the vibrant crystals surrounding her.

Cold air pressed in on her, and she rubbed her arms to keep warm. The bark on her forearm had long since disintegrated—her wound completely healed—and she said a quick thanks to her crafting. Bad enough that she was captured, it would've been worse if she was still injured. She hoped Oryn's head wound was still doing okay after that fight. And that someone had bound their leg from the arrow wound.

But really, if she was hoping for anything, it was that she'd be able to see her sibling soon. Worry gnawed at her stomach, making her nauseous.

"Worrying does nothing," she muttered to herself. "Do something productive."

"I like the sound of that," a voice floated to her. It sounded close. Rougher, but female with a curious lilt that sounded almost musical.

Zayla clasped the bars once more. "Who's there?"

The scraping of boots filled the space. From Zayla's peripheral vision she could just see dark fingers wrap around the bars beside hers. A lock or two of curly black hair fell into view as the person inside leaned tight against the bars of their cell. "Name's Orenda Silverstone. I'm with a friend of mine—"

"I'm Misti Eildelmann. Who are you?" The interruption came from a high-pitched voice with a Northern accent that cut around the edges.

Those names tickled the edges of Zayla's memory. "My name's Zayla. Do I...know you two?"

"Zayla," the one with the Northern accent muttered. "I'm not sure. It's easier for me to remember faces than names."

Someone snapped their fingers. "Zayla! You're the one who was being chased by sun goddess worshippers in Wyrtig Grove."

The memory of flowers, vines, and shrubbery bloomed in Zayla's mind. The plants glowed bright under the night sky. She felt the slash of panic, of running, while a trio of sun goddess worshippers chased her down.

"And you—Orenda. You saved me that night." A dark-skinned Elu woman and two Divus had come along. They'd killed the worshippers chasing Zayla. She'd been male presenting then, too, and had been so scared, she'd cried in the Elu's arms.

"I did," Orenda replied. "Well, we did. It was a group effort."

"Are the two Divus with you?" Zayla asked.

"No, we parted ways for a bit back in Marion." Her voice took on a hint of sadness before she cleared her throat. "You gave me some leaves that you had said wouldn't hurt me. I've always wanted to ask…what did you mean by that?"

"I felt vines growing in your shoulder, and I knew they hurt you. The leaves I crafted were from the bryiuu forest." Zayla had been so scared back then, she'd crafted Orenda a few leaves from her mother's home offshoot—trees grown deep in Dara Grove and meant only for protection. She wished she could see Orenda's face. The woman had been so brave that night, a bravery Zayla wished she could emulate.

"Ah, for protection. I understand." Orenda's voice sounded like a smile.

"Did those leaves happen to be spiny and red?" the other woman asked.

"Yes, why?" Zayla replied.

"Then you gave me some as well. When we met at Ingo. You told me to find a Divus to help remove my pendant. Your voice is deeper than I remember."

"I'm male presenting right now," Zayla explained as the memory brightened. Misti was a Vagari woman with dual-colored eyes—one orange, one blue. Zayla remembered short brown hair and a burning white pendant around Misti's neck. She'd been brought in to Ingo, unconscious, when Zayla was doing her walk through that Grove. A sunkissed vulnix had watched over her.

"Your advice helped," Misti replied before quickly hurrying on. "You were just brought down here. Before they covered your eyes, did you see anything? A vulnix? Or a neades? Did you see a dark-skinned woman with horns?"

"No, sorry." Zayla frowned. "I was blindfolded ages ago. I didn't even see Ratnaa Grove as we walked through it."

"Ponuriah's ass!"

"Dylori's been rubbing off on you, Misti," the Elu muttered.

"We've been locked in here for nights, Ren. Multiple nights," Misti snapped, aggravation clear in the sharp edges of her voice. "If those sun goddess worshippers lay a single hand on Zora, I'm going to have more than foul language for them."

"Can't you sense your companion animal…and other animals, like the neades you mentioned?" Zayla asked slowly, trying not to make the woman any angrier. Neades were massive bovine-like creatures, with a thick stocky body, rippling muscles, thick fur, and a roar that could crack the very stone they stood on. Vagari could connect with the beasts in the world, could give and take life energy from them, could even command them. Their companion bonds were legendary, some even spanning continents.

"Of course I can sense Zora, and Dis, but Vagari communicate via touch, and these sunbaked idiots obviously won't let me close enough for that," Misti grumbled. The bars shook with a clanging noise, and Misti cursed again under her breath. "They're the only two natural beasts that I can sense, aside from a tiny blushtoe riding around in that man's pouch. The one who came down to talk to you."

That must be Chip's companion animal. Zayla had never seen a blushtoe before. "And you're sure it's gone with him?"

"Yes. It almost never leaves the man's side. All the other animals fled when the sun goddess worshippers attacked Ratnaa Grove, even the damned insects," Misti continued. "There's something about these sun goddess worshippers that drives the natural animals away. It must be some kind of device, because Zora and Dis wouldn't come close."

Zayla twisted the ring on her finger, again and again and again. The motion didn't help quell the anxiety rising within her. "They came prepared."

"Too prepared." Orenda sighed. "Why are you here?"

"I was walking the path through the Cinder Forest toward Ratnaa and discovered Shadre. I trusted her, but she isn't who she said she was." Zayla's throat tightened around the words, and tears prickled the backs of her eyes. *Not here. Not now.* She shoved the rising tide of feelings away.

"The woman who brought you down the tunnel?" Misti asked.

"That's her," Zayla replied. She hoped they wouldn't ask any more questions, thankful when Orenda changed the topic.

"Is it true your friend is a Gale Nemora?" she asked.

"My sibling," Zayla corrected, her stomach twisting with guilt again. "And yes, they are."

"Maybe a Gale Nemora isn't as powerful as—"

"Oryn is everything you think of when you imagine a Gale Nemora...powerful...deadly...a true crafter, but the hunters bound my sibling with some device that nullified their powers. We were captured, and now I'm here talking to you." A surge of protectiveness had overtaken her. She'd get Oryn out of this. She had to. Until then, she'd defend them.

Silence followed her words, like a slow, spreading fog seeping into every crack of their crystal chamber.

"Gods. A nullifier. How awful." Orenda sounded subdued.

"I know." Zayla didn't want to imagine the terrible things the sun goddess worshippers could do with something as powerful as that. "What are you two doing in Ratnaa?"

"My goddess told me there's a moon goddess shard here," Orenda said simply.

Shock pulled Zayla's spine straight. "I thought they were a myth," she whispered. "The shards, not the gods," she corrected. Obviously, the deities existed, and in the presence of a holy woman who received commands from a literal goddess, she didn't want to be disrespectful.

Orenda chuckled. "The shards are much more than a myth. They're powerful artifacts from history, created when the goddess sisters battled. They're said to be imbued with the very forces that held the sisters together. Anyone who believes in the goddesses and wields their shards can only get immensely more powerful. Aluriah has tasked me with looking for her moon shards so we can better prepare for the coming battle. The journey guided me here...to Ratnaa. Misti's been traveling with me. We got here after the sun goddess worshippers took over. We probably should've turned back after seeing what they did—crystals shattered, scorch marks everywhere. Ruined enough to make a solid gods-damned point. They didn't like us poking around."

A rushing sound ran through Zayla's ears. The sun goddess worshippers had captured Ratnaa Grove. The Nemora knew the worshippers were after their Groves, but to hear it happen shook Zayla more than she cared to admit. The war was here. Now. All around her.

"I'm looking for my sister," Misti admitted quietly. "My goal isn't as important to the war as Orenda's quest, but she's been helping me for a while."

"With what she's become, finding your sister might be ridiculously important to the war, Misti," Orenda replied. "Don't downplay her role in what's happening."

Misti didn't reply, and Zayla had too many other things on her mind to ask for clarification.

"Did you see the sacred tree?" Zayla asked.

"Burned," Misti replied.

"Burned?" Zayla repeated, asking clarification on something that, somehow, she'd already known. Hearing it aloud as truth cut her deep to the core, severed something inside of her. Not because she couldn't complete her Choosing Ritual—but because of the Nemora who had defended and protected that tree and the history behind it. The Ratnaa people were kind and generous, always willing to give an extra meal or lend a hand. They were finders and caretakers of gemstones, minerals, and the like. Not warriors. She was almost afraid to ask the next question.

"Do you know where all the Ratnaa Nemora went?" She couldn't imagine any of them fighting back. A part of her hoped they had scattered before even thinking of picking up a weapon, but if their sacred tree was destroyed... "Did they all die?"

"No, though some were killed. And there were some in cages crafted aboveground—noxlings and adults. I'm not sure how many people lived here, but there wasn't much bloodshed. It seemed like a lot of them fled long before the fight got here," Orenda replied. "Or maybe hid?"

"They would've fled." A rush of sorrow filled Zayla, warring with relief. Her people had died at the hands of these sun goddess worshippers. The same worshippers who were tearing through the Groves, trying to capture and burn them to the ground. At least some of the Ratnaa Nemora had escaped. Maybe they'd gone to Ingo for help. A thread of worry pulled through her. "What are they doing with the young ones, the noxlings?"

"I overheard the sun goddess worshippers talking, when we were sneaking around," Misti said slowly. "It sounded like they needed to use the Ratnaa Nemora to find rare gemstones for them. They were forcing the older Nemora to find the crystals and killing the noxlings if they disobeyed."

A sickening wave of disgust swept through Zayla. How could Shadre be working with these people? Helping them? Bile rose in her throat. "That's horrible!"

Orenda and Misti must've had a few nights to digest the information because Misti just continued, her voice low and steady. "I only heard the colors when we passed them by, but they seem quite specific. White crystals that could be smoothed into orbs. A yellow-orange geode that sparkled with black dust. Any goddess shards that could be close by. I bet a season's worth of coin that even the adult Ratnaa Nemora are having trouble finding them."

A flash of memory burned within Zayla, of fear shimmering in Misti's eyes. "A white crystal orb like the one around your neck?"

"The one that *used* to be around my neck. And yes, I highly suspect that's the one. It can absorb life energy like a Divus and heal the wearer. Mine was unstable. A test."

An unstable gemstone that could steal life energy. Zayla leaned against the bars, feeling like her knees would buckle under the weight of all this information. "Do we know what the other gemstones are used for?"

"The goddess shards are obvious. The only gemstone they actually named was lazicon. It's a blue-green gemstone that I've gotten from the Ratnaa Nemora before, for one of my trading jobs, but I don't know its use." Zayla could hear the annoyance in Orenda's voice that she didn't have more information. "And I don't know what the other crystals and geodes might do, but—"

Zayla was about to ask why the Elu had suddenly paused, when the faint crunching of footsteps caught her attention. Someone was coming down the tunnel.

She pulled away from the bars and sat against the wall. It would be foolish to think the prisoners wouldn't talk to one another, but they didn't have to make it so obvious. A few scuffles from beyond the gemstone wall told her Orenda and Misti must've done the same.

Is it Shadre? A horrible bubble of hope swelled inside Zayla. Not that she wanted to see the woman—her heart hurt just at the thought of it— but she did want to talk to her, to ask her why she'd ever work with such ghastly people. Why did she call them family? A smaller more selfish part of her wanted to ask why she'd ever become Zayla's friend.

And why she seemed to want to become more.

The gentle looks, the flirty behavior, the soft touches. Was it just plain cruelty, a ruse to get Zayla to trust her? It must've been.

The footsteps grew louder, closer. Finally, a figure emerged from the dark tunnel and into the flickering light.

And Zayla's bubble burst.

Chapter Fifteen

A WILLOWY MAN STEPPED into the prison, moving with the fluid grace of a fighter. Belts of crimson leather studded with metal wound in a crisscross pattern over his entire body. They wrapped his chest, cinched his waist, and continued downward to clasp his cream-colored pants tight to his lower legs. The belts almost looked like chains around the man's body. One belt curling around his wrist had a crusty brown stain that looked like blood, and Zayla's body went cold at the sight.

The man drew closer. The umber skin of his bare shoulders and arms seemed to absorb the firelight. A white tattoo curved from atop his bald head and down his forehead to his cheeks, before disappearing under a brilliant crimson scarf covering the lower half of his face. Zayla couldn't see the entire design, but the flared circle of rays was obvious. *A sunburst to honor Ponuriah.*

The man gave her a gentle but low nod, and the circular sun design, that many sun goddess worshippers wore, glinted pale in the flickering light.

Zayla tilted her chin up, staring at the strange man. These sun goddess worshippers might've killed some of her people, imprisoned others, and forced nearly the entire Ratnaa Grove to flee... but she would not cower in their presence.

Lowering his scarf to rest around his neck, the man gave her an empty smile that matched his pale, empty eyes. Her stomach turned over. Something was decidedly off with this man. Something felt wrong, but she couldn't put her finger on what it was. Even this close, Zayla couldn't see any distinguishing features that would identify his kin—not the pink-scaled flesh of the Vagari, and certainly not the dots and leaves, like hers, of the Nemora. She didn't see any scars, so that probably ruled out Elu, unless he never used his crafting ability. Maybe Divus?

The man wrapped the long fingers of one hand around a prison bar, then tilted his head as if listening to something in the distance. He stayed silent. Too silent. Eerily silent. Fear dripped down Zayla's spine.

The man blinked, slow and sure and obviously waiting. His eyes locked onto the female-marking flower pinned to Zayla's tunic. *What does he want from me?* Perhaps merely to unnerve her, she didn't know, but she refused to give him any satisfaction.

It took every ounce of willpower not to fidget under this man's unwavering stare, but she waited as well.

"Hello." The man's voice was a mere whisper, like water sliding over rocks. "Chip and Shadre have been working under me for quite a few seasons now, delivering people to help our cause, but I must say, you and Oryn are the most interesting offerings we've had in a long time."

Unease coiled in her stomach. "Deliver people to you. Why?"

Again, the man waited several moments longer than necessary to reply, his pale eyes an abyss of emptiness. He seemed to cherish the moments of silence. "To glean information, mostly. We've been at war for numerous seasons now, and information is the most powerful tool we can utilize. Where the Moon Knights are stationed. Where exactly the Nemora Groves are located. How many Nemora live there, and what their defenses are like. Shadre and Chip usually deliver high powered people to us, t'zils of the Moon Knights, guards of royalty, and the like. Having a Gale Nemora in our hands is wonderful, of course, but you…well, Shadre mentioned you were unique as well, and I had to come see for myself. I haven't seen a hybrid Nemora in quite some time." His strange gaze raked over her markings, and Zayla shivered. "Dara and Myceli. Such a unique pairing. Your parents must have been very much in love to cross-hybridize like that. I'm surprised your precious nature even allowed the blend."

Zayla didn't rise to the jab, though the barb still stuck. Nature allowed hybrids to be created, but the lack of other bitterroot Nemora made her feel like an oddity all on her own. She certainly wouldn't tell this man her insecurities.

"Shadre thinks you know things about the Gale Nemora, but Chip's told me you don't want to talk. While I admire your loyalty, you're only as valuable as the information you provide." His pale eyes started to glow pure white, and Zayla's breath caught. *A Divus.* They were able to cause pain—able to kill—just by touch. "I could make you tell all." A slow, predatory smile curved his lips.

Instinctively, she stepped back from the bars, pulse racing in terror.

The glow faded from his eyes, and his smile faded as well. "But I have better places to expend my crafting, such as extracting information from the Gale Nemora themself." The soft, easy way he said those words slithered into Zayla's soul, and her hands started to tremble. She knew exactly how this man would *extract* information from her sibling. He continued, "They'll break, eventually, and tell us everything we need to know about the Nemora defenses. Then we can use them like the powerless pawn they are. I'm sure the Seventh Circle leaders would gladly trade a Grove in exchange for the most powerful Nemora around."

Trade? These worshippers didn't seem like the trading type, not when they were taking over the Groves by force. Zayla's gut clenched. Oryn was important, but the Seventh Circle leaders would see through that ruse in an instant. They'd do anything to save their Groves...but would that include sacrificing Oryn?

The man tightened his hold on the bars. "But since we're diving ever deeper into the cave ruins soon, the Nemora might need more motivation. That motivation can be you."

Misti's words came back in a rush, and Zayla's mouth went dry. They were killing noxlings to force the older Nemora to do their bidding. Zayla was still a noxling herself, the perfect tool for this man's sunsick endeavors. Her whole body began to tremble, and her crafting rose to answer her anxiety. A warm vibration spread from her core to the very tips of her fingers. The sensation gave her the courage to speak. "You can kill as many of us as you'd like, but you won't win this war. Nature overtakes everything and everyone, even you."

The Divus man grinned, showing yellowing teeth, unnaturally sharpened yellowing teeth, like he'd filed them down somehow. Why in all the wyvern shit would anyone want to do that?

"Not if we burn everything with Ponuriah's cleansing fire first," he said.

He inclined his head to the cell next to her where Orenda and Misti were imprisoned, then strolled back up the tunnel and finally disappeared from view. Only after the steady crunch of his footsteps faded completely did Zayla exhale and press a trembling hand to her forehead. That Divus was terrifying.

"We need to get out of here," Zayla muttered. *I need to get Oryn out.* "Misti, Orenda, have you two tried to escape?"

"Obviously," Orenda grunted. "I knocked out a guard, but that was useless since we can't break these bars. They're a strange kind of metal."

"Duskiron," Zayla supplied.

"Duskiron," Misti replied, slowly like testing the word on her tongue. "How do you know that?"

"Shadre..." The explanation died on her lips. Curse every root and spore; even *talking* about the woman made her feel awful. She forced the words out through trembling lips. "The woman who put me in here—she's an Ingo Nemora from a duskiron offshoot."

Wrapping her hands around the cold bars, she remembered how easily Shadre had created the barrier in the cave, keeping everyone safe for the day—until the suncreature burst through the rock wall behind them.

"She said that no one else from her offshoot has ever left. She's the only one." Zayla's voice dropped to a whisper, the realization like pouring acid on an open wound. Her hands tightened on the bars, knuckles turning pale. "Shadre created these cages. She's the only one who can easily alter them."

"She seems pretty lockstep with these people," Misti replied, her voice low as well.

Tears welled in Zayla's eyes, but she shoved her emotions down. Those feelings could stay locked away, trapped just like she'd been in her dreams. She could let them out later, when they were free of this place and Shadre's hold on her. Right now, she had to act. "Have you tried anything else?"

"I used my Animal crafting on the blushtoe to get his companion's set of keys, but Chip caught me, and he bragged that he doesn't have them anymore. Shadre only made one set, and now, only person who has them is Tor, the Divus who just left."

Tor. Zayla burned the name into her memory. "He seems like the one in charge. Is that true?"

"As far as we know, yeah," Orenda replied. "Gods, I can't imagine trying to steal the keys off him."

I can still try. Zayla pressed her forehead to the bars, letting the coolness of the metal ebb into her skin. The vibrant-blue crystal floor shimmered in the firelight. Tor and the other sun goddess worshippers were looking for gemstones. Going deeper into some cave ruins, he said. Curiosity sparked within her. "Do you know anything about the caves Tor mentioned? He said they were going to head deeper into them."

"Only that he called it Alastra," Orenda said.

"Alastra." Suddenly, Zayla was back in her room in the sobsky offshoot, studying for an upcoming exam covering the history of the ancients. The word was a key to a locked door that suddenly flung wide open. "Of course. Ratnaa Grove was formed on top of Alastra. It's an ancient underground city of our nymph ancestors. It's said to have an expansive, web-like network of tunnels that interconnect the buildings and structures, but nobody has used it in ages."

"Tor's been sending his guards down there this whole time. Now it makes sense that his people are getting so lost," Orenda muttered.

Misti scoffed. "Or that someone would want to hide something valuable in there."

Gemstones wouldn't help them escape. Zayla needed trees and mushrooms to do that. Her eyes riveted to the dark vein of dirt that ran across the walls beyond her duskiron bars. *Living dirt.* Another thought rapidly grew into something like a root pushing away from its trunk. She wished she could press her fingers into the dirt, feel for the life around her. The sun goddess worshippers might've burned Ratnaa in the battle, but they couldn't have injured the living nature below the dirt. The roots of trees. The mycelium of mushrooms. Surely...surely something had to have survived. If she could just get to the surface and touch the dirt there...if she could just find a tree or two to command. "If I can get outside, I might be able to free us," she whispered.

"How?" Shock flared behind Orenda's words.

"My Nature crafting," Zayla explained. She shrugged, forgetting momentarily that the others couldn't see her. "I have to try. Otherwise, I'm just motivation, and we all know what that means."

The silence that lingered after her words felt as thick as smoke.

Zayla continued, trying not to think about the consequences of failure. "I'll say that I can help them. Prove my worth by demonstrating my crafting. If I can just get outside, I'm sure I could command roots and mycelium to break us free. It's risky, I know, but I have to do something."

"Well, it's not like we have any other plans right now," Misti said, voice soft. "But you know, if they discover what you're doing, they could just kill you anyway."

"I know, but it won't come to that." Zayla infused as much confidence as she could into her words. The idea had already taken root in her mind, unshakable, even with the threat of death looming in front of her. "I'm going to get us out of here."

Chapter Sixteen

FOOTSTEPS JARRED ZAYLA AWAKE. Goosebumps prickled her skin, as cold ebbed into her back from the gemstone wall. Her thin tunic did next to nothing to keep her warm. Her clothes felt uncomfortable, the cloth a bit too tight across her chest. She glanced down, and a ripple of relief spread through her at the sight of her curved form and softened features. She was presenting as female once more. The nox must've shifted her form in her sleep. *Even here, in this horrible situation, the natural cycle of growth continues.*

They were so far underground, with no natural warmth or light. She didn't know how much time had passed since she dozed off. Firelight from the crystal torches glinted off the gemstone floor and walls. She pushed herself to her feet, clamping back a groan as her body ached at the movement.

The footsteps came closer. She hoped they belonged to Tor, or even Chip, so she could put her plan into motion. The faint, familiar jingle of instruments told her otherwise.

Shadre stepped out of the dark tunnel that led aboveground, a heavy bundle of blankets in her arms. Two flasks perched precariously atop the blankets, and a large, cloth bag hung low across her shoulder. A pan flute dangled off her hip, gently tapping the double-headed axe hooked onto her belt. On the other hip, two small, unlit lanterns bumped together.

Zayla hated how her gaze drifted to Shadre's toned arms. Hated the kick in her stomach at noticing that even carrying such a cumbersome load, the musician seemed to move with grace and ease. The firelight shimmered off her silvery skin. When her rust-orange eyes locked onto Zayla's, a blush crept up the back of Zayla's neck, and her body reacted, even when her mind screamed otherwise.

The woman was gorgeous—and a betrayer. Like Zayla's bitterroot or the veincap mushrooms, beautiful, but poisonous.

Shadre slipped two of the blankets and the two flasks through Misti and Orenda's bars. "I thought you all could use these. It gets cold in here at night."

"Took you long enough," Orenda muttered.

Shadre's lips thinned to a line. "Tor doesn't usually let his prisoners last long enough to need comforts like this."

Zayla didn't say a word as Shadre slipped the third blanket through her set of bars. Didn't blink as the musician tipped over her bag. A third flask and cloth-wrapped packages about the size of her palm thudded to the ground. Shadre pushed a couple of the bundles through Misti and Orenda's bars then shoved a few through Zayla's as well. A flask followed soon after. So many words clogged Zayla's throat, clawing at her tongue like a feral animal, but she couldn't force them out. It felt like her body was rimmed in ice.

Shadre didn't say anything to Zayla either.

Horribly, that silence felt like a dagger to Zayla's gut. Even after everything they'd been through, Shadre could simply ignore her.

Shadre carefully lit the two small lanterns and hooked them onto a rung in the duskiron bars—one in Misti and Orenda's cage and one in Zayla's. A curious purple flame flickered from inside. Zayla had never seen fire that color.

Eyes riveted to the purple flame, Shadre finally spoke. "Tor woke something in his exploration of the caves that attacked the explorers. These will ward against the creatures in the ruins."

"What kinds of creatures?" Misti asked, as if in mild curiosity. Hope flared in Zayla's chest. If there were creatures—natural beasts—perhaps Misti could call on them with her Animal crafting.

"I haven't seen them," Shadre paused. "But I heard reports that they're suncreatures, so they're no use to you."

Zayla's hope winked out.

"Suncreatures don't normally attack worshippers of Ponuriah," Misti said evenly. "Why are they attacking your people?"

Shadre ran a thumb down her axe. "These are different. Volatile."

"Perhaps they're reacting to the device you're using to drive the natural beasts away. Perhaps you're *making* them volatile," Misti commented softly, with more venom in her tone than Zayla expected.

Shadre narrowed her eyes. "And perhaps I should take away your lantern, Eildelmann. See how you fare against them."

No! Zayla couldn't let that happen. They were already trapped in these cells; she didn't want to see what would happen if suncreatures tried to attack them. "Why aren't you carrying a lit lantern?" she blurted, trying to take the heat off Misti.

"There are some lanterns by the openings, so we don't need to carry them around. These are just a precaution." Shadre kept her eyes on Misti and Orenda's space. "I put one by Oryn's cage as well."

Zayla scoffed. "I understand why you'd want Oryn alive. They're the most powerful Nemora in the world. Your people could use that power—power even beyond whatever you're trying to find in the ruins, but why do you care if I get attacked? Or Misti and Orenda, for that matter. Curse every root and spore, why would you bother giving us anything?"

The purple firelight lit up Shadre's soft features, dancing in her eyes and gleaming on the sharp Ingo markings that decorated her throat. She didn't answer. Still didn't even look Zayla's way. She opened her mouth to speak, then clamped it shut again, pressing her lips tightly together as if wanting to keep the words at bay.

Anger kindled inside Zayla, heating up her core. "You have to keep us alive so your... your *family* can use us as motivation aboveground, right? Take over homes. Destroy lives. Some family you have, Shadre." Zayla spit out the sour words. Her throat tightened with each syllable, but she had to know. "How could you ever associate yourself with these people?"

For a long moment, Shadre didn't say anything. Her gaze flicked to the duskiron bars, then finally locked with Zayla's. The answer came in a quiet voice, so low Zayla almost had to lean in to hear. "They saved me, Zayla."

A chill rippled down Zayla's spine. That wasn't what she'd expected to hear at all. The sun goddess worshippers were murderers, not saviors. "Saved you? How? From what?" The words tumbled from her.

"From a lifetime of bad decisions." Shadre sighed. "I'm banished from Ingo Grove."

"Banished?" A chill passed through Zayla. Shadre must've done something horrible. Banishment was a sentence only reserved for criminals who couldn't return for pain of death because of a crime they'd committed. Word traveled fast, so if Ingo banished Shadre, then likely Ratnaa, Dara, Myceli...all the other Groves would as well. Most of the time, the offshoots wouldn't even allow the Nemora back in. Zayla had even heard that if the banishment was strict enough, all the other cities on the continent would follow suit. There would be nowhere for the banished one to go. A lifetime in the deadly wilds of nature teeming with suncreatures and sun goddess worshippers was a death sentence, but only for those who deserved it. She pressed closer to the bars, a sickening sense of curiosity winding through her. "What did you do?"

"It's a story," Shadre muttered. "A long one."

"I have time," Zayla replied coolly.

"So you do." Shadre hooked her thumb through her belt, her eyes going distant. The lanternlight flickered its strange hue against her silvery skin. Finally, she took a deep breath. "After finishing my walk of the path and officially leaving my home at the duskiron offshoot, I tried being a Moon Knight and didn't enjoy it. After that, I connected with a group of musicians. They became my friends. We traveled together, performed in taverns, bars, outdoor venues. We called ourselves The Starless Ones. I was their primary flutist." A flicker of emotions danced through her eyes—joy, hope, nostalgia. She barked out a laugh. It sounded hollow and twisted her lips into a scowl. "My group weren't the people I thought they were. Thieves, the lot of them. When we got to Ingo Grove, I was the only Nemora in the troupe, so I vouched for them. Then, in midday when most of the city was sleeping, they tried to steal the Sphere—a relic in the center of the Grove."

Zayla had traveled through Ingo when she'd walked the path; she knew the exact relic Shadre was talking about. Twice the size of her head, formed entirely of a rare copper ore. Priceless. "Your friends weren't very bright to try to steal the most important artifact in the entire Grove."

Shadre shook her head. "They were bright enough to let me take the fall for it."

"How?" Zayla asked.

"I used daggers back then, and they used one to kill the three men guarding the Sphere. The Sphere was too heavy for them to carry, so the rest of my troupe ran while I took the brunt of the punishment. I tried to plead my case, but of course no one would listen to some wandering musician from the group who tried to steal the Sphere, even one who was originally from Ingo Grove. I'd vouched for the others and had duskiron daggers hanging off my belt." Shadre took a long breath and barreled on, like she had been wanting to tell this story for a long time. "None of the seven Groves would take me in anymore. None of the surrounding cities or offshoots outside the Groves would, either. I had a few awful seasons out in the wilds, being chased by suncreatures, hunted by other banished ones who wanted my supplies, and attacked by sun goddess worshippers." Her hand slipped off her belt to land on her hand axe as if on instinct. "I was young, past my Choosing, of course, but still naive. I didn't know how to survive in the wild. How to fight. I resorted to stealing food, supplies, clean water. Had to do some awful things. Hurt people to get away. I nearly died, Zayla. Multiple times."

Zayla wrapped her hands around the duskiron bars. She barely felt the cold anymore. Her anger had dissipated like fog burnt away by the sun. A smaller, shorter, younger Shadre smiled at her in her mind's eye. Filthy, hair tangled, stealing clean water from a nearby town. Struggling to survive because of crimes she didn't even commit. Zayla actually felt a pang of sorrow for Shadre. For the younger version of her.

She shoved that feeling under the thoughts of treachery. The woman before her didn't deserve her empathy. Not with everything she was willingly doing right now.

"Why did the sun goddess worshippers help you?" Zayla asked.

"Chip found me half-starved and trying to steal from his pack," Shadre replied. "He took pity on me. He'd been working for them as a sellsword mercenary. He convinced the sun goddess worshippers that I'd make a good addition to their group. The worshippers gave me a job to do, a roof over my head, hot meals every day, coin to last a lifetime, all the supplies I could want. They took care of me, Zayla. Saved me."

Saved her, or corrupted her? Possibly both. Zayla crossed her arms. "You do realize that you went from one bad situation to an even worse one, right?" Her voice was as hard as the gems surrounding her. "What did you think Tor was doing with the people you delivered to him?"

Shadre licked her lips, not meeting Zayla's eyes. "At first, Tor only needed people for information. I thought he was letting them go."

Disappointment washed over Zayla at Shadre's response, and anger flowed with it, like the ebb and crash of water. "You can't feign ignorance like that, Shadre. You just mentioned that folks don't usually last long here. And you know what they're doing aboveground. I think you just don't want to fully acknowledge what Tor is doing or jeopardize the coin, meals, or roof over your head. You've obviously made some terrible choices, Shadre, but I didn't think you were that oblivious."

Features hardening into a stoic mask, Shadre took a step back. "I'm not stupid, Zayla. I know what they are and what they're doing, but they gave me a place to belong when no one else would open their doors. They became my family—or the closest thing to a family I could ever have again."

Shadre's words had no inflection, no emotion. Calm like open waters, as if they were merely talking about the weather and not about working with a group of ruthless killers...and it annoyed the hells out of Zayla.

"No, they became your employer, Shadre. You said so yourself, they give you coin in exchange for a job. You *work* for them." Zayla pinned Shadre with her gaze, wanting her to see the truth. Wanting her to be the strong, intelligent woman Zayla had hoped she was when they first met. "You don't need to pledge some sick sense of loyalty just to keep a damned roof over your head."

"Hells, Zayla, I had nowhere else to go," Shadre said.

"Why didn't you try to go home, to your duskiron offshoot?" Zayla asked.

Shadre shook her head. "I didn't want to face them if they banished me."

"You could've pled your case there instead of getting wrapped up with sun goddess worshippers who literally murder people." Her stomach felt queasy as she thought of her own offshoot, of how much she'd give to go back home, even under Shadre's circumstances. "At least you have a home to go back to, Shadre."

Shadre sighed. "It was just easier if I didn't know what they'd think."

Coward. The thought jabbed Zayla's mind, as clear and sharp as broken glass. She clutched the bars tighter, words flying from her mouth like arrows. "But you didn't even try! No, you decided to run right into the arms of the enemy. Every night you stay with this group, every moment, every heartbeat you spend in their presence, doing what they ask, you're agreeing with what they're doing. *Everything* they're doing. Even the war on the Groves." With each word, Zayla's voice grew louder until she was shouting at Shadre. *Stupid stubborn sunsick woman.* Zayla's heart felt like it was cracking inside her chest. "You're on the wrong side of the war, Shadre, and I think you know that. You just don't want to jeopardize what you have in order to do what's right. And that's honestly more disappointing than everything else I've learned about you tonight. I thought you were the bravest person I'd ever met. I didn't realize you were actually a gods-damned coward."

Shadre blinked a few times, her eyes bright. Then she scowled and stalked out of the prison without another word.

Zayla shouted after her. "How could you do this to me and Oryn? We trusted you!"

No one replied, not even Orenda or Misti.

Zayla let go of the bars, her hands aching with how tightly she'd been holding them. Her whole body was trembling, but she didn't know when the shaking had started. Tears welled behind her eyes, and she blinked hard to keep them from falling. It felt like a gaping hole was slowly forming inside her chest, a void that sucked her inward, curling her up until her knees hit the hard gemstone floor. *Stupid stubborn sunsick woman.* The thought echoed in her mind, but this time, she didn't know if she was thinking about Shadre...or herself.

Chapter Seventeen

THE BREAD ZAYLA NIBBLED was stale, so she followed it up with a deep drink of water from the flask. Two more wrapped slices of bread sat on Zayla's lap—the last of what had been left during Shadre's visit. Zayla had wanted to reject the comforts out of principle, but eventually gave in out of necessity. *I need energy to escape. To put my plan into action and get us all out of here.* She tucked her knees under the thin blanket, grateful for the small bit of extra warmth. Soft snoring came from the adjoining cell, Orenda and Misti obviously satisfied with the scant meal.

She ate the second piece of bread. When her stomach growled, she sighed and unwrapped the third slice. *How long have I been down here, to be so hungry?*

When she shifted, the blanket gave off a nutty, earthy scent that reminded her of Shadre. *Was she even hurt when I called her a coward?* It certainly didn't seem like it. The scowl painted on Shadre's features had looked genuine. A hollow feeling grew in Zayla's chest. *How could I have been so wrong about her?*

Her gaze flicked to the dark dirt veining the walls opposite her cell, thinking of her plan. If she could just get her fingers into the fresh living soil aboveground, she could command mycelium and roots to burrow into this space and bend the duskiron bars, setting Orenda and Misti free. Then the three of them could find Oryn.

Before any of that could happen, she'd have to get out of this prison. It seemed like the only thing Tor cared about were the gemstones and goddess shards in the ruins. Surely just her saying she could help wouldn't be enough. He'd need proof.

Closing her eyes, she rested her head against the gemstone wall, letting the cold seep into her body. *How can I prove to be valuable? Crafting is the only thing I really have.* A part of her was proud that she was planning on using her crafting to set Misti and Orenda free, but she was also surprised. She'd never reached for her Nature crafting before walking the path and heading into the Cinder Forest, never wanted to draw nature's gaze to her. She feared retribution just for being alive, that her crafting would kill the sole survivor of her bitterroot offshoot, but ever since her crafting had healed her, a deeper, calmer, more centered part of her told her she shouldn't be frightened of her powers. Hells, even her nightmares had subsided.

Sighing, Zayla opened her eyes. She had to find a way to get on the other side of the sunsick duskiron bars and get aboveground.

Footsteps echoed down the darkened tunnel, and the snoring from Misti and Orenda's cell immediately stopped. A steady glow of a lantern's yellow flame flowed into view, the refraction of the firelight bouncing off the gemstones and brightening the prison area to near daytime. A female guard with brilliant blue eyes approached the cells and looked inside, as if satisfying herself that they were still occupied.

"Nice seeing you again," Orenda said, voice thick with sleep. "Must be daytime."

The woman didn't respond. Tucking her white cloak around her, she leaned on the gemstone wall in front of the prison bars, watching Zayla, Orenda, and Misti. The guard didn't seem fazed by the purple lanterns, and she didn't carry one herself, but she frowned at the bread and flask on Zayla's lap for a moment before shifting her gaze away to stare into nothingness.

Zayla rose. "I need to talk to Tor."

The guard ignored her.

"He's looking for a goddess shard in the ruins, right?" Zayla pressed. "I can help him find it."

A lie, but she just had to get aboveground.

The guard arched an eyebrow. She looked over her shoulder and bellowed, "Chip!"

A few moments later, Chip meandered down the tunnel, munching on a blue tuber the length of his forearm. "What?" he grumbled. "This better be good. We were eating."

A small reptilian creature about the size of the man's palm scurried out over his shoulder. With pink scales that turned crimson at the feet, it almost blended in with Chip's mottled skin. His blushtoe. Large yellow eyes took in the space in an almost frantic, panicked state. When Chip broke off a small piece of tuber, the creature snatched it and scurried over his shoulder again, out of sight.

The guard canted her head in Zayla's direction. "She says she can help Tor find the goddess shard."

Chip scratched his beard, then lumbered over to Zayla's cell. She sensed the power coiled within the short man. "Who says we're looking for goddess shards?"

"Don't play dumb." Zayla crossed her arms. "The Ratnaa Nemora can't seem to find what Tor is looking for, because the tunnels are confusing, but twists and turns won't matter to me."

Chip arched an eyebrow. "The Ratnaa Nemora live here. Why do you think you can do better than them?"

"Because goddess shards aren't naturally made gemstones." She frowned, daring him to contradict her. "They're shards of deities. Ratnaa Nemora are powerful; they can sense gemstones from great distances, but shards made from the essence of goddess sisters? That's something different entirely."

Chip scoffed. "And your crafting will find it?" His gaze raked over the dots and leaf markings on her skin. "Last I heard, Dara Nemora and Myceli Nemora weren't finders. They're growers."

"More growth happens below the dirt than above it," Zayla replied simply, hoping she'd figure something out once she could access her crafting aboveground.

"Prove it."

"Take me to Tor," Zayla pressed. "Let me prove it to him."

A cruel grin curled up Chip's lips. He snapped another bite off the tuber and, with blue mush dribbling from his mouth, muttered, "Fine. We need some new entertainment anyway."

Zayla suppressed a shudder, wondering what kind of entertainment they normally had.

Digging around in his pocket, he withdrew a duskiron key and unlocked Zayla's cell.

So, Chip actually does keep a key on him. Zayla tucked that information for later. If push came to shove, it would be far easier to steal something off Chip than Tor.

The guard pushed off the wall and stepped inside, gripping Zayla's arm hard enough that her mottled skin turned pale. Zayla gritted her teeth at the pain but didn't say a word. The guard bound Zayla's wrists in front of her with a length of rope, then slipped a cloth bag over her head.

As darkness encased her, Zayla's heart rate quickened, and her pulse pounded in her ears. Each breath drew the cloth against her mouth in a suffocating way, sending her back to her nightmares of being pulled under the dirt. She closed her eyes against the panic roiling within her and walked forward when the guard's hand yanked on her arm.

The guard led Zayla up the tunnel, turning this way and that. The further away she got from her prison, the more her body hummed. Suncreatures. She felt them around her from all directions. *Are they working with the sun goddess worshippers, or are they the creatures from the ruins?* Of course, she couldn't tell.

Eventually, the air warmed against her skin and the earthy, swamp scent she'd grown accustomed to faded into a different, yet familiar smell...smoke. Someone yanked the bag off her head. Sunlight speared Zayla's eyes. She winced. After living in the glow of firelight for so long, the midday sun was painful. After a few blinks, her eyes adjusted.

Her breath caught.

The Ratnaa Grove that lay bare before her was nothing more than chunks of blackened gemstones, and empty, open space. A single multicolored, crystal spire towered above them, but the matching ones lay broken on the ground. Fires smoldered on the wooden beds and tables inside homes, smoke clouding the sky like the whole Grove had been set aflame.

This...this was nothing like the paintings she'd seen of its crystalline towers, homes constructed of brilliant orange geodes, bustling markets to sell and trade their precious, multicolored jewels. The sun goddess worshippers had razed Ratnaa Grove entirely to the ground. Even the soil had been torched at such a high temperature that it had changed color to a charred yellow-red.

There's no life in this soil. The realization sent a chill down her spine. *But there has to be fresh, unscorched dirt deeper down. I have to go into the ruins.*

She could command the mycelium and roots from there...but how would she pinpoint where Misti and Orenda's cells were? Ratnaa Grove was built on top of the ruins, but she didn't know where the tunnels actually were in relation to the prison area. Worry constricted her lungs until her breaths came in short, shallow gasps.

"That's not even the best part," Chip muttered, motioning behind them.

Her gaze followed a charred root as it splintered behind her to a jagged, blackened stump, the only remnant of Ratnaa Grove's sacred tree. A slippery sense of disappointment threatened her resolve. Her walk ended here in Ratnaa Grove. She was supposed to complete her Choosing Ritual in the sacred Ratnaa Grove tree. Now, she'd never have that honor.

An even more horrific display stood nearby. Planks of burnt wood had been bound together to support silvery metal branches in a crude mockery of the sacred tree. From those branches hung nooses, tight around bruised necks.

Ten small bodies.

Ten young Nemora noxlings, faces swollen and black in death.

Lifeless bodies, swaying slightly in the breeze.

Bile rose in Zayla's throat, and she pressed her bound hands to her mouth, trying to keep the stale bread from rushing past her lips. She forced her gaze away, but the sight of the young noxlings remained burned into her memory. Tears welled behind her eyes.

Chip chuckled. The sound did nothing to quelch the bile in her sour stomach.

Butted up against one of the shattered gemstones, more silvery metal had been twisted and warped to create bulbous prisons. A handful of guards stood at attention, gazes riveted to the people inside the cells. In one, a handful of adult Ratnaa Nemora waited to be put to work by the same people who had murdered the Grove's young. The second cell held a group of noxlings huddled together, crying.

Zayla's breath seized when she spotted the occupant of the third smaller cage. *Oryn!*

As if drawn to her by instinct or love, by a bond only siblings shared, Oryn's head turned toward Zayla. Their eyes widened.

A cut marred Oryn's blue cheek. A slash cut across their neck trickled blood down their bare chest and arms, flowing across old and new bruises welling on their skin. Their wrists were still bound by those strange cuffs that cut Oryn off from their crafting.

The urge to run and grab hold of her sibling's hands filled Zayla like a swelling wave.

But she didn't move. Doing that might ruin any chance to escape.

Oryn was alive. That's all that mattered. Tor mentioned needing Oryn for a greater purpose, so the sun goddess worshippers would keep her sibling alive, as long as they had Oryn under their control.

And at least Oryn is aboveground. Zayla latched onto that thought. She'd only need to push roots through the strange burnt soil to get to her sibling's cell, not hard-as-rock gemstones like with Misti and Orenda. It seemed like fate had finally twisted her way.

Only if I can get myself into those ruins. She turned toward Chip, who continued munching on his tuber and grinning, teeth stained blue. "Where's Tor?"

Chip's gaze lifted somewhere over her shoulder, and Zayla turned.

Tor stood a few paces away, eerily close and just as eerily quiet, tossing a starry black crystal back and forth between his hands. "Hello, noxling." He grinned, an empty smile matching his empty, pale eyes. "My guard tells me that you have something to show me."

Just seeing the man caused her heart to pound faster and her palms to slicken. Ignoring the pulse of fear, Zayla lifted her chin. "I know about the goddess shard you're looking for. I'm here to help you find it."

Chapter Eighteen

TOR TOOK AN ETERNITY to respond. Would he believe that she could help him find the shard? *Do I believe it?* A small breeze blew a cloud of smoke and ash between them, spiraling up and away into the clear blue sky.

Tor rolled the black crystal between his palms. "How?"

"Give me some fresh dirt and a tree seed or a living mushroom, and I'll show you."

He chuckled. "Do you think I'm a fool, giving you access to your crafting sources? Besides, look around you, there's no uncharred dirt here. My followers made sure of that."

"Then I guess you can keep endlessly looking in the ruins—and your followers can keep dying to the creatures you set loose," Zayla replied.

Tor pressed his lips together. She'd obviously hit a sore spot. *Good.* Brushing past her, he headed to the metal cells.

Chip shifted closer to her. "Don't even think about running," he muttered.

Zayla ignored him, watching Tor and the prisoners.

Tor struck up conversation with an adult Nemora woman with striking red skin behind the bars. Her long robes woven with circular patterns indicated she was a Seventh Circle. The leader of the Nemora in Ratnaa Grove.

It struck a chord within Zayla that the Seventh Circle hadn't fled when the Grove was attacked. This woman was the most important person in this Grove, one who should be protected at all costs, yet she stayed behind with the others.

The Seventh Circle glanced toward the noxlings, before her whole being bent toward Tor and she snarled something at him.

Tor pointed toward an archway, and one of the prison guards left his post, trotting beneath the crimson crystals to disappear from view.

Judging from the archway's position, it had to lead into the tunnels and the underground prison area where she, Misti, and Orenda were being held. Zayla made a mental note of the location in reference to where she stood.

The Seventh Circle stared daggers at Tor, as if trying to send a gemstone flying right into the man's forehead.

But Ratnaa Nemora's crafting didn't work that way. They could find gems and crystals, create them sometimes with the right materials, but

Ratnaa couldn't fight with the crystals. Not like how Dara Nemora could spear their enemies with roots and Ingo Nemora could create metal swords. Each Grove was different, and Ratnaa was always the gentler sort, a Grove for conversation and trade, not battle.

The realization burned like a hot coal within Zayla's gut.

That was why Tor and his followers had captured Ratnaa Grove first. These people, try as they might, couldn't really fight back.

The guard returned from the archway carrying a small, yellow-green pot, which he handed to Tor. A muttered word sent the guard scurrying to the noxling cage. The noxlings sobbed as he hauled out a little one with pale, red skin and bright, pink eyes. The noxling resisted, screaming, as the guard yanked them toward the grotesque hanging tree.

No! Zayla's mouth went dry.

"I was only keeping the Seventh Circle alive so she could watch when we murdered her people. It turns out there's yet another reason to not kill her. She withheld information about some dirt our fire hadn't reached." With a malicious grin, Tor gestured to the sobbing noxling, though his gaze locked with Zayla's. "I will give you what you need, but if you do anything stupid, that one will hang."

Zayla gulped and nodded, wondering how she was going to accomplish her mission when a noxling's life was on the line. Still, she held out her hand, proud that it didn't shake. Tor tilted the pot. Fresh, clean, uncharred dirt fell into her palm, cool and moist and smelling of life.

Tor threw the empty pot over his shoulder, letting it smash onto the ground.

"I need more than just dirt," Zayla pressed.

"Luckily we had some seeds below as well." Tor held a single pod up between them. Dark brown and wrinkled, the pod was no bigger than the tip of his pinky. "I assume this tree seed will do."

Though she hadn't really seen a tree seed like that before, Zayla nodded. Their fingertips touched for the briefest of moments, and her body chilled. She realized a moment too late that she had just willingly touched a Divus. Flesh on flesh. He could've killed her right then. Flicking her gaze to his face, she half expected to see his eyes glowing a Blood crafter white.

Only those pale, empty eyes looked back, and a slow smile curled his lips.

Fear clawed for space in her thoughts, but she pressed it to the back of her mind. She couldn't let panic control her. She couldn't let him know how much his mere presence made her skin itch. She had a plan...and it involved working with Tor, for the time being.

"Watch closely," she said, though she hadn't needed to.

Everyone was watching her. Tor. The guards. Oryn. The other prisoners.

Catching the gaze of the Seventh Circle, Zayla gave her a small smile, a thanks for the fresh soil in her hands. The Seventh Circle nodded in return.

Holding the mound of dirt in one open palm, she pushed the seed into it, then placed her other hand on top, cupping the dirt between her palms. Trying not to think of the backlash, she summoned her crafting and focused her energy on the tree seed. A lush crimson tree bloomed in her mind's eye as she called on the power of Dara Grove.

Her crafting hummed, and a brown glaze hazed her vision. She watched the leaf markings on her forearms glow bright copper. Power flooded through her as if released by a dam. She pushed it toward the seed, imagining the tiny seed growing and spreading its roots wide.

When she opened her palms, a delicate shoot pushed from the dirt then sprouted a trio of leaves, its natural growth cycle accelerated by her crafting. A small thrill of elation fluttered in Zayla's chest. The tiny sprout glowed a steady copper as Zayla focused on the roots tendrilling through the handful of dirt, emerging between her fingers to grow down, down, down so long they brushed the scorched ground beneath her boots.

A wild thought entered her mind. She could command the roots to puncture Tor. Kill the guards around her. Free Oryn and the others. She could do it, right now.

Before she could even glance up from her work, the cold sensation of a blade against her neck froze that thought.

One of Tor's hands clasped the knife, though his pale eyes were still locked on the growing tree. "Don't think I would hesitate to kill you, too, noxling, if you decide to do something...rash."

"No!" Oryn's frantic voice ripped through the air.

Terror swelled inside her, but Zayla shoved it down. As much as she wanted to allay Oryn's fears, she couldn't chance a look at her sibling in case retribution was on Tor's mind. She concentrated on her crafting. The vibrations within her body grew, chattering her teeth, shaking her bones. Pain lanced her forearm as a thin sliver of crimson bark pushed through the skin. She groaned. Her Nature crafting was lashing back.

She was still a noxling after all.

"I'm just showing you my crafting, like you requested," she said.

"I already know you can grow things, noxling, but how does this help me in the ruins?" Tor growled, frustration clear in his voice.

How will my crafting help in the ruins? Zayla's thoughts spun. *How will trees and mushrooms help find things? How can roots and—*

Mycelium. Her recurring nightmares of being caught by thin white strands of mycelium gave her a sudden flash of inspiration. "If I focus long enough, I can sense anything the roots can. Rocks, bugs, water. Even goddess shards."

In her nightmares, the white strands of mycelium had seemed to come from everywhere and seemed to connect to everything around her. The same could be said for roots. They spread far around their tree, both on the surface and deep, deep underground. Since she could command roots and mycelium, it stood to reason that she *should* be able to sense the things they touched.

"Prove it." Tor's eyes glinted.

Zayla nodded. "It'll be easier if I have mushrooms to work with. Mycelium is thinner and can travel farther than roots."

"I'm not going to give you a fungus, noxling." Tor scowled, pressing the blade until it bit into her skin. A warm drip of liquid carved a path down to her collarbone. "Prove it with the tree."

"Fine." A burst of recklessness awakened. Maybe she couldn't kill Tor, but she could see how hard this scorched dirt was to work with. *If I'm going to save Oryn, I have to know.* Commanding the roots to grow far past their usual expanse, she willed them to dive into the yellow-red dirt. It was like trying to dig into a brick wall. "It'll work better if I know the rough shape of the thing I'm looking for."

"How about this." He removed the dagger from her neck and showed her the weapon's thick handle wrapped in leathers supporting a curved, black blade.

Zayla burned the image of the dagger into her memory then nodded.

Tor flung his weapon somewhere behind Zayla, so far away she barely heard the thud of it hitting the scorched dirt. "Go ahead. Find my dagger, noxling," Tor sneered.

Zayla clenched her teeth, focusing on the roots above ground and commanding them to search behind her. Shoving her senses along the roots, she felt the tendrils wind over scorched dirt and stones, curl around something that that was too thick to be the dagger's hilt, push around shattered crystals, and expand farther and farther away from her until...

There. The roots touched something smaller. Twisting the tendrils around it, she got the approximate size and shape. A thick handle. A sharp curved blade.

Another sliver of bark tore through her arm. Blinking back tears, Zayla pulled her senses back and stared at Tor. "I found it."

His shocked expression told her what she said was true.

Pride surged through her. She'd actually found an item. *I've never done that before!*

She met his gaze. "If you let me go into the ruins, I'll find your shard."

"Impressive," he said with a nod.

I have to see how hard this soil is. She refocused her attention on the roots trying to burrow into the scorched soil by her boots. The fire must've changed the soil's density. Her roots finally pushed through the top layer of burnt yellow-red dirt. *Yes!* But below the top layer of soil and stone was another layer and another and another still. Worry niggled the back of her mind. It took too much time and effort to force her way through. Hers wasn't the only life on the line. She couldn't risk Tor hanging the innocent noxling.

"You've proven yourself, noxling." Tor stepped back. "End your crafting."

She blinked the brown haze away, just as another burst of pain tore through her. A thick layer of crimson ripped through her skin around her neck. She groaned.

"I said end it!" Tor yelled, pulling his hand back.

His punch landed hard across her cheek. Sharp pain exploded in her jaw. Stars shattered her vision. She barely noticed the sting when she landed hard on her knees. The tree toppled next to her. Fresh dirt scattered.

"I told you to stop," Tor snarled.

Catching her breath, Zayla pressed a hand to her throbbing cheek. Warm blood oozed between her fingers. She lifted her head to meet Tor's pale eyes. "I did. I ended it right when you told me to. My crafting was lashing back at me."

"As it should, noxling. Take her back to the prison," Tor ordered, but Zayla saw the glint of greed in his eyes. He believed her. Believed she could find his precious goddess shard. "And burn her tree."

The tree's copper glow faded as Zayla's Nature crafting ebbed away, revealing a pale-green trunk, off-yellow leaves, and light brown roots. *What sort of tree is that?* It was nothing like she'd seen before.

Before Zayla could look closer, Chip shoved a bag over her head. He grabbed her arm and hauled her to her feet, pulling her forward. Blood dripped down her chin.

Though muffled, Tor's voice still managed to reach her ears. "And hang that one."

The noxling's scream followed Zayla the whole way to her prison cell. *I caused that.* Tears burned behind her eyes.

The noxling's cry was cut short in a sudden, horrible jolt of silence, and something deep, deep inside Zayla stilled with it.

After Chip took off her blindfold and bindings, locked her in the cell, and lumbered up the tunnel, Zayla wrapped her hands around the duskiron bars. She heard voices coming from the tunnel that led aboveground, probably Chip talking to the next guard in the rotation.

"You okay?" Misti asked.

"No." Zayla let the cold of the metal bars seep into her skin. She'd had enough. Enough betrayal. Enough torture. Enough killing of innocent people. "I'm going to free us and the Ratnaa Nemora by any means possible. I'm going into the ruins."

Chapter Nineteen

"HE COULD'VE KILLED ME multiple times," Zayla whispered to Orenda and Misti, after filling them in about what had happened aboveground. Laughter bounced down the tunnel as Chip and the other guard chatted. Zayla spoke freely, if quickly and quietly. Her cheek throbbed from where Tor had punched her, so she poured some water from her flask onto a corner of her blanket and pressed it to the wound. The damp cloth eased some of the pain. Thank every root and spore that it was so cold down in the prison. At least the swelling had gone down a little.

"It's a blessing from Aluriah that Tor didn't kill you," Orenda replied.

A blessing. A sour taste filled Zayla's mouth. *If the goddess was really watching, how could she let the little one get murdered like that?*

"No, I found his dagger." Her fingers feathered the thin band of crimson bark around her neck. She could almost feel the blade pressing into her neck, the pinch of pain as it bit into her skin. Her crafting had formed a protective choker over the wound, and Zayla knew it would eventually heal the slice he'd made. Until the bark flaked away, she could call on her Dara crafting and use the wood covering her wounds to defend herself. It wasn't as good a source as having a tree seed, but it was something. She wasn't entirely defenseless. "I proved myself. When I showed him my crafting ability, I could see the greed clear in his eyes. It's why he killed the—" the word caught, snagged like a thorn scraping her throat on the way up. The noxling's scream echoed in her ears. She forced the words out. "—the younger noxling."

A chill rippled down her skin, and she rubbed her arms, fingers brushing against the thicker slice of crimson bark on her forearm. At least the backlash of her crafting only covered her neck and forearm—not most of her body as it had after the suncreature attack in the Cinder Forest. *I'll have to be mindful of using my crafting in the ruins.*

"I wonder if I could volunteer to go into the underground ruins?" Misti's quiet voice filled the space. "You could use backup, and perhaps they'd need another Vagari."

"Much as I'd love that, Shadre said there are suncreatures in the underground ruins. Vagari aren't able to control them," Zayla replied.

A soft chuckle came from the other cell. "Misti's able to do a lot of things that aren't common knowledge," Orenda replied.

A spark lit Zayla's curiosity. She leaned against the bars, wishing she could see Misti's face. "You can control suncreatures?"

"It's not something I can do often," Misti replied, "but I can bend their will at the right moment."

Some ability indeed. Before Zayla could ask more about Misti's power, footsteps echoed down the tunnel. By unspoken agreement, they ended their conversation. A guard they hadn't seen before took up a post next to the exit. He didn't say a word to them, merely crossed his thick arms and scowled. A scar pinched the skin across his forearm. After a few shuffling sounds, Misti and Orenda's cell was silent.

Zayla settled on her back on the gemstone floor, watching the firelight flicker off the walls. She twirled her bitterroot ring—her only trinket from home. While she couldn't use it as a source for her crafting, the constant motion helped take the edge off her nerves.

Her thoughts drifted to the purple fire lantern that was hanging off her cell. She wondered how it could keep the creatures in the underground ruins away. She'd never heard of such a defense, and part of her wanted to know how the fire was even purple to begin with. Another part of her whispered that she shouldn't be so curious, shouldn't prod into things the guards might not want to talk about. She needed to work with Tor and his people. Perhaps she should be a bit more docile for a while. *The Ratnaa Nemora are being docile, and they're being murdered for it.* The bile returned in her throat at the thought.

As the day slowly passed, her thoughts drifted back to what she'd discovered aboveground. The Ratnaa Nemora were grouped in those metal cells, while Oryn sat alone in theirs. The scorched, hard-as-stone dirt took a surprising amount of her crafting power to push through, and there were so many layers. The image of the decimated Ratnaa Grove was scarred into her memory. *Burned into history, just like the war would be.* She turned her discoveries over and over in her mind.

She pressed her hand against the cool, smooth gemstone beneath her. At least only the aboveground part had been destroyed. Minerals and crystals and gemstones were usually found far beneath the soil. The roots of the sacred tree must've grown too deep to be completely destroyed. Even this space—this prison and the tunnels and whatever else was around—this was part of Ratnaa Grove as well. The sun goddess worshippers hadn't destroyed it all. It's why the Ratnaa Nemora still lived. The small, quiet thought gave Zayla some hope.

"I hear you gave Tor quite a show. Wish I had been there."

Shadre's voice startled Zayla, and she flicked her gaze from the shimmering walls to see the musician standing in the tunnel opening.

Firelight danced across Shadre's features as she moved closer to the prison bars. "Didn't think you'd be one to help their—" She paused, frowning as she took in Zayla's bruised cheek. "You're injured."

Anger pushed Zayla to her feet, burning like a hot coal. Anger at Tor for punching her, at the senseless murdering, at this beautiful betrayer of a woman who had the nerve to act surprised about her injuries. She tilted her chin up, showing off the choker of bark in an air of defiance. "I'm fine."

The silence that followed her words spread through the prison, so thick it felt like a weighted cloak across Zayla's shoulders.

Shadre's hand drifted to the duskiron axe hanging off her belt, her rust-orange eyes darkening. "Who hurt you?"

"Who do you think?" Zayla challenged. Shadre might be a coward, but she wasn't stupid.

"Tor." Shadre lowered her gaze to the floor. "Wyvern shit."

"Apparently I did put on quite a show for him." Zayla threw Shadre's words back at her. "Too much of a show."

Shadre pressed her forehead against the bars and sighed. "Why would you help Tor after what he's done to Oryn, after what he's done to you? Why are you going into the underground ruins?"

Was that a concerned edge to her tone? Zayla couldn't be sure. Shadre could just be fishing for information to give Tor, trying to figure out the real reason why Zayla was going into the ruins. *Well, I won't fall for that.*

"I don't want to sit around and wait for death," she replied coolly.

"The ruins are dangerous!" Shadre spat back before turning away with a huff. "Tor just lost another wave of people to the suncreatures inside. Ten people, gone."

"Did the Nemora come back alive?" Zayla asked.

"Yes, but they're bleeding from wounds on their arms and screaming about being attacked." Shadre's hand tightened around her axe once more. Her shoulders bunched, as if preparing for a fight. "It's not safe for anyone down there."

Fear squeezed Zayla's chest. Of course going into the ruins wasn't safe—and not only because of the suncreatures lurking inside. She'd be surreptitiously trying to break Orenda and Misti and Oryn free, but she didn't want Shadre knowing how scared she truly was. Breathing in and out, she carefully schooled her features. "I'll manage."

Footsteps crunched down the tunnel to the entrance of the prison. Another change of the guards?

"You shouldn't go down there," Shadre hissed, spinning back around to face Zayla again. "You shouldn't be helping Tor."

Zayla scoffed. She couldn't help it. "You're one to judge."

"My circumstances are different," Shadre snapped, scowling.

"If you're so concerned for her, why don't you just go into the ruins and protect her?" Orenda remarked from her cell. Her voice took on a teasing lilt. "Unless you're too scared…"

Shadre snapped her head in Orenda's direction. "I'd be careful what you say, Elu, I don't see you volunteering to do anything."

"I'll volunteer," Misti replied, almost too quickly. "If you need more hands in the ruins, I mean. It beats being cooped up in here for another night."

"We don't need any more prisoners down in the ruins, Vagari," Tor's voice floated down the tunnel. Chip lumbered along next to him.

Shadre pressed her lips together. Her eyes grew cold.

Tor gave Zayla an empty smile, then gestured to Chip, who no longer drooled blue mush. "Chip is the only Vagari you'll need. He'll lead you into the ruins and oversee the followers I send to accompany you."

Zayla swallowed, trying desperately to ignore how sweaty her palms just got. Nausea nearly swayed her. *I'm going into the ruins. With Tor's followers. Without any help.*

It was what she wanted, but curse every root and spore, the idea terrified her.

Tor moved toward Zayla's cell with the smooth grace of a predator, wrapping his long fingers around the duskiron bars. He kept his strange pale eyes on Zayla, but his words were directed at Shadre. "I want you to gather some food for the whole party before they go, Shadre. Tell the Seventh Circle I want more of these crystals." He gestured to the purple flame lanterns.

Realization dawned on Zayla. Crystals must be what made the purple fire. Crystals found here in Ratnaa Grove. Zayla had a niggling sense that perhaps there was another reason the Nemora came back alive with only scrapes on their arms while Tor's followers hadn't survived. Perhaps an even better reason than the device the sun goddess worshippers activated that scattered all natural creatures away. *Are the suncreatures in the ruins…defending the Nemora who live here?* She tucked that thought to the back of her mind and focused on the conversation at hand.

"—find some additional weaponry, too," Tor was saying. "We don't want our precious Nemora being attacked before she can find our shard."

"Of course," Shadre murmured. Her demeanor had completely changed when Tor arrived. Her fiery exterior had melted away, replaced by quiet submission, but Zayla didn't miss the tightness in the woman's jaw. Shadre nodded once to Tor, gave Chip a guarded grin, then headed up the tunnel and out of sight.

"The goddess shard isn't yours," Orenda called from her cell, her voice cold.

"Finders keepers, Elu." Tor didn't bother to look at Orenda, like she wasn't even worth the words he uttered. No, Tor kept his gaze riveted on Zayla, staring at her—staring through her, as if trying to judge her soul.

I don't need to worry. I passed his little test. Proved myself. Zayla pulled back her shoulders. She'd free Misti and Orenda and Oryn. "When do we leave?"

"As soon as Shadre gathers all the necessary items, of course. Won't be long," he replied. "And since you said you needed a point of reference, the goddess shard you'll be looking for is from Ponuriah—the edges will be jagged, the surface smooth, and it will be very, very hot."

Zayla nodded. Hope and dread warred inside her. The first part of her plan had worked perfectly—she was going into the ruins. She hoped the rest of her plan would work just as well.

Chapter Twenty

A HAND CLAMPED DOWN on Zayla's arm as soon as she stopped walking, blindfolded and bound once more. *It took one thousand three hundred and eighty-five steps to get here.* She had counted her footfalls from her prison cell, up the tunnel, out into the open air of Ratnaa Grove, and finally…here. The cloth hood pressed against her nose as she breathed slowly, in and out, trying to calm herself.

Something crackled nearby, and the scent of smoke wafted toward her.

Unfortunately, the smoke couldn't mask the sharper scent of sweat that lingered right beside her. A guard. Even though their hand clamped tight around her arm, their palm was sweaty against her skin. Twitchy, too, the guard constantly shifted their weight from side to side.

Nervous, Zayla realized.

Nerves skittered under her skin, as well. She clasped her hands together and felt the familiar press of her bitterroot ring between her fingers, wishing she could spin it…if only to pass the time.

A determined set of footfalls came from behind, circling to her front.

"She's going to have to be able to see to do her work, you know," Shadre muttered.

A hand yanked the bag off Zayla's head, bringing her face-to-face with the musician.

Dusk had already fallen. Darkness clung to the ground like fog. Firelight from a torch standing nearby threw light and shadows over Shadre's features. A few more standing torches ringed a large, jagged hole in the ground behind her. Four backlit figures stood staring into the rift, their black-scaled armor shimmering in the dusky light.

The entrance to Alastra. Zayla itched to head inside the ancient, underground nymph city. The faster she could get underground, the faster she could break her friends and sibling free, but suncreatures lived in the ruins as well, and dread soon blanketed her like a thick cloak.

"Here." Shadre pushed a wrapped piece of bread into Zayla's bound hands. "Everyone gets a fresh loaf."

Warmth seeped into her hands, and a nutty, earthy scent wafted from the bake. The same scent that Shadre carried with her.

"Don't eat it all at once." Shadre's jaw tightened, and she turned away from Zayla, addressing the group. Chip, two Elu, and one Divus turned to look at her, each holding a fresh loaf of bread. "You don't know how long you're going to be searching for the shard."

The male Elu gripping Zayla scoffed. Scars from using his Moon crafting crisscrossed his thick arms. He jerked her closer to the hole, like she was some animal for him to control. "Shouldn't be too long with this one around, yeah?"

"Not at all." Chip tucked his bread into a large rucksack thrown over his shoulder. In his other hand, a long-bladed spear glinted like the wink of an evil eye. Zayla gulped, noting all the guards had weapons of some kind—spears, daggers, swords, dual spiral blades called ruk'shas. *To fight the rogue suncreatures if they attack.*

Zayla suddenly felt very exposed. Her body hummed in response, the vibrations settling toward her spine. She glanced over her shoulder into the deeper shadows.

Multiple sets of large crimson eyes stared at her. A pyrewolf suncreature lifted its muzzle to the sky and let out a howl that reverberated through the silent, empty space, joined by the howls of its two companions. The thunderclaps ruffled their feathers at the noise, and the scaled wyvern growled. Crimson light poured from beneath their white fur, feathers, and scales.

Zayla felt like she'd been dunked in ice-cold water. "Are...are they coming, too?"

"No." Shadre slipped a large bag off her shoulder and plucked out five curved, duskiron daggers, passing them to Chip and the guards. "The suncreatures help guard the Ratnaa Nemora at night."

Just beyond the suncreatures, Zayla made out the glint of the hanging tree. A small sense of elation rolled through her as she realized she now had her bearings. *One thousand three hundred and eighty-five steps....*

Chip clapped his hands. "Time to go."

He picked up a coil of rope Zayla hadn't noticed before and looped one end around his body, securing it tight, then handed the other to Shadre. Without a moment's hesitation, he stepped to the edge of the hole and fell in.

Zayla's breath caught.

Shadre grunted as the rope grew taut, slithering between a series of thick metal spikes lodged deep into the scorched dirt, and Zayla realized she was looking at a simple and effective pulley system.

Shadre breathed heavily, her hands gripping the other end of the rope. Her muscles strained as she slowly lowered Chip, then the other guards, into the hole. Finally, only Zayla and the sweaty Elu guard remained.

"How deep is it?" she asked Shadre.

Shadre opened her mouth, but the guard jumped in. "Don't know, noxling," The guard smirked. Malice glinted in his green eyes. He undid Zayla's wrist bindings and stepped back. "But I hope you aren't afraid of heights."

"Your turn, Zayla." Shadre had crossed the distance between them in a heartbeat and slipped rope over Zayla's head and shoulders, securing it around Zayla's waist. She was so close, Zayla could see every detail in the sharp edges of her Ingo Nemora markings. When Shadre lifted her head, the firelight shimmered like a glowing shield in her rust-orange eyes, blocking her true feelings from view.

Zayla's heart skipped. Despite her resolve to remain angry, she wished the musician were coming with her. The woman radiated protectiveness, and try as Zayla might to ignore it, she felt safer with Shadre around. *Betrayer.* She forced herself to remember. *She's why Oryn is captive. She's why I'm in this situation right now.*

Zayla pressed her lips together and wrapped her hands around the thick, scratchy rope. Scooting closer to the edge, she peered over the lip into inky blackness. Far, far below, a trio of flickering lights caught her eye, moving like firebugs. Torches. Zayla's stomach dropped. Damned every root and spore, those flames were far down. She never considered herself afraid of heights…but maybe she'd just never been this high before.

"I got you. Lean back and let gravity do most of the work." Shadre leaned closer, cinching the rope tighter around Zayla's waist. "This'll make it a little easier for you." Shadre deftly wound some loops between Zayla's legs, affixing them to the rope cinching her waist to create a sort of sling. "And don't forget, some things need to be burned in order to blossom."

"What?" Zayla asked, confused by the comment.

Without elaborating on her cryptic phase, Shadre walked away and lifted her end of the rope, nodding once to the remaining Elu guard. With both of them staring at her expectantly, Zayla stepped to the edge. She hesitated. This seemed too easy, and a small part of her didn't trust it.

"Have a fun drop," the guard muttered. He put a hand on her back and shoved her into the darkness.

Weightless. Her stomach lifted. Wind rushed past her face.

As she plummeted downward, she heard Shadre cursing angrily. The rope snapped taut, and Zayla suddenly jerked to a stop. Pain pinched on her waist, thighs, and back as the harness pressed against her.

The shadows grew deeper, pressing in on her for a few moments before the torchlight below rose up to meet her. She came to a stop with enough room to comfortably touch her boots onto the stone below her.

In the torchlight, an expanse of smooth, pale stone curved up like a shallow bowl around them. In the deeper recesses, what appeared to be the craggy ceiling loomed overhead, held by thick stone beams. The hole she'd come down was merely a hand's width large from this distance, and Zayla suddenly felt very, very small.

"Took you long enough, noxling. Get out of the way." Chip tilted his chin to the guards.

For a moment, a wild urge splashed through her. *I should run.* But with no light, little crafting, and no way out except for the hole above them, Zayla had no choice but to obey. She crossed the short distance between her and the other three guards. The two lanky Elu muttered to one another, eyes alert, and the shorter Divus glared into the darkness as if she expected something to leap out at any moment. They each held a torch in one hand, and a weapon in the other.

Zayla felt tingles of uncertainty seep into her body. She felt so utterly defenseless, with not a single friend in sight.

To distract herself from the worry, she took the time to assess her surroundings. The torchlight barely flickered against crumbling archways nearby. Beyond that, darkness loomed. Water dripped somewhere in the black. Wind curled in from the hole above them, bringing the ashy scent from aboveground.

As soon as the twitchy Elu guard reached the bottom, Chip wasted no time in ushering them along. "Come on, then, it's this way," he said. He took one of the guards' torches and lumbered forward.

As they walked, Zayla flicked her gaze up to the stone beams. One jutted the direction they were headed—back toward the hanging tree above her—and hope sparked in Zayla's chest. *I can count my way back to Orenda and Misti.*

The Elu guard walked beside her with a tight grip on his curved duskiron dagger. He didn't grab her arm again, and for that she was grateful. The guards probably thought the same way she did. Even if she did run, there was nowhere to go.

They stepped over an ankle-high, curved edge of stone. When Zayla looked back, she noticed wave markings had been carved into this side of the stonework. Had they been standing in a large fountain or pool? As they walked further, the firelight revealed more and more of the space around them. They reached a section of raised stone pots with dry dirt and long-dead plants, then dipped under more smooth pale stone. Some of the archways were crumbled, others held fast through time.

She'd expected tunnels, tight corridors of stone and dirt, not a wide-open area. Yet it made sense to have a space like this, a place to breathe and stretch and run. A courtyard.

As she walked, Zayla counted her steps, taking note of some benches around a rocky firepit.

Fifty steps closer to Misti and Orenda so far. One archway they passed was decorated with the curved writing of the ancients. Zayla couldn't read it, but she touched the stone and paused. The hum always within her body quieted, as if pausing as well. A surprising sense of awe washed over her. She was standing in Alastra. A city of the ancients—her ancients.

The nymphs of Alastra had lived underground, because they wanted a defensible position from the battles constantly raging overhead. Zayla recalled learning that a large, salty lake had situated directly over this area and protected the city even further. It was thought that, after the war between the goddess sisters ended, the lake seeped into the ground and created the minerals and crystals of Ratnaa Grove.

The Divus guard bumped her on the shoulder. "Keep moving."

As they walked farther, the torchlight caught on something white. As they drew near, Zayla realized it was a cracked skull, jutting out from the stone. A few paces later, a femur glinted. The firelight washed over an archway above a small pile of bones. Everywhere Zayla looked, she saw skeletons. Bones worn clean by time. A chill raced across her skin.

"It's like a graveyard," the Divus muttered.

"But it's been hundreds of seasons since the nymphs lived here. Could these bones belong to them?" Zayla breathed, running her fingers over a broken femur.

"I doubt they're that old," Chip called back over his shoulder. "Probably belonged to one of our guards. The creatures must've got to them."

The suncreature attacks. Zayla's eyes widened, and panic clawed up her throat. The thrumming in her bones prickled uncomfortably.

They moved on, following Chip's lead. Soon, the ruins seemed to fall away and the stone path beneath their boots crumbled away to fresh dirt. Zayla breathed deep. The clean scent of soil calmed her. At three hundred steps, they reached the edge of the cavern. The walls were still pale stone curving upward. A triple set of tunnels led deeper into darkness.

Never breaking his stride, Chip headed down the center tunnel. The beam pointed in the same direction, and Zayla kept that in mind as she followed. The passage was wide enough that three of them could walk side by side, not rough hewn, but carved into the substrate with stone supports arched overhead. Moisture ran in rivulets down the rock. A few more bones littered the ground, kicked aside or crunched over by the guards' boots. Zayla skirted around them, stomach queasy. *How many of Tor's guards died down here?*

She ran her hand across the tunnel walls, feeling the veins of damp dirt between the stone supports. *I can definitely use my crafting here.* She could use the bark covering the wounds on her skin, but she knew deep down that she couldn't grow the length of roots she needed from that scant amount of wood. For that, she needed a living tree seed. Or a living mushroom. So, she dutifully followed Chip and hoped he'd give her some materials soon. At least this tunnel was leading them closer to Misti and Orenda's underground prison cells. *Four hundred and seventy-five steps. Left turn. This one is parallel so no need to count. Right turn, leading closer. Eighty-six more steps.* She twisted her ring as she counted, helping her remember.

They reached a small circular area with tunnels that led every direction like the spokes of a wheel.

Chip turned to her, rummaging through his pockets. He pulled out a single brown mushroom no bigger than his finger. "You're up, noxling. And be warned, this is the only crafting material you're going to get, so you'd better take care of it."

Taking the tiny brown mushroom, Zayla nodded and sank to her knees. A surge of excitement rushed through her. She was too far away from Orenda and Misti, but another idea grew inside her. She could use her mushrooms like markers in this tunnel system. If she got lost, she could connect with them and find her way back. She pressed the mushroom into the fresh dirt in front of her and closed her eyes. *Myceli.* She called upon the grove of mushrooms, recalling the purple veincap fungi of her mother's offshoot. *Grow.*

Her crafting surged and hummed within her. When she opened her eyes, a brown glaze pulled over her vision, and the dots scattered about her skin glowed bright copper.

She stared at the brown mushroom, commanding it to search. It glowed with the same copper light as her markings. Thin strands of mycelium immediately sprouted out of the stem and pushed easily into the fresh dirt beneath it. Within a few heartbeats, the mycelium had spread to the very edges of the small space, creeping into the many tunnels.

The humming within her intensified.

She focused on the ends of the mycelium, sensing what it touched, searching for a crystal hidden within the dirt and stone. Searching for the goddess shard. Pain blossomed in her arm. She knew without looking that a sporebruise had formed. Gritting her teeth, she kept pushing, feeling, sensing. Dirt, rocks, tunnel walls. No shards.

She relaxed her concentration, blinking away the brown glaze. "The shard isn't around here, but I wouldn't expect it to be, this close to the courtyard." She pointed at the tunnel entrance that went Misti and Orenda's direction. "I think we need to go deeper into the ruins. That way."

Chip nodded. Instead of leading, he gestured for her to go ahead.

Leaving the living mycelium buried in the dirt, she plucked the tiny brown mushroom from its base and pocketed it. Even if she never needed her mycelium markers, it felt good to leave something living in this desolate city. She moved toward the tunnel and resumed counting her steps. *I'm coming, Oryn. I'm coming.*

Chapter Twenty-One

"IT'S THAT WAY." ZAYLA plucked the brown mushroom from its base and pointed down yet another tunnel. Massaging her breastbone, she picked the second tiny mushroom that she'd grown alongside the main one and snuck it into her pocket before following Chip down the tunnel that her mycelium had told her swerved sharply to the left. The guards stalked behind her, bringing up the rear.

So far, she'd created eleven extra fungi and planned for more. She thumbed the mushrooms in her pocket. After the first spoke, she had the idea to create a second tiny mushroom each time she used her crafting. If she ever needed a larger amount of power, she could plant all of her mushrooms and have a greater expanse of mycelium to use.

Inspecting her hand, she sighed. The deep brown skin of her fingers didn't look like her own—dark sporebruises spread across her flesh. She coughed, and sharp pain pierced through her like a piece of glass was lodged in her lungs. Since she had continued to call upon Myceli during her time underground, the spores had sunk past her skin and into her tissues.

Fear crept into her as well.

She'd never used her crafting so often in such a short amount of time. She knew if she called too much of her Myecli power, the spores could begin to multiply tenfold. They'd grow in her lungs, sprout from her eyes and mouth, kill her if she used too much without resting. She was still a damned noxling after all; her crafting lashed back far too harshly. Although she preferred presenting as female, a small part of her regretted she no longer presented as male; they could withstand the price of crafting better.

Still counting her steps, she ran her fingers across a smooth, stone archway as they passed under. She remembered the statue of the Hallr Nemora woman from the Cinder Forest. Her look of fear, captured forever in stone. Sometimes, even for adults, nature simply demanded its price. It wouldn't matter if Zayla was male or female or anything in between—if she used too much crafting, nature would simply reclaim her.

That won't happen to me. I'm going to save Oryn, and the others.

"Get a move on, now." The twitchy Elu guard shoved her forward, forcing her to quicken her steps.

Tiredness pulled at her, so much so that it felt like she was walking through mud, not over soft, clean dirt and smooth stone. Her stomach growled. The brief walk wasn't enough to motivate the guards to take a break. They weren't using their crafting, draining their energy.

Zayla had been using her crafting at every fork and spoke, pushing the mycelium farther away from her each time, but they still weren't close enough for her to command the mycelium into Misti and Orenda's underground prison. Zayla began to wonder if they'd ever be close enough to do what she planned. She always picked the tunnels that took her closer to her friends, but the routes twisted and often doubled back on themselves or ended in a collapse she hadn't sensed with her crafting. She had the mycelium to help orient her, yet frustration simmered. She kept mentally counting her steps. So many tunnels led away from her friends that they were still over a thousand steps away from Orenda and Misti. So many steps. So many dead ends.

A putrid rotting scent snaked past Zayla's nose and made her gag, warning her they were about to stumble upon another dead body. They'd passed at least fifteen so far. Sure enough, Chip's torchlight washed over the mangled corpse of another of Tor's followers. Jagged gashes cut along the woman's face and torso, so deep that white bone poked through the split flesh in multiple places. Blue blood seeped onto the stone and into the dirt. The lower half of the Elu woman had been ripped away, leaving only a shredded mess of shattered bones, leaking organs, and ruined clothes. Stomach flipping, Zayla put a hand over her nose as they quickly walked by.

A scrabbling noise—like claws over rocks—echoed down the tunnel from behind them.

Zayla stopped, her skin immediately prickling at the sound. The hum within her body amplified, settling toward the tops of her shoulders and the back of her neck. Suncreatures. It wasn't the first time they'd heard the sounds. That scratching noise had gotten more and more intense as time passed.

Chip spun around, eyes wide in the firelight, spear at the ready. "Show yourself. Go on, face me!" His voice pitched up in a yell that reverberated down the tunnel.

"Yeah, that'll show 'em." The Divus rolled her eyes, but kept her longsword at the ready.

Everyone was on edge. Zayla's skin itched each time she heard the sound. She hoped the rogue suncreatures would consider her as one of the Ratnaa Nemora and leave her alone if they ever came face-to-face, but even some of the Nemora had been wounded. Her palms grew slick at the thought.

"If those suncreatures ever decide to show themselves, I'll cut them in half," Chip muttered, lumbering down the tunnel again.

As they continued, Zayla kept her eyes on the Divus. Suncreatures were nothing compared to that woman's Blood crafting. A Divus could kill her with a mere touch if she wanted to. Zayla pressed her lips into a thin line. She needed all of the guards' protection, Divus included, but as soon as they reached the surface again…well, these guards would just be people to fight through to reach Oryn. And Misti and Orenda. To reach freedom. These guards had willingly razed a Grove, kidnapped its inhabitants, and murdered its noxlings.

As much as she wanted to, she couldn't possibly face all these guards, not with how exhausted she was already feeling, not with only the mycelium and her small pieces of wood to command.

But I'll need to fight them eventually.

They reached another fork, tunnels twisting every which way around them. One even opened up above them. *It heads straight up! What's that even used for? No wonder so many people get lost down here.*

The guards looked expectantly at Zayla.

"Can we eat first?" She pulled the cold loaf of bread from her pocket. "I need the energy to keep on crafting."

Her stomach growled again, as if to prove her point if the others could hear it.

Chip worked his jaw, glancing down the tunnel with the dead body, then nodded once. "Only a short while. I don't want to be down here longer than we have to." He motioned to the Divus guard. "Keep watch."

Zayla sat and pressed her back against the smooth stone archway that held this open space aloft. Her feet ached from all the walking, but her mind was still sharp. She mentally traced the twists and turns and doublebacks they'd been through, reaffirming the number of steps still left to get below Misti and Orenda. Over nine hundred to go.

She sank her teeth into her loaf, the thick crust breaking with a satisfying crunch. The bread itself was equally crunchy. A sweet nutty flavor filled her mouth. Whole nuts and slivers filled the hearty bread. Surprised by how good it was, she immediately took another bite.

The rest of the group munched through their loaves, and a low, crunching noise filled the space as they ate.

Zayla took another bite. Her teeth grazed something hard. Too hard. She plucked a whole shell out of the bread. It was the same color as the small brown pod Tor had provided for her test. Her fingers tingled with the sense of life within the shell. *This is a living tree seed.*

Shadre's cryptic words came back to her. *Some things need to be burned in order to blossom.*

Shadre gave her this bread, told her things needed to burn in order to blossom. Shadre knew Zayla could use both Myceli and Dara crafting. She already had Myceli covered with the brown mushrooms grown along the way, and she could only access a little of her Dara side with the bark covering her wounds. If this nut could sprout...Shadre had just given her a way to access a powerful, renewable source: a whole tree.

Shadre's helping me.

The hope blossomed in Zayla's thoughts, soon burned with a flash of anger. *Why is Shadre helping me now? Not earlier?* Zayla wanted to hurl the pod away. Common sense told her to keep it. No matter who gave it to her, the tree seed could help free Oryn. Zayla quickly pocketed the treasure. *Giving me the tree seed was the least Shadre could do.*

"All right. Enough relaxing," Chip barked. "You're up, noxling. If you lead us into another dead end, I'll start cutting your fingers off, one by one."

They'd had this conversation numerous times before, and Zayla still had all her fingers. A lie fell easily past her lips. "You were the one to pick the smallest mushroom with the shortest mycelium reach, Chip. I can push its growth cycle further, but that'll burn me out faster and we'll have to rest more often. You know it's better to walk a little bit then let me investigate."

In truth, the size of the fungi didn't have any effect on how far the mycelium could spread. Chip had no way of knowing how far she'd been spreading the mycelium, since it was all underground. That wasn't even considering the other fungi she had in her pocket.

But she wouldn't sacrifice too much of her crafting until she was closer to Misti and Orenda's prison cells.

Pressing her fingers and the original tiny brown mushroom into the dirt, she closed her eyes and called up her crafting. Her power immediately filled the room with a soft copper glow, and the mushroom brightened to match. The mycelium spread beneath their boots. She pressed thin strands out farther, extending them deeper into the tunnels around them. She concentrated on what those strands discovered. Dirt, stone, a small pool of cool water, a curious set of smooth scales—

Vibrations, like someone had plucked a note on a string, immediately spread through the mycelium. A warning. She pulled the mycelium back in a burst of panic. Suncreatures. She'd just found the suncreatures who'd been following them. She knew it as certainly as she knew every strand of mycelium in the tunnels.

Swallowing hard, she commanded the mycelium to skirt the area, through more soft dirt, past a larger slab of rock that was probably a support beam and into a strange area of cold, empty space, then—

Zayla gasped, but the glass-like feeling in her lungs made it hard to breath. The vibrations within her body shook in a deeper chord, a darker melody, resonating to her core.

Focus. She wrapped the mycelium strands around what she'd discovered. A smooth surface. Jagged on one end. The whole thing was no bigger than her hand. An intense cold seeped into the mycelium so fast the strands froze in place. A cold so strange it could be nothing else.

Curse every root and spore.

She'd actually found a goddess shard.

And not just any goddess shard. Tor had told her the goddess shard he was looking for would be hot, burning to the touch. He sought a shard of Ponuriah, the fiery sun goddess.

The cold air she sensed indicated this one had to belong to Aluriah, the moon goddess, the protector. *Are there two shards in these ruins?* It didn't matter. Not only was it unlikely Tor could use Aluriah's shard, the moon goddess shard was the opposite direction of Misti and Orenda's cell.

But what if I could get the shard into Orenda's hands? Such an artifact could turn the tide of war in their favor.

Somehow, she had to get the shard without allowing Chip and the guards to find it. She couldn't let something so powerful fall into Tor's hands. If she headed in the direction of Misti and Orenda, she could break them free. Maybe they could sneak back to the ruins later on. No, that would be too risky. And what if Tor and his followers found Aluriah's shard in the meantime? If he couldn't use it, he'd destroy it.

She had to get the shard now, tuck it away, and continue "looking" for the Ponuriah shard.

"Well?" Chip's gruff voice interrupted her thoughts.

Her eyes popped open, the deep golden glaze still filling her vision. Blotches of brown sporebruises spread on her arms as the fungi spores sank deeper and deeper within her.

Chip paced back and forth in the small area. "Find it?" All the guards had risen, eyeing the dark tunnels as they gripped their weapons.

A truly horrible idea came to her.

"Yes, actually!" Zayla replied, infusing as much shock into her voice as possible. Truthfully, it wasn't that hard to do. Using her crafting, Zayla commanded the mycelium closer and closer to those slippery scales she'd discovered earlier.

Chip grinned.

She nodded to the tunnel by the twitchy Elu guard, one that twisted away from the shard but toward the scales. "The goddess shard is that way."

Chapter Twenty-Two

THE STENCH OF ROTTING flesh got stronger with each step Zayla took, until it nearly made her gag. Her eyes started to water. The unending vibrations had settled in her chest, just behind her breastbone, pulling her forward and pulsing at a steady beat in a counter tempo to her racing heart. The suncreatures were ahead of her. Directly ahead.

Over the pounding in her ears, she struggled to hear any sound of claws scrabbling on the stone. Only the distant sound of running water, their footsteps, and the heavy breathing of the guards made it past the steady thump-thump-thump of her heart.

She followed close to Chip's heels, urging him forward. The tunnel narrowed to only allow one person through at a time. The ground transitioned from soft, smooth dirt to a rocky and uneven surface. Her eyes snagged on a trio of claw marks dug into one stone archway. Swallowing her fear, she kept walking.

The suncreatures had only killed Tor's followers, not the Ratnaa Nemora that had come with them. Would the suncreatures see her as a friend as well? She could only hope.

"It's this way?" Chip glanced over his shoulder at her, doubt wrinkling his features. Purple firelight glowed from the small lantern dangling from his hip. That firelight was supposed to keep the creatures away, but right now, she desperately hoped that strange glow would do the exact opposite.

"Yes." A cough rattled its way up her throat. "It's not far now." The sharp pain in her lungs brightened with each breath she took. Her energy wavered.

"You'd better not be lying or I'll—" Chip's words died on his lips. The narrow tunnel opened into a wide oval space supported by thick stone arches. The space was so big, it could easily hold forty people. And it sort of did. Cracked white bones were piled in the center. Atop the grisly hill lay a male body, still mostly fresh but decomposing. Blood and intestines and some kind of goo Zayla couldn't place oozed from the corpse's gashed abdomen.

A fresh stream poured through the base of one of the arches into a smooth, carved bowl clearly made to hold the water. Ripped clothing and a strange, gray moss bunched along the base of one wall. The guards' torchlight dipped into multiple impressions in the moss like something had recently curled into the soft beds. Another tunnel yawned open on the opposite side—but only one.

Oblivious to the gore, Chip continued forward and stepped into that other tunnel. He turned to glare at Zayla. "You said it's this way?"

Zayla barely heard him. Her curiosity piqued at this strange, obviously inhabited space. Running a hand over a stone bench that curved along one wall, her fingers caught on the spiderweb-like cracks in the rock. Blue-green gemstones patterned into the bench glittered in the firelight. Wooden bowls filled with dried worms, dead insects, and purple gemstones rested on the stone. A strange loop of leather curled next to one bowl. She picked it up, feeling the soft, supple material between her fingers, as she opened the various loops. A leather harness, one that would fit a young noxling.

This space was clearly made by the nymphs of old, but judging by the wooden bowls and worn leather harness, someone had been using it recently. Maybe the Ratnaa Nemora? The thought jolted through Zayla, followed by a realization as clear as glass.

"This is a den," she breathed. She set the harness back down.

Chip grunted. "I don't give a dragon's ass if this is a den. This isn't what we're looking for. Let's. Go."

The vibrations flooded into Zayla's left side, then her right, the hum diving down to the soles of her feet then flying to the top of her head. It spread through her entire body. *Curse every root and spore, they're everywhere.*

Before she could prepare herself, the dirt that formed the walls of this space suddenly exploded outward. Blurs of white lunged from the walls. A barrage of rock and clumps of soil flew around the room like a storm.

Yelping, Zayla lifted her arms to cover her face, the dirt and stone pinging off her skin.

The guards shouted, Chip's yell louder than all the rest. One after another, red-eyed creatures burst through the dirt and attacked the guards. One lunged for Chip, while a second engaged two of his guards as they scrambled for their weapons.

Suncreatures.

Zayla stumbled back until her shoulders hit the stone archway. She wished she could blend in with the rock. *Please don't notice me.* A blur of white streaked between her and the Divus guard directly in front of her. The tops of its shoulders barely reached her hips. Its sinuous body was covered with overlapping layers of white scales. The creature crouched on four muscular legs, its long, thin tail whipping back and forth.

Her breath caught when it turned its long, narrow muzzle in her direction. The firelight glinted red in its beady black gaze.

Glinting red. Not actually red.

Shock tingled across Zayla's skin.

That isn't a suncreature.

As if dismissing Zayla, the creature turned back to the guard, sank low to the ground, and screeched. The Divus lifted her weapon too late. The creature leapt, easily dodging the sword, and sank its black claws into the guard's shoulder. The creature pierced the guard's armor as though it were merely paper.

Dropping her weapon, the woman screamed. Her eyes flared white as her Blood crafting emerged.

Zayla's stomach lurched.

The guard's hands scrabbled across the thick scales covering the creature's back, her fingers pulsing white with her Blood crafting.

The creature screeched again, seeming to ignore the deathly pull of the Divus's crafting. It wrapped its long tail around her leg, pulling the woman into a gruesome embrace by digging its claws deeper into the woman's flesh.

Beyond the Divus, Chip and the other guards were battling the beasts on all sides. There had to be at least ten creatures, their white-scaled hides reflecting the torchlight and the purple glow from Chip's lantern. One of the guards lay in a pool of blue blood, and his attackers joined the battle against Chip and the remaining guards. What would happen once all the guards were dead? Zayla's hand crept to the mushrooms and the seed in her pocket, wondering if she'd need to call on her crafting. She slid against the wall, heading for the tunnel exit that would lead her back the way they'd come.

As if sensing her thought, a nearby creature pivoted to look at her and shrieked, spitting crimson saliva past its twin rows of teeth. It snapped its long narrow jaw shut and hunched low to the ground, its tail whipping back and forth in anger. The creature flexed purple-tipped claws that glistened wetly at their pointed tips. *Poison?* Zayla bit back a scream as glowing crimson eyes locked with hers.

The vibrations within her body only confirmed what she already knew.

This one...this was a suncreature.

How many of these creatures are natural and how many are suncreatures? And why are they working together? The thoughts skittered through her mind in a heartbeat and left just as fast.

Praying her theory about these suncreatures was right, she lifted empty hands, showing she had no weapons. No drive to fight. The bark on her forearm caught the firelight, and she lifted her chin to show the bark choker as well. Her pulse pounded in her ears, and the shouts and shrieks of the fight continued around her.

The suncreature blinked. Intelligence shimmered behind its eyes as its gaze flicked between her Nemora markings, the crimson bark on her skin, and her open palms.

Zayla didn't move, standing so still it was as if she was made of stone. She waited.

After a heartbeat that could fit an eternity, the suncreature huffed, cocked its head in a curious gesture, then lunged.

Throwing her arms over her face, Zayla braced for impact, for pain, for the creature to land on top of her and wrap its tail around her like it did to the Divus.

A strangled scream came from beside her. Chip.

Zayla peeked between her arms and saw the creature wrap Chip in that deadly embrace, sinking its teeth and claws into his flesh.

The suncreature attacked him! Not me.

Zayla skirted the edges of the space until she reached the tunnel they'd come through. Barreling through it, she left the fight behind, plunging away from the torchlight into darkness. The screams and shrieks echoed in the underground passage, urging her to move on even in the inky blackness. She stumbled, nearly tripping over her own feet. With each heaving breath, the pain in her lungs spiked.

Her steps slowed as the sounds of the battle softened behind her. No footsteps or scratching claws followed her as she reached the area where they'd stopped for their meal. Leaning on the stone archway, she gasped for breath, trying to slow her racing heart. One, two, three deep lungfuls of air.

Finally, she pushed away from the archway. *I have to find the shard before Chip and the others get to it, then I can save Oryn and the others.*

Digging her hands into the fresh dirt, she called on her Nature crafting. Though her mycelium had grown beneath the dirt, some copper light shone through, brightening just enough for her to see a path twisting down the tunnel to her left.

She followed the dim light, first left, then straight, then a sharp right turn. She ran as fast as her legs would take her, keeping her hands against the dirt walls and stone archways, stumbling through the nearly pitch-black tunnels with only her mycelium leading the way.

A few turns later, a strange, pale-blue light brightened the tunnel ahead of her. Cold ebbed into the tunnel, making her skin prickle. She stepped into another open area and nearly slipped on the glass-like surface covering the floor. A jagged-edged crystal, no bigger than her hand, rested on the ground by the far wall. Its brilliant azure glow washed the surrounding stone and dirt.

The moon goddess shard.

The air grew colder, like she was stepping over the threshold of a warm house into a crisp winter's day. Her breath fogged, and she immediately began shivering. She kept moving forward, inching closer and closer to the shard. Closer and closer to a thing of legends.

As she crouched down next to it, waves of icy air washed over her like the shard itself had a heartbeat. The vibrant-blue shard was wrapped with thin, white mycelium strands, frozen in place by the sheer cold. *My mycelium. My crafting. I found this when no one else could.*

Zayla tore off a piece of her tunic and folded it so layers of cloth could protect her bare hands from the shard's frigid surface. When she picked up the shard, her palm felt like she had dipped it in ice water…but not painfully so.

"Noxling!" Chip's voice echoed down the tunnel, sourceless but coming closer. "Come back here!"

Zayla's stomach plummeted. She immediately pocketed the shard. *How many of the guards survived?* Not wanting Chip to see this strange room and know what she currently had in her possession, she darted back into the tunnel. She ran toward Chip, toward danger, if only to keep her secret for a little longer. One turn, then another, then—

She met Chip in a straightaway.

He held a torch aloft, the firelight throwing his features into stark relief, but the purple lantern on Chip's belt was shattered, its fire gone dark. The sight gave Zayla a vicious sense of joy that Tor's plan to keep the creatures at bay hadn't worked. Blue blood splattered Chip's face. A trio of long gashes ran across his chest, oozing orange. His breathing came labored, but anger clearly pushed him forward. "You led us into a trap!" he growled.

She stepped back, keeping some distance between them. "No! Those creatures could've killed me, too."

"You got my people killed, noxling." Chip drew the duskiron dagger from his belt. "You think I'm going to let you live?"

A rebellious anger flared in her chest. "Tor knew about the suncreatures. He got your people killed, not me. He's the one who's ordered this useless hunt for a goddess shard that isn't even here."

"I'll kill you!" The man roared, dropping the torch and closing the distance between them in a heartbeat, and Zayla's anger vanished against a swell of fear.

Chapter Twenty-Three

ZAYLA CLOSED HER FIST around a mushroom in her pocket a heartbeat
before Chip barreled into her. Both of them crashed to the ground, and
pain spiderwebbed through her back. Air left her in a sudden rush.

Chip's full weight pressed down on her like a heavy, restricting blanket
smelling of blood, sweat, and a damp musk.

"Those creatures ate my companion animal!" He growled in her ear,
hot breath fanning her cheek. "And if the shard isn't here, I guess Tor
doesn't need you anymore."

The duskiron dagger Shadre had given him glinted as he twisted and
lifted it high above his head. The smirk crawling across his face said she
was too weak to fight back, too limited in crafting sources, too young a
noxling.

He was wrong.

Zayla pressed the mushroom into the wall next to her, fingers grating
against the rough dirt. The familiar brown glaze pulled over her eyes as the
fungus glowed with her crafting, casting shadows across Chip's shocked
expression.

Restrain. The command, ushered from her body, spread through the
tiny fungus. In a breath, thin strands of mycelium burst from the
mushroom and wrapped around Chip's wrist, holding the dagger back.

Vibrations shuddered through her, the spores spreading over her skin.
Her chest seized with a new pain—searing and swirling on one single spot,
like all the spores were centering themselves. No, not centering. Growing.
Fear flashed through her. *I need to end this. Now.*

Grunting, Chip ripped his hand free and plunged the dagger toward
Zayla's face.

She yanked her head to the side. The blade sliced a burning line from
her cheek to her ear, slamming into the dirt next to her head. A scratching
noise echoed down the tunnel. The vibrations within her body hummed to
her left. The creatures were coming to fight Chip, but not soon enough.

Chip drew back his other hand and punched her.

Her head slammed to the side. Pain burst through her cheek, and hot
blood spurted from her nose. White spots swam in her vision. She
groaned. Her heart pounded, like footsteps running toward her.

Chip lifted the duskiron dagger once more.

In the dim crafting light, a figure suddenly appeared behind Chip. A woman grabbed hold of Chip's arm and threw him bodily to the side. He landed hard against the opposite wall.

"Shadre?" Chip growled, pushing himself upright. "The hells are you doing—"

Sitting up, Zayla used Chip's moment of confusion. She commanded the mycelium once more. The strands burst from the dirt, wrapped tight around the Vagari's arms, and pinned him to the wall.

The spot of crafting within her chest ached, its fire searing her lungs. Air came in like a trickle instead of a rush. Her lungs wouldn't work properly, couldn't expand. The fungi had finally taken root. A flash of horrible inspiration came to her. *Take his breath.*

He struggled against the mushrooms, thrashing this way and that, but her strands held him back.

Forcing the thin mycelium strands down Chip's throat—one after another after another—Zayla commanded the mycelium to dive into him until his airway was completely blocked. Suffocating him. He gurgled and choked, the mycelium so thick not even a scream could pass through.

Chip's wide eyes met hers. Shock. Fear. He tried to move again, but the mycelium kept him restrained, the thin strands bolstered by Zayla's crafting.

Slowly, the light in Chip's eyes ebbed away.

His body slackened, and his duskiron dagger clattered to the stone beneath him.

Zayla slumped away from the corpse, a long, jagged breath releasing from her constricted lungs.

Blinking her crafting light away, Zayla nodded at Shadre and shoved Chip's dagger into her belt. It wasn't like he needed it anyway. The vibrations warning her of the approaching suncreatures dimmed to a dull hum. Her body ached, both from the fight and from using her crafting. She pushed herself to her feet. Each breath stabbed like a knife wound. An imaginary band cinched tight around her lungs, forcing her to take small, shallow breaths. Cold worry crept over her. *Do I have fungi living inside me now?* Her skin was tight and painful, like she'd been burned, and she knew the sporebruises now covered most of her flesh. Just standing felt like a monumental effort.

"Wow. Are you okay?" Shadre said in the way of a hello. "I thought you might need help but—"

Anger, disappointment, a deep aching tiredness, and something that felt like relief stormed through Zayla. She clenched her jaw—and punched Shadre. Pain flashed through Zayla's knuckles.

Grunting, Shadre's head snapped to the side. Righting herself and rubbing her chin, she muttered, "Okay, yeah, I deserved that."

"Hells yeah you did. How'd you even find me, Shadre?" Zayla pressed a trembling hand onto the wall to hold herself upright.

"I've been down here before, but mostly, I just followed the screaming," Shadre admitted. Her eyes roamed Zayla's body, as though checking for injuries. "Are you able to walk?"

"Not very fast." Her legs trembled uncontrollably, slowly going numb beneath her. Afraid she'd fall over, she sank to the ground.

What would Shadre do, now that Chip and the other guards were dead? Chip, at least, seemed to have been her friend. *I have to keep moving. I have to free Misti and Orenda. I have to help Oryn.* Desperation clawed at the edges of her mind, but sleep would be a sweet relief, and she might not be able to resist. She closed her eyes and breathed as shallowly as she could, but even that sent stabs of pain through her lungs. The sweet scent of clean, damp dirt filled her nose, blessedly covering the stench of Chip just across the way from her.

"Why?" She forced open eyelids that felt weighted like stones.

The lanternlight flickered across Shadre's features, deepening the worry lines on her forehead. Kneeling down, she rummaged in her pack, handing a bag of jerky and dried berries to Zayla. "I came down here not just to help you, Zayla, but to warn you."

"About?" Zayla unceremoniously shoveled a few handfuls of food into her mouth, knowing it would help her regain her strength. The jerky filled her senses with spices and smoke, and the sour berries cut the richness. She followed it all with a few deep pulls of water. *I have to free my friends.*

"Tor's getting desperate." Shadre lowered her voice, as if she feared Tor could hear her. "He confided in me that he was only supposed to mine for specific gemstones. He fears that he lost too many guards to these underground ruins, looking for a goddess shard that might not even be here."

Zayla fought the urge to check her pocket for the shard. Hurt from Shadre's betrayal and gratitude from her coming down to the ruins were fighting a battle nearly as intense as when the goddess sisters fought. She'd trusted Shadre once. Could she ever trust her again? Zayla tightened her jaw, refusing to release the secret.

"He thinks he's going to get into trouble with his higher ups." Shadre sighed. "He plans to kill the Seventh Circle today."

Surprised, Zayla met her gaze. "What? Why?"

Shadre pushed her hands through her hair. "If he can show he overthrew Ratnaa Grove completely, taking out their most powerful person...well, maybe it won't matter how many guards he lost in the process."

"But he didn't lose the guards to the Ratnaa people. Why punish and blame them?" Zayla argued.

"Because he's a sunsick—"

"Wait," she interrupted Shadre. A thought almost too terrible to share flashed through Zayla's mind. "If Tor thinks that killing powerful people will help get him out of trouble...what's stopping him from killing Oryn?"

Shadre's lips pressed into a grim line. "Exactly. We need to get back up there, and quickly." She let out a sigh, blowing a strand of silvery hair from her face. "I don't know how we're going to get out of here, though. I'd planned on leading us back to the courtyard, so we could climb the knotted rope I left, but I got turned around."

That would be easy to do, for anyone that wasn't Zayla. She pressed a palm flat onto the dirt next to her, expanding her mind and sensing the mycelium webbing outward. If she followed her mycelium, she'd get them both out. "I know the way back."

"After only your first time down here? Amazing," Shadre murmured, her brows pulling together.

A sudden feeling of uneasiness and dread twisted through Zayla. Something was happening. Something bad. *Oryn?* Horror gripped her mind. Was something happening to them? Every part of her wanted to run to her sibling, but it would take too long. She needed help from people aboveground. She needed to free Misti and Orenda. "Let me free my friends first."

"The two women in the prison? Misti and Orenda?" At Zayla's nod, Shadre backed away, giving Zayla more space. "Are you sure you have enough energy to do that?"

"I'll have to. They can get to Oryn the quickest." Pulling all but three of the remaining eleven mushrooms from her pocket, Zayla peered at them. *How will I find the prison cells from so far away?* An idea sparked through her, and she quickly set the duskiron dagger next to her. She wouldn't be looking for stone or water or scorched dirt. *I can look specifically for the duskiron.* They weren't directly underneath the prison cells where Misti and Orenda were being held, but if she could find duskiron bars, she'd find the cells.

Even with the food, her energy was waning. She could barely stand. How could she dredge up enough energy to craft?

Chip's dead body lay before her, and she stared at his slackened jaw, his forever open and empty eyes, the blood on his clothing. *I killed Chip. I don't have enough energy, but maybe I can use his.* Placing the mushrooms onto Chip's corpse, she commanded the fungi to feed off the Vagari. Through her crafting, Zayla sensed a small, if steady, wave of energy flow into the mushrooms. Just enough to command the mycelium to grow, to spread and link with the other mycelium she'd left behind in the tunnels. The threads of mycelium found each other and connected. A pulse of energy rippled through them. A few threads became hundreds, then thousands, then more, until the entire underground network of mycelium she'd created was at her fingertips. A surge of cool energy crashed into Zayla, banishing the exhaustion and pain away like she'd been doused in frigid water. She gasped at the raw living power at her fingertips.

I can find them. I have to.

Closing her eyes, she commanded the mycelium to move again, not outward like ripples, but up.

Up.

Up.

 The mycelium spread faster and farther than ever before, propelled forward both from Zayla's fresh energy and her determination, angling toward where she believed the prison cells were. She threw her senses outward. Her threads pushed through layers and layers of smooth soft dirt, tiny streams of fresh water, small rocks and insects, until the dirt grew tough. Rocky. Hope flared within her.

She'd hit the layer of burnt ground. *Only a bit more now.*

She shoved the mycelium through the rougher terrain. Her body hummed. The sporebruises crawled like burns across her skin. The spiraling center mass of pain in her chest sharpened once more, pulsing like a heartbeat out of sync with her own.

Ignoring it the best she could, Zayla concentrated. Her mycelium hit a smooth stone surface. *A rock? No.* Zayla tried to wrap the mycelium around the foreign object, but it was too big. The angle. The distance.

This has to be it. The gemstone prison.

But she had to be sure.

Zayla spread the mycelium across the gemstone until she found what she was looking for. Cold, solid, smooth metal.

Opening her eyes, Zayla's brown-glazed vision riveted to the duskiron dagger she'd set in front of her. At her order, a single strand of mycelium grew from the fungi on Chip's body and wrapped around the duskiron blade.

The connection sang. Duskiron meeting duskiron—blade connecting to bars. And Zayla knew, immediately, that she'd found the prison cells. *Yes!* Her idea had worked.

Agony spiked in her hands, distracting her. Her fingers flexed instinctively. Thin white tendrils pushed from beneath her fingernails, diving into the ground. Zayla gasped. A sudden fear tore at her concentration. *My crafting, lashing back. Nature will claim me as its own.* The spot in her chest flared, and her breathing seized. *No, not yet. Please, not yet.* Zayla pressed on. She couldn't stop now. Couldn't let her fears for her own life get in the way of freeing her friends.

Commanding the mycelium far, far above her, Zayla forced her strands to travel up the duskiron bar, using the imperfections around the metal to shove their way to the surface. The strands burst through, and Zayla sensed cool, empty air. Movement became so much easier and faster.

She had to be so, so fast. A thread of worry pulled through her, hot and fast. She could only assume a guard was standing watch. *I have to bend the bars.*

Keeping the mycelium close to the ground, she commanded them to loop around two of the bars and pushed more of her crafting into them. More and more and more of her newfound energy flowed through the thin strands, bolstering them, making them far stronger than only nature allowed, strong enough to bend the bars.

Vibrations thundered through metal.

An intense, white-hot pain sizzled through the mycelium into Zayla.

Blistering, searing, agony.

Fire.

Zayla felt it as clearly as if she'd stuck her hand into a burning inferno.

Someone was actively burning her mycelium. Stopping her from freeing her friends.

She released hold of her crafting, blinking back tears and sucking in as deep a breath as she could.

"Someone's burning my fungi," she blurted. The words seemed to rip her throat on the way out, and she started coughing. Heaving.

A guard must have seen. Someone had burned her plants. She had meant to free Misti and Orenda, meant to give them a way out. Instead of helping, she might've just gotten her friends into more trouble. *I might've just gotten Orenda and Misti killed.* "I have to get to the surface, Shadre. I have to get above ground right now!"

Zayla pushed herself to her feet, but her legs couldn't hold her weight, and she immediately collapsed.

"I was thinking, if you can't walk on your own, I—" Shadre paused, then drew in a sudden breath as if overcoming a bundle of nerves. "I can carry you."

Discomfort prickled under Zayla's skin, remembering the last time Shadre had carried her, after the fight with the hunters in the Cinder Forest. The woman had carried her right into a prison cell. Who's to say she wouldn't do it again? Gathering all her scraps of energy, she pushed herself to her feet again, leaning on the wall for support. *I have to get aboveground.*

Her vision canted to the side, and her gaze locked onto Chip's dead body. Mushrooms had sprouted from his wounds. Mycelium had spread beneath his flesh like he had a new set of veins. Even though she'd just killed him, his body cavity had already sunken in. His eyes were sucked dry as the fungi broke down his body. It was almost too easy, killing him. Using him. Would she have to use Shadre the same way? The thought sickened her.

She leaned over and patted his pockets, pulling out the key to the duskiron cells. *Just in case.* Turning away, she stumbled down the tunnel, Shadre following close at her heels. "Why should I trust you, Shadre?"

"Because I gave you food and water and blankets when you were in the prison cell," Shadre began. Zayla barked out a laugh—like providing survival items would really heal the rift between them? But Shadre pressed on. "I gave you the purple lanterns when I shouldn't have. I tightened your harness before you came down here to make sure the drop didn't kill you. I snuck you the living tree seed for your crafting, and I came down to help you." Exasperation strangled her words. "I stopped Chip from knifing you back there! I just...I don't know how else to show you that you can trust me. That I want to help you. Help you both, hells, help you all! You, Oryn, Misti, Orenda, the Rantaa Nemora. I want to help you all."

Zayla didn't look back at the musician. "Sure. That's why you locked us up in the first place, I suppose."

Her foot snagged on a stone, and she tripped, tumbling to the ground. The impact jarred her hands and knees, but she shoved herself back onto her feet.

"Let me help you!" Shadre stepped in front of her, blocking her path.

"You're working with them," Zayla muttered. Her vision blurred. After a couple of quick blinks, the world sharpened once more. A soft hand lifted her chin.

Shadre's expression was full of resolve and sorrow and something else that Zayla couldn't quite put her finger on. "I'm not. Tor and his followers...they're horrible. I...I can't look away anymore. I won't look away anymore. I'm not working with him any longer." She lowered her hand. Wetness glimmered in her eyes, and her bottom lip trembled as the words tumbled out. "And I'm so sorry for what I did. For my part in your and Oryn's capture. You're right, it's my fault that you're here. It wasn't right. And I'll spend the rest of my life proving how sorry I am. I'll spend as long as it takes—as long as you'll let me—to prove that you can trust me again."

The genuine apology broke something in Zayla, and some of her anger slipped through the cracks. Some, but not all. "Well, that's going to take a long time." She gave Shadre a tired grimace she wasn't sure was a smile or pain. "But I think you're stubborn enough to see it through."

"Hells right I am." Shadre grinned, then offered a supporting hand. "So, can I carry you?"

Doubt still weighed heavy on Zayla's mind, but her worry for her sibling was far heavier. She needed to get to Oryn. As tired as she was, it wasn't as if she had a choice. "Fine."

Shadre gathered Zayla up into her arms, gingerly and slowly, as if she feared Zayla would break under the pressure. Shadre's rust-orange gaze flicked to hers. "Okay. I've got you. Tell me which way to go."

Zayla wrapped her arms around Shadre's neck, holding tight. Shadre's warm, nutty scent filled her senses. Cognizant of the strange mycelium sprouting from her fingers, she closed her hands into fists and nodded toward the tunnel that led in the direction of the courtyard. "That way."

Shadre started to run down the passage in a smooth jog that, surprisingly, didn't jostle Zayla much. The musician moved so easily, and so quickly, it was as if Zayla weighed nothing to her.

Silence followed them, but worry kept pace. Were Orenda and Misti suffering now for her attempt to free them? Was Oryn still alive? It was unbearable, not knowing what was happening aboveground. To distract herself more than anything, she filled Shadre in about the creatures who lived in the ruins.

"I can't believe you called the suncreatures to you." Shadre quickened her pace as she backtracked through the winding passageways at Zayla's direction. "What a sunbaked idea."

"It worked, didn't it?" Like this woman could talk about sunbaked ideas.

"Much better than the purple fire lanterns," Shadre admitted.

"I think it's their food," Zayla replied.

Shadre glanced down at her. "What?"

"There were some purple crystals in bowls in the creatures' den. I think the Nemora were feeding them. Taking care of them, maybe even like pets."

"The suncreatures?" Shock rippled through Shadre's words.

"There were a mixture of natural creatures and suncreatures in the horde that attacked us. I think that's why the suncreatures didn't attack the Nemora...why they didn't attack me. The suncreatures and the natural creatures were living together. The Ratnaa Nemora must have cared for them, so the creatures protected them in turn. Protected me."

They came to a split path. Shadre held Zayla close enough to one wall to press a palm to the dirt. The mycelium pointed to the left path. "Suncreatures and natural creatures living together," Shadre breathed, continuing their run. "That's some theory."

"I came face-to-face with a suncreature during the fight, and it didn't kill me. I have no other reason why I'm alive right now. It was a terrifying and exhilarating experience," Zayla admitted quietly. She hadn't felt great in the moment, but looking back, the experience had been...amazing. Unheard of. Something for the history books even. She couldn't shake how intelligence had gleamed so clearly behind the suncreature's eyes.

Shadre slowed, then stopped. "Aw, hells."

Zayla blinked, coming back to the present. She stared at a solid wall of dirt and rocks. The main tunnel leading back to the underground courtyard had collapsed.

"Hells," Zayla agreed.

Chapter Twenty-Four

LEANING ON A STONE archway for support, Zayla stared hopelessly at the wall of crumpled dirt and stone ahead of them. Her mycelium hadn't warned her about this, and her crafting was next to useless here. Growing something large enough to move dirt would probably just collapse more of the tunnel around them.

At least being carried had given her a chance to rest, and as much as she hated to admit it, the food Shadre had given her also helped. That, and probably gaining the energy from Chip's corpse. Her legs felt stronger, and her breathing came a little easier. Instead of a dagger stabbing her with each inhale, it felt more like a thorn scratching her lungs. She still couldn't get a full breath, and she knew, deep inside, that the spores really had grown into her lungs, taking over space where air should be.

Shadre lifted a stone and set it aside, causing soil to sift down around her feet as she tried to see how far the collapsed tunnel went. "This is such wyvern shit! I keep hitting more dirt and stone. I think we'll have to double back."

"We don't have time." Zayla searched the threads of her mycelium for an alternate route. Misti and Orenda needed her help. The Seventh Circle might already be dead. She gulped thickly. Oryn might already be dead. She quickly shoved that thought away. She'd know. If her sibling had died…she'd know. The sudden sense of dread earlier had to mean something else. Anything else. Not that.

But any of the other routes through the tunnels would add too much time to their journey to the surface. Time they didn't have.

"We're so close!" Zayla said, her nails digging into her clenched fists and the mycelium. "The courtyard is directly on the other side of this."

"Is it a straight shot?" Shadre glanced at Zayla for confirmation, then turned back to the collapsed tunnel. "Okay. You got us this far. Let me see what I can do."

Soft, golden-brown light brightened the angled Ingo markings on the back of Shadre's bare shoulders, then poured into the ones circling her arms. She unhooked her lantern from her belt, her duskiron lantern.

Zayla hadn't noticed before, but the lantern was made of the blue-black metal from Shadre's home offshoot instead of the silvery lanterns she'd seen on the other guards.

Shadre met Zayla's gaze over her shoulder. "It's going to get dark," she warned, pushing the metal into the dirt wall. The duskiron melted into the soil, sending the glass panes shattering to the floor and extinguishing the yellow flame. Only the weak, golden-brown glow of Shadre's Nature crafting permeated the inky darkness.

Zayla pressed her shoulder into the dirt wall, finding comfort in the scent of fresh soil.

The sounds of shifting dirt and crunching rocks echoed Shadre's concentration as she created a duskiron tunnel only wide enough for one person to wiggle through. The metal glowed with Shadre's Nature crafting, pushing farther and farther away from them.

Zayla gaped at the sheer amount of power Shadre could wield. She'd never seen Ingo Nemora crafting used this way.

The duskiron tunnel punched out the other side. It had to be the courtyard.

"You go through first," Shadre rasped, her words nearly disappearing under a coughing fit. "I'll hold it up."

Zayla scooted past Shadre, glancing at the musician as she did. Her Nemora markings glowed, casting shadows across her features, but Zayla still caught the thin line of blood trickling out of Shadre's nose. The price of her crafting.

"Go!" Shadre kept her palms flat against the paper-thin metal holding back the collapse.

Hefting herself up, Zayla slipped into the small duskiron tunnel. Her elbows touched the metal walls, and her head scraped the ceiling as she scooted her way through. Thank every root and spore she didn't mind tight spaces.

Once, Shadre's duskiron had been bars, keeping Zayla locked away, and now the metal was a way out. A way back to her sibling. To her friends. Her worries gave way under a surprising rush of gratitude.

The closer she got to the courtyard, the brighter the tunnel became, until even the dark metal glinted at her. She finally came to the end of the duskiron tunnel and dropped out the other side, the soles of her boots crunching against the stone. Far ahead, a bright column of sunlight filtered down from the hole. It was daytime aboveground. They were so close. Relief and dread spiraled within her.

"You out?" Shadre said.

"Yes!" Zayla answered.

After a bit of swearing and scooting, Shadre made her way through. The moment her boots hit the ground, she blinked her Nature crafting away. The golden-brown light faded, and the duskiron tunnel behind her collapsed in a scream of metal and crunch of stone. She leaned on the wall, eyes closed, and wiped the blood away from her nose.

"Are you okay?" Zayla grabbed hold of Shadre's hand.

"I'll be fine." Shadre gave her a weak smile, then coughed into her elbow, the sound like rocks grating against one another. After a bit, she straightened and wiped a bit of blood from her lips. "Let's just keep going."

Zayla tightened her hold on Shadre's fingers. "Thank you," she whispered.

"Anytime," Shadre replied. "But I might need some help getting to that hole."

Zayla nodded.

Leaning on one another for support, they limped to the column of sunlight. Past the bones littering the ground. Past the broken archways. Over the lip of the fountain. Soon, they were directly below the light, peering up at the hole.

The sounds of commotion floated down from above. Someone was shouting angry, indistinguishable words. They heard the sound of beating wings, a wyvern's shriek. The vibrations within her body migrated to the top of her head. Suncreatures, above them, the ones guarding the prisoners. A person screamed. The sound cut short.

Zayla's chest tightened. She looked around for the knotted rope Shadre had used to get down.

"We can't use the rope," Shadre said from behind her, her voice tight.

Zayla turned. "Why? You said—"

Shadre held the severed end of a long length of knotted rope. "Tor must've found out I'm down here and suspected something was up."

Another scream pierced the air. The voice sounded younger. A child.

Zayla's blood turned to ice. It wasn't just her friends and her sibling in danger. Not just the Seventh Circle. The rest of the Ratnaa Nemora were in trouble, too. The other prisoners. The other noxlings.

Clenching her jaw, she pulled the living tree seed from her pocket with one hand and looked at Shadre. "Stay close to me."

Shadre gave her a curious expression but moved within arm's reach.

Zayla gathered her energy and took as big a breath as she could, heedless of the sharp twinge against her ribs. She closed her eyes and imagined the lush, green-capped trees of Dara Grove, the sturdy blue trunks of sobsky offshoot, Oryn's home, the tall crimson trees of her mother's offshoot. When she opened her eyes, the familiar brown glaze filled her vision.

Dara. She summoned her crafting, pouring her energy into this wrinkled tree seed and willing it to bloom. The shell cracked open, and the tree sprouted. A tiny shoot glowed with her crafting.

The familiar hum within her body intensified, drawn inward to the center of her power. She ignored her shaking limbs. She was harnessing Dara crafting—not Myceli—so the backlash should be slower. She hadn't called on Dara since the fight with the hunters in the Cinder Forest. Not for a few nights at least. Nature should—no, nature *would* give her more time.

Grow. She commanded her little sapling. *Now!*

With a creaking sound, the glowing sapling doubled in size. Soon, the trunk stretched taller than Zayla's head, its roots spilling past her hands to tickle the stone pavers around her feet. She set the young tree on the ground, allowing the roots to burrow deep into the cracks. Keeping hold on a small branch no wider than her finger, she wrapped one arm around Shadre, hugging her close.

Shadre rested one arm around Zayla's waist, chin tilted up to watch the burgeoning canopy of wide, feathery leaves spreading above them.

As if time itself was racing forward, the trunk thickened. First only as wide as Zayla's arm, then as wide as her body. Then suddenly the tree grew, two, three, five people wide.

The limb Zayla held grew five times its size. She could hardly hold on to it as she and Shadre were lifted off the ground. Shadre clung to her, her weight nearly tearing Zayla's grip from the branch. Zayla gave a brief nod of attention to her feet, forcing another branch to push out of the trunk below them, easing the burden and bearing them both aloft as the tree stretched to the sky with dizzying speed. Her stomach plummeted as she watched the fountain disappear into darkness below.

Vibrations chattered her bones. Crimson wood tore through her shoulder, bursting through her skin, burning like fire. She gritted her teeth and tightened her grip on the branch. *I have to get aboveground.* She pushed more of her energy into the tree, commanding it to keep growing. The bark beside them split, oozing sap. Tri-petaled flowers bloomed around them, their petals quickly falling away and buds swelling to deep, dark orbs of fruit.

"Hells, Zayla," Shadre yelled.

"We're almost there," Zayla replied.

A familiar screech came from overhead. A thunderclap. Its cry cut short, too.

In a needle of pain, another sliver of bark burst through the back of Zayla's hand then dove into the branch she clung to. It held her palm against the bark, keeping her steady as the tree stretched upward.

Higher and higher the tree grew until, with a great cracking sound, the trunk burst through the hole into the aboveground air. Wood shards rained down as branches snapped on the way out, peppering Zayla's arms and legs with splinters. Shadre's arms tightened around her waist, small trickles of brown blood marking her skin where the splinters had hit her. The familiar scent of ashes mixed with the sweet sap of broken wood.

Blinking in the daylight, Zayla shuddered and let her crafting go. The brown glaze vanished, and the tree's glow faded. Zayla clung to a familiar, green-barked branch tipped with off-yellow leaves. Between the gaps in the foliage, she could see the burned, yellow-red dirt of Ratnaa Grove.

An explosion rocked the air. Cracking fire. A billow of smoke plumed into the sky.

"No." In a burst of energy and anxiety, Zayla ripped her hand free, tearing bark and flesh. She grabbed several seed pods closest to her, and ran the length of the branch, leaping to the ground below.

Chaos had erupted aboveground between here and the shattered remains of the center of Ratnaa Grove. New fires burned around them, sending thick clouds of smoke into the air. One massive wall of flame blocked the view of the hanging tree and the cages beyond. Bloodied dead bodies lay strewn about. She scanned frantically for her friends or Oryn, eyes watering from the smoke. Both Ratnaa Nemora and Tor's followers lay with tangled limbs and bloodied faces. None of them her friends. Large piles of smoldering ash sat between her and the wall of flame. She could just make out a few white feathers and scales among the crimson cinders. The wyvern and thunderclaps? It seemed some of the suncreatures guarding the prisoners had been killed.

What happened here? Zayla could hardly make sense of it before her attention snapped to two adult Ratnaa Nemora racing in her direction. Heading for her, or for the hole, or for the outskirts of their Grove, Zayla didn't know.

Three pyrewolf suncreatures emerged from the smoke behind them in pursuit, their long legs closing the distance. A pyrewolf slashed one of the Nemora's legs, sending brown blood gushing into the air as the Nemora toppled over. Another beast used its long muzzle to rip the second Nemora's back open, vicious teeth clamped hard around their spine. The third pyrewolf howled and bit one of the Nemora's arms. As they tore into their fresh kills, the suncreatures' white fur rippled, showing the crimson glow of their skin.

Zayla's stomach turned over. Though her heart ached, there was nothing she could do for those Nemora. Nothing except pray to every root and spore those pyrewolf suncreatures wouldn't see her as she moved toward the wall of flames. Her legs shook and her already tortured lungs burned with smoke, but she forced herself to keep moving.

Shadre put her hand on Zayla's arm, offering support, but Zayla shook her head. "Be ready to fight."

Shadre nodded, hand going to the axe at her belt.

As they skirted the flames, Zayla covered her mouth with her hand to block the smoke. Her lungs ached, bucking at each inhale. Heat penetrated her clothes and tightened her skin.

As she rounded the massive fire, she saw Tor standing directly in front of the hanging tree, clutching a dagger that dripped brown blood. The Seventh Circle lay dead on the ground in front of him. A dark, brown stain bloomed over her heart, her eyes open, unseeing.

Ten guards wearing wyvern scaled armor flanked the man, and three of them held prisoners with daggers at their necks.

Misti, Orenda, and a dark-skinned woman with short horns jutting from her black hair and a deep gash on her arm who Zayla didn't recognize were all gagged and bound.

Zayla searched the silvery prisons nearby. Each one had gaping holes. It looked as if the metal had melted somehow. And all the cells were empty. "Where's Oryn?"

Tor's gaze met Zayla's through the smoky air. His lips curled into a sneer as his attention flicked between her and Shadre. "We had an incident while you were below," Tor said, ignoring her question. "You know part of it, I assume, as you were trying to break your friends free."

He gestured to the archway. Tendrils of black smoke curled from the entrance. The fires they'd set to stop Zayla's mycelium. To hold her off. "But there was also another prison break…led by that one."

The guard holding the dark-skinned woman shook her roughly. She bared her teeth at him, but the guard merely pressed his dagger closer to the woman's neck. Orange blood seeped around the blade.

Zayla's gaze flickered across her friends.

Orenda had a wide cut on her forehead that oozed blue blood into her eyes. She swayed in her guard's grip. Misti clutched her stomach, breathing hard, while the dark-skinned woman glared at her. No, not at her, at the guard holding Misti. If looks could disembowel a person, that woman's stare would do just that.

Tor chuckled. "Trying and failing to set the Ratnaa Nemora free." His eyebrow twitched as he looked at Shadre. "I assume you were also involved, Shadre. Heading into the ruins against my express permission. How disappointing."

Shadre lifted her chin, placing a hand on Zayla's arm.

Tor raked his gaze over Zayla as if he could see clear through her. "I assume Chip and the others have died. By your hand or the creatures in the ruins?"

Zayla lifted her chin. "Both."

"Very well." His pale eyes crinkled at the sides. "But your hunt was successful."

Zayla stilled. The goddess shard in her pocket felt a thousand pounds heavier. He couldn't know that she had it. He had to be fishing for information, and she wouldn't give it to him.

Shadre jumped in before Zayla could reply. "There was no goddess shard in the underground ruins. You got your people killed for no good reason."

Tor pursed his lips, then wiped the Seventh's Circle's blood off his blade with a corner of her robes. "Is that what she told you, Shadre?" At Shadre's silence, Tor laughed. "Then it seems like you betrayed me just to get betrayed yourself. Zayla has the shard."

Shadre's hand slipped off Zayla's arm, then warm breath feathered her cheek. "Is that true?" Shadre whispered.

Green eyes flashed as Orenda ripped off her mouth gag. "Don't give it to him!"

The guard delivered a swift hit with his dagger's hilt, and she crumpled to the ground.

Misti and the dark-skinned woman pulled uselessly against their guards, eyes wide with fear.

Zayla kept her focus on Tor. "I don't have your precious sun goddess shard, Tor."

It was the truth. She didn't have his goddess shard, a crimson shard from Ponuriah, his fiery deity. She had a blue shard, one from Aluriah, the moon goddess.

Scowling, Tor gestured in one sharp hand movement to one of his guards.

The woman broke rank, disappearing behind the hanging tree for a moment. She returned hauling a bloodied, gagged, bound figure to Tor's side.

Oryn.

Oryn kicked at the woman, trying to yell something around their gag. A second guard—a Vagari with long fingers that looked more like claws—pinned Oryn's legs, holding them in place. The strange metal bands still circled Oryn's wrists, cutting them off from their crafting. Blood oozed from fresh cuts on their chest.

Zayla gasped, and her hand automatically sank into her pocket, feeling the three remaining mushrooms and trio of tree pod seeds. The dirt here was scorched and ruined, but she could force some mycelium to grow from the mushrooms. Grow three trees from the seed pods. Hells, even use the bark covering her wounds if it came to that. Command enough nature to kill Tor, at least, before her crafting took its final toll on her life.

Shadre gripped her arm—to hold her back or for comfort, Zayla couldn't tell.

"Give me the goddess shard, Zayla." Tor lifted his hand to her, palm up, as if he expected her to simply hand it over. "Now."

At the words "goddess shard," Oryn's wild gaze caught Zayla's, the sky-blue color darkening with anger and worry. They shook their head.

Zayla's heart pounded. She couldn't give up the goddess shard. It was too powerful, a legendary artifact that could turn the tide of war. She'd never hand it over to Tor.

But she couldn't let her sibling die.

"Oryn's too valuable to kill, Tor, and you know it," Zayla said. "Your higher ups wouldn't like you killing one of the most powerful crafters on the planet. Not when the sun goddess worshippers would want to use Oryn's powers."

For the first time, Zayla saw worry flash through Tor's eyes.

Her crafting swelled within her. The vibrations swirled in her palm, making her hand clench, closing over both the mushrooms and the tree pod seeds. Chip's dead body flashed in her mind's eye, and realization tingled down her spine. She pulled her shoulders back. A memory came, unbidden, of a thin, deep-red root that sprouted vibrant, glassy-green fungus. A bitterroot. Her poisonous offshoot, a home she couldn't return to because a suncreature had destroyed it. A hybrid crafting she rarely considered. The power seeped into her, waiting for her command.

A plan unfurled in her mind as she realized she didn't need to use just Myceli or Dara crafting. I could do so much more.

Tor grabbed Oryn by the nape of their neck. "I've already lost too many people. If I'm going to die for my actions, I might as well take as many of you fools with me as I can."

In a decisive thrust, he sank his blade into Oryn's gut.

Chapter Twenty-Five

"NO!" ZAYLA LURCHED FORWARD as Tor pushed the knife deeper into Oryn's abdomen.

Oryn. She had to do something. Zayla reached for her power. The steady hum and nature's full, vicious anger surged within her. The world turned brown as her crafting took hold. Dara and Myceli, her two Groves, filled her imagination—lush crimson trees surrounded by purple capped mushrooms appearing in her mind's eye. Neither was strong enough alone to defeat Tor.

Tor caught Zayla's gaze and started to laugh. "What? Are you going to fight me, noxling?" He sneered. "You won't even come close to saving them."

The ten guards closed rank around them, putting themselves between her and Tor, even the three holding her friends. Blocking her view of Oryn.

Zayla stopped moving. A cold, even calmness spread through her. She opened her fist, sensing the raw potential inside the mushrooms and tree pods resting on her palm.

Not Dara. Not Myceli. *Both.*

Bitterroot.

Her hybrid power—her true power—expanded within her with a sudden gasp. The combination of Dara and Myceli power had been anchored deep in her soul, just waiting to be embraced and released by her. It had been so long since she called upon her bitterroot offshoot. Since she called upon her home. She always feared doing so. While her hybrid crafting was much more powerful, it also backlashed more quickly, but the backlash didn't matter now. The only thing that mattered was Oryn. The mushrooms and tree seed pods glowed with her crafting.

Bitterroot.

She imagined a splintered crimson root woven with lively green mushrooms and oozing purple sap. It was the only thing she remembered from her offshoot home, but her crafting sang with the memory. The vibrations of her power deepened until they became a low rumble in the pit of her belly.

The mushrooms and tree pods fused together on her palm, then exploded outward in thick crimson roots woven with green veins. A bitterroot. A plant entirely and only hers as the last remaining survivor of the bitterroot offshoot.

One, two, three—the roots pierced the front three guards' wyvern scaled armor and sank into their flesh. Poisonous sap shot through their veins, and the guards went stiff before they could even lift their swords. Paralyzed. Zayla pushed the roots deeper, through flesh and muscle and bone until the roots reached their hearts.

One, two, three—dead.

The ground might be scorched beneath her feet, but she didn't need fresh dirt, just bodies. Her spores spread through the dead guards, turning their flesh brown. Their chest cavities sank inward in a gruesome exhale. They decayed instantly before her eyes, and a burst of frigid energy flowed to her. Fuel for her crafting.

Tor and the remaining seven guards gasped in admonishment, while Zayla braced herself for the backlash—the sporebruises from Myceli or thick bark bursting from her flesh from Dara or a horrible combination of the two from her bitterroot. None came, at least not yet.

Emboldened, Zayla grasped the bundle of roots in her hand and commanded the bitterroot once more. She lashed the roots like whips.

She aimed a root at Tor. A nearby guard cut it in half before it could pierce Tor's flesh, but a small puff of vivid-green spores drifted across Tor's face. Her spores couldn't outright kill living flesh, but they could muddle his thoughts and freeze his muscles.

"You can't defeat me, noxling!" Tor slunk back, dragging Oryn with him, and sank to the ground. One arm was wrapped around Oryn like an embrace, the other hand still gripped the dagger. Tor stiffened, as her spores seized his muscles.

That has to be enough to stop him.

Two more guards rushed at her, but Zayla embedded her bitterroot into one of the guard's foreheads and sent the other through the second guard's throat. Their deaths happened almost without thought. It was easy, killing them.

A glint of metal to her right caught her attention. A guard had circled to her side, his spiral-bladed ruk'sha held high. His jaw seemed unhinged. It opened wider than it naturally should and revealed glowing orange teeth that his Vagari crafting sharpened into deadly points.

Heart thudding against her ribs, Zayla tried to yank her bitterroots back from her most recent victims, but their thorns caught on flesh and bone. She gasped as the man brought down the spiral blades, aiming for her face.

With a clang of metal, Shadre's duskiron axe blocked the ruk'sha with a parry to the side.

His momentum carried him forward, and he sank his teeth deep into Shadre's shoulder in a vicious bite.

Yelling, she twisted free and slashed with her axe, keeping him at bay. Blood seeped from the wound on her shoulder. Ignoring the wound, she said to Zayla, "I've got this one."

Zayla exhaled in relief, thankful that someone was on her side. Though her crafting hadn't lashed back, her muscles trembled, her strength ebbing. She turned her gaze to the newly fallen guards and commanded, *Feast.* Spores spread through the guards' dead bodies, feeding their energy to her.

Howls echoed through the air, and padfalls thudded toward her to her right. The pyrewolf suncreatures that had torn down the Ratnaa Nemora as they were trying to flee emerged through the smoke, eyes glowing and lips pulled back with bloodlust.

"I've got them, too. Focus on Tor!" Shadre cut the guard down and turned toward the incoming suncreatures.

Zayla barely spared the woman a glance, her attention now focused on the blue shield that had shimmered into existence between herself and the rest of the guards and Tor. An Elu guard held her hands up, eyes glowing a vibrant blue. Moon crafting.

Just beyond the woman, Oryn's limp body lay half across Tor's lap. Tor had yanked the blade free and dazedly stared at it in his loose fist. Oryn's blood seeped into the scorched dirt beneath them.

No.

The trio of guards holding Misti, Orenda, and the dark-skinned woman were shouting and gesturing at Tor to get up.

He blinked furiously but couldn't move.

Zayla swore she saw fear in his eyes, but that might just be wishful thinking. *Those spores have to be enough to stop him for a little while. Please be enough.*

Shadre grabbed Zayla's arm, her axe slick with orange blood and covered in burning cinders. The cinders ate away at the metal, and she dropped it. Grabbing the spare duskiron blade from Zayla's belt, she shouted something. Her mouth was moving frantically, but all Zayla could hear was a buzzing sound.

The vibrations of her crafting were drowning everything else out.

Shadre pointed at the Elu guard and began to move forward.

Zayla didn't know what she intended, but she glared at the shimmering shield separating her and Oryn. Her and Misti and Orenda.

Not for long. Concentrating, Zayla forced a fourth bitterroot to burst from the fused pod in her palm, replacing the one that had been cut down. She pushed it into the Vagari guard Shadre had just killed, filling herself with a fresh, cool surge of energy.

A fierce yell tore from her throat. Fortified, she walked toward Tor, heedless of the remaining four guards in front of her. Demanding more from nature itself, Zayla pushed her hands outward. Her fingers seemed to multiply in front of her eyes, reforming and splaying outward like mycelium threads.

Her bitterroots surged forward and dove into the scorched dirt. They moved through it like water. Like a geyser, they burst upward on the other side of the Moon shield.

A bitterroot pierced deep into the Moon crafter's chest, killing and decaying her so instantly it was like she'd disappeared in a cloud of ash.

The guards shoved their prisoners to the ground, moving in front of Tor in a last-ditch attempt to save him. Bound tight and already injured, Misti, Orenda, and the other woman couldn't do anything to stop them.

One guard slashed into a root, cutting it in half and sending a spray of purple sap onto his face. He pulled back and screamed, dropping his blade and covering his face with both hands. Angry boils sprang up beneath his fingers.

In the same heartbeat, the other guard's nails extended into glowing, bright-orange claws. The guard ripped the second root in two, flinging it to the sides before it could release any spores or sap.

A duskiron dagger flew through the air and sank into the man's forehead. Shadre had flanked the group and now moved in from the side. She tackled the remaining guard and the two went tumbling out of sight toward the bonfire.

Only Tor remined.

And Zayla only had one remaining bitterroot left to kill him. *It'll be enough.*

Zayla tried to move, but she couldn't. When she glanced down, she realized, in horror, that bitterroot had grown around her feet, locking her in a net of crimson-green roots. She tried to direct the roots to move, but they didn't listen. Her energy suddenly flagged, ripped away like wind tearing leaves off a tree. Her world canted to the side. Each shallow gasp came with a flash of pain. Her flesh burned like she stood in a raging fire. The buzz within her body was nearly deafening. Something was wrong. *My crafting, lashing back.* Would she be rooted here like a tree for the rest of her nights?

She locked her eyes onto Oryn. Her future didn't matter. The only thing that mattered was saving her friends. Saving the Ratnaa Nemora, the best she could. Saving Oryn.

Tor's eyes started to glow a dull white with his Blood crafting. His power oozed like sap through his veins, creating crazed lines around his eyes.

Her last remaining bitterroot had fallen to the scorched ground, waiting for Zayla's command.

Move. Zayla willed her bitterroot to attack, but only its tip stretched tiredly toward her goal. She didn't have much time. Her spores had frozen Tor's muscles and slowed his crafting, but the glow crept in lightning-like lines across his cheeks and down his neck.

Focusing all her energy, Zayla drove her bitterroot forward. It curled closer with maddening slowness, like it moved through thick sap rather than over stone.

Tor's crafting reached his wrists, slowly but determinedly moving to his fingers. With obvious effort, he lifted his hand and pressed his fingers to Oryn's cheek, casting a white light over Oyrn's pale skin. If Oryn wasn't already dead from the blade, Tor's Blood crafting could finish the job.

No! Desperation spawned a wild, feral yell. She commanded her crafting again. Just once more. *Kill!* she ordered.

She knew, in the deepest, darkest part of herself, that the root wouldn't reach Tor in time.

The glowing white power pushed through Tor's fingertips.

Shadre burst from the smoke behind Tor, her face a bloody mess and her eyes alight with the power of her crafting. Chest heaving with coughs, she grabbed hold of Oryn's body and yanked them away from Tor.

A heartbeat later, Zayla's bitterroot sank into the leader of these sun goddess worshippers. Like a candle snuffed out, the white glow in his eyes and veins vanished. He toppled backward to the ground, staring sightlessly toward the smoke-filled sky.

Together, she and Shadre had accomplished the impossible.

Zayla desperately wanted to move closer to Oryn, to see if her sibling still lived, but she couldn't. She wasn't even certain if her own legs still held her upright, or if it was the roots now twisting from her ankles to her hips.

Breathing heavily and bleeding from the wound on her shoulder and another on her brow, Shadre carried Oryn toward Zayla. Her rust-orange eyes met Zayla's, expression full of concern and sadness.

Zayla's already laboring heart trembled as if about to give out. Was she too late? She stared at her sibling's limp body, willing them to breathe. Surely, they had to come back. They had to be alive.

Oryn didn't move.

No. Zayla's chest seized. Tears burned behind her eyes before falling in quick hot lines down her cheeks. *Oryn's dead.*

Sounds rushed back to her. The crackling of the flames behind her. The excited yells of the Nemora rushing out from the smoke-filled archway. Orenda struggling with her bindings, cursing up a storm. The dark-skinned woman kicking free of her ropes and running to Misti.

At least I saved some people here. Her gaze went back to Oryn, her sibling, not by blood but greater in her heart. *Just not the one who mattered most.*

Zayla lowered her arms—or tried to. She couldn't put them down. *I can't move.* Thick strands of bitterroot lashed tight around her arms, holding them in place. It felt like the roots had wrapped around her whole body. Had the bitterroot merged with not only her flesh, but her bones as well? She breathed shallowly, feeling the sting of air in her ruined lungs, and took stock of herself and her surroundings. Numb from shock, from exertion, from something else entirely, she couldn't quite tell.

Nature pressed in on her—she could sense every tree and fungi and thorn, metal deposits and gemstones, fresh water deep underground, stone even deeper. It was almost...calming. The press of nature didn't scare her anymore. She'd asked for too much. Demanded too much. She knew that. Nature was simply righting that wrong—not because she was different, or that she shouldn't be alive—but because that was what nature did. Nature equalized itself.

A soothing kind of darkness narrowed her vision, tunneling what Zayla could see until only Oryn and Shadre remained. Zayla breathed shallowly in and out. *Is this what dying feels like?* Closing her eyes, she let the darkness take her completely.

Chapter Twenty-Six

A FEATHER-LIGHT TOUCH drew Zayla back to consciousness. *Shadre?*
Expecting to see the musician, Zayla opened her eyes. Warm, golden-
brown light surrounded her. Rivers of purple and green spiraled closer.
Each time they touched her, she felt feather-light tickles across her skin.
Where am I? Exhaustion dragged her eyelids closed again.

A moment later, blinding sunlight pierced through her eyelids, and a
headache throbbed at the base of her skull. Forcing her eyes open took
everything she had. The golden-brown light had vanished. It was so cold—
bone cold. She lay shivering on the ground as shadows moved around her,
gesturing. Muffled shouting tried to penetrate past the buzzing in her ears.
A crimson tree with feathered, purple leaves and vibrant, green
mushrooms sprouting from its trunk towered over her. A bitterroot tree,
split in the center, oozing purple sap. Her bitterroot tree. Darkness washed
into her vision. Tired, she willingly fell into it.

She woke over and over, always only for a moment, enough time for a
single breath.

Arms wrapped around her, carrying her as the world swayed. She
inhaled a comforting nutty scent. *Shadre.*

A campfire flickered at the edge of her vision.

The ashes of Ratnaa Grove gave way to a rocky pathway.

She felt the press of a blanket on her skin, hard stone beneath her.

Fur tickled her nose as her face pressed against something...a
creature whose muscles rippled underneath her.

The gentle pressure of Shadre's hand on her neck. The musician's face
floated in and out of sight, brown blood leaking from the corner of her
mouth that she quickly wiped away.

Between those glimpses, time became nothing but a dark, buzzing
void.

Finally, Zayla's eyes drifted open and stayed, taking in the silvery
webbing above her that partially blocked out the night sky speckled with
stars. She turned her head and saw a daygem on the table beside her, and
beyond that, the webbing reached the pale, stone floor.

I'm in a prison. Tor's aboveground prison. Her chest seized, and her
hands clenched instinctively. Smooth sheets crumpled in her fists.

Sheets and a soft mattress underneath her.

Wait. Where am I? Zayla pushed herself upright, surprised she could move so easily after being encased in the bitterroot. The metal webbing formed a high dome around her, but directly across from her the metal pulled to form an archway. Beyond that, daygems lit paths between her and other silvery domed structures. Movement inside them told her that people were nearby. Soft music floated through the air—a familiar melody that Zayla couldn't quite place.

"Oryn?" she called, surprised by how deep her voice sounded, then equally surprised that she could hear again. The buzzing in her ears had subsided to a soft vibration. She held her hands before her, examining her arms and outstretched legs. The bitterroot encasing her body had vanished, but so had her curves and soft supple skin, replaced by the sharp lines and hard muscles of a more masculine form. The nox had shifted her gender once again. Her usual mottled, purple-green coloring caught the light. The dark brown sporebruises were gone. She took a deep breath. No pain. No tightness. *So, my crafting took care of that as well. Healed everything.*

Oryn's lifeless body came back to her, and tears sprung to her eyes. *No. Not everything.*

A strange tunic made of black material pulled tight across her chest, but someone had pinned the carved flower with a swirling cloud of pale, yellow-white smoke petals to the fabric. *Shadre remembered.* More tears pricked her vision.

"Shadre?" She called out again, her deep voice filling the space. "Misti, Orenda…anyone?"

Footsteps came from behind her, and she twisted just in time to see a thin, diminutive figure step through the open archway and into the light.

Her heart stopped beating for a moment. "Oryn?"

"I thought you'd never fully wake up, noxling." Oryn's sky-blue eyes met hers and her sibling grinned.

Zayla couldn't believe it. She'd seen her sibling die. Yet, there they stood. Zayla leapt up and threw her arms around their shoulders. "Oryn!"

"Zayla." Oryn's reply was muffled, their face crammed into her chest.

She held Oryn tight, and a joyful sob shuddered through her. Her sibling was alive. All the worries she carried with her since her time in the underground ruins broke away. "You're okay! You're okay. You're okay."

"I am." Oryn laughed, arms wrapped around Zayla's waist.

The more she said it, the more she believed it, but even with Oryn in her arms, every time she closed her eyes she saw their death. The dagger in their gut. Blood on the ground. Their body going still. She pulled back, gaze raking over her sibling's form, taking in every detail. Fresh, billowy clothing. Smooth skin. No blood or bruises or cuts that she could see. Even the shackles around their wrists were gone. "How—are you okay? I—I watched you die."

Oryn shook their head. "I think I did die. Or came very close to it anyway." They gave her a cocky half smile then grew serious and pulled Zayla over to the bed to sit. "Nature must still need me, I guess. After I regained consciousness, one of the Ratnaa Nemora was able to stabilize me so I could travel. He used some of your bitterroot mushrooms to help."

Zayla straightened. "But...they're poisonous." She felt dumb for saying such an obvious thing.

"They can be healing, too, under the right circumstances." Lifting their loose, blue shirt, Oryn revealed a thick white bandage wrapped around their stomach. A green stain bloomed in the middle, right over the wound. The same vivid green as the mushrooms growing from her bitterroot.

Zayla gaped. Poison...and healing. Death and life. I can make peace with that.

"You were encased by a bitterroot tree, Zayla." Oryn admitted quietly. "I thought you died as well, that nature had claimed you."

Shivers ran down Zayla's spine as she recalled the roots jutting through her flesh. "I guess...nature decided it wasn't my time, either."

"I'm grateful," Oryn said. "The other two women you rescued from the prison were able to bring us here, and a Divus who was traveling through here was able to heal most of my wounds."

"Here. Where is here?" Zayla asked. Nothing of her surroundings looked familiar.

"Ingo, of course."

Ingo. That was eight nights of hard travel away from Ratnaa, at least. She'd visited this Grove of metals before, one of the first Groves she'd journeyed through while walking her path. She'd even met Misti near the copper Sphere, the Ingo Nemora's treasured relic.

The lingering melody drifting through the darkness finally sparked Zayla's memory. Shadre had played the tune when they were walking through the Cinder Forest. Shadre, who couldn't step foot into Ingo or any of its offshoots, or really...anywhere in the Nemora homelands. Banished for something she didn't even do.

"Where's Shadre?" Zayla asked.

Oryn's gaze drifted to the west. "She's safe. Outside the Grove's boundaries."

Zayla cocked her head, listening to the far-off string of notes. "She's playing her flute."

Oryn nodded. "She's been playing all night. She said that she wanted you to hear something nice when you woke up."

Zayla's heart ached. A curious warmth slowly spread through her. She peered into the darkness, wishing she could see through the distant night.

"Shadre removed my shackles on the way here," Oryn commented thoughtfully. "The bands were made of some strange metal, and it took a lot of her crafting to remove them. She coughed for nights, even while she insisted on carrying you." Oryn paused, then nodded as if to themself. "I think...I think deep down, she really is a good person."

"I think she is, too," Zayla replied quietly, remembering the blood on Shadre's lips. Her crafting had lashed back because she used too much of it. "What happened to the shackles?"

"The Seventh Circle here is looking at them."

The elderly Nemora that Zayla had met during her walk. His soft-spoken nature and kind eyes came back to her. He might be the oldest person Zayla knew, but his mind hadn't dimmed at all. If anyone could figure out how the shackles worked, it would be the leader of Ingo Grove.

"Good. I understand why Tor and his followers captured Misti and Orenda, and I also understand why they kept me around. But..." She looked at her sibling. "What was he going to do with you?"

Oryn's expression darkened. "At first, Tor tried to break me for information. Where the other Groves were, what their strengths and weakness were, how much did we know about the Ponuriah worshipper's movements." Oryn's jaw clenched, their eyes going dark as if remembering the pain. Zayla squeezed Oryn's hand, and they breathed deep—in and out. "When I didn't give anything up, Tor said he was going to hand me over to someone he called an Ember Elect. I never found out who or what that is."

Ember Elect. Zayla tucked that phrase to the back of her mind. She could ask more questions later. This should be a time for celebration. *Oryn's alive!*

"Well, it doesn't matter now. They don't matter now." Zayla grabbed Oryn in for another hug. "We escaped. We're alive. That's what matters."

Oryn pulled away, scanning Zayla's face before grinning once more. "What matters is you're a badass, sibling." They punched Zayla on the shoulder. "You saved an entire Grove!"

"I had help," Zayla replied, a blush heating her cheeks. "Shadre fought, too."

Oryn waved her words away. "We already knew Shadre's a skilled fighter. I'm talking about you, Zayla." Oryn poked her in the chest, their eyes filled with awe. "You are a badass. I didn't realize how powerful the bitterroot offshoot was. How powerful you are!"

Zayla preened under the compliment. She always looked up to Oryn, so the words warmed her to her very core. "I always knew my hybrid power was strong," she admitted, "but I was shocked by how easily it came to me. It was almost like...like breathing."

"That's how crafting is for me, too." Oryn patted her knee. "I'm so, so proud of you."

"I'm proud of myself, too." Zayla laughed, letting the feeling sink into her. She'd done so much in the last night or so, she hadn't fully processed all of it. "How are the others?"

"They're okay. I can show you where we're all staying, if you'd like?" Oryn gestured to the archway. "I think the Seventh Circle would like to meet with you."

"Tomorrow." Filled with nothing but love and joy, Zayla curled up on the bed. Sleep still tugged at the corners of her mind, calling her to rest. "Can you show me around Ingo tomorrow?"

"Of course." Oryn settled onto the bed next to her, their forehead nearly touching hers. Dimples formed in their cheeks. "Badass."

Zayla laughed. Soon she'd see the others and visit with the Seventh Circle. For now, she'd rest with her sibling. She'd finally be a peace, at home, with them. She twined her fingers with Oryn's, just like they had in their youth, and allowed herself to finally, fully relax.

Chapter Twenty-Seven

ZAYLA STARED UP AT the giant boulders jutting from the ground, marveling at how metal ores embedded into the rock glinted in the daygem's light. Red, green, yellow, even gray—ores of all kinds. Each boulder had a different ore in it, a signpost for the Nemora working and trading there. Next to each of the boulders, a hole burrowed deep into the ground, so deep and dark she couldn't see the bottom. Shouts echoed up from holes—Ingo Nemora, doing their daily tasks.

"Pretty impressive, isn't it?" Oryn knocked their shoulder into her elbow.

"It is. When I came here for my walk, I didn't really get to see the quarry, just the Sphere." Zayla looked behind her at the winding pathway lined by spiraling columns of metal that led to the copper Sphere. Daygems hung off metal hooks, illuminating the space even though it was the darkest part of the night. Thick, heavy clouds obscured the moon and stars. "It's nice to see where the Ingo Nemora actually work."

Three young Ingo Nemora clambered out of the hole in front of them, chatting excitedly and clutching handfuls of pearlescent metal ore. Dust covered every inch of their clothing, and the scent of dirt and stone clung to their silvery skin. With mirroring silvery-blue hair, rust-orange eyes, and soft angled markings, they looked like they could be siblings. They stopped when they saw Oryn. Eyes wide with awe, they gestured with hands hovering over their hearts. A motion of respect.

Oryn returned the gesture with a smile.

The Nemora glanced between themselves, grinning wide, then dashed off.

Feeling refreshed after a few extra nights of rest, Zayla led her sibling down the pathway toward the outskirts of the quarry. "Who's the badass now?" she teased.

Oryn chuckled, but then they rolled up their sleeves, displaying the unique curled markings of a Gale Nemora in a way Zayla had never seen before. It suddenly struck her. Loose clothes, rolled up sleeves, pulled back hair, Oryn wasn't hiding anymore. The sight gave Zayla hope.

"I'm glad you feel comfortable now," she said, tapping a wind curl on their forearm.

"The hunters think I've been dealt with." Oryn gave her a cocky grin, but their sky-blue eyes held a seriousness that Zayla rarely saw. "I'll prove them wrong."

Zayla's stomach dropped, but she nodded all the same. *Prove them wrong.* That probably meant Oryn would go to the front lines, blow straight into the battle headfirst to defend their people. She couldn't bear to see her sibling in danger and couldn't force herself to confirm her fears. *Not yet.*

The air felt thick and cool, as if on the edge of a downpour. When they passed by a sturdy brown tree with hard green needles, a sweet scent permeated the air. Not many trees grew at Ingo, but the ones that forced their way through the stone grew hearty and thick. The color of the needles made her think of the bitterroot tree she'd grown—she'd become? She remembered the feather-light touches of green ribbons of light that had curled around her when she was unconscious. "What happened to the bitterroot tree I grew in Ratnaa?"

"The tree withered and died almost as soon as you walked out of it. It's just a husk now," Oryn replied quietly, running their fingers over the needles as they passed by. "It was pretty, though, while it lasted."

Zayla nodded and hummed a reply, thinking of the bitterroot's purple feathered leaves, the bright-green mushrooms, the crimson bark. It was beautiful. "I wish I could've seen more of it," she finally said.

Oryn looped their arm around hers and patted her arm. "I do, too," they admitted. "Meeting more of your kin would've been nice. I wonder if they were all as badass as you are."

Zayla shook her head, laughing. "Maybe."

"Zayla!" Misti's voice drew their attention. The pathway continued on, but a small stone and metal paddock had been erected nearby. Misti leaned over the paddock wall, waving at them. "I'm glad to see you're up and about!"

Zayla waved back. The scent of manure and fresh dirt filled her nose as she and Oryn drew closer to the paddock wall.

"I'm glad you're okay, too, Misti," Zayla said. The Vagari looked as good as Zayla felt—clean, well-rested, wearing a new set of traveling clothes.

In a blur of bright feathers and fur, a small vulnix flew over to Misti and landed delicately on her shoulder. The female, vulpine-like creature chirped and butted the side of Misti's head with her own in greeting. The beast tucked her bright-orange wings to her back, then settled onto Misti's shoulders like a scarf. Orange paws dipped in crimson and a trio of orange-yellow tails curled on one side of Misti's neck, and the creature's head and front paws curled on the other. Wide, dual-colored eyes blinked at Zayla, one orange and one blue, just like Misti.

"Zora, I take it?" Zayla asked with a smile. That vulnix had to be Misti's companion animal.

Misti nodded, reaching up to scratch Zora's shoulder. "She's pretty happy, too."

"I bet." Warmth filled Zayla at the sight. They both looked so content. "How are the others?"

"Not bad," Misti replied, looking over her shoulder. "Dylori, Orenda, come here!"

Zayla peered into the paddock. Daygems were set into the wall, brightening the area in a soft, white glow. In the far corner, a large mass of dark fur shifted slightly, but Zayla couldn't make out what kind of beast it was. Low rhythmic rumbling shook the ground—snoring. Orenda sat next to the mass of fur, scratching it, while the dark-skinned woman Zayla remembered from Ratnaa dropped thick stalks of white grain next to the snoring beast. At Misti's call, both women ambled over.

"I don't think you've officially met Dylori Clyofis," Misti said as the dark-skinned woman stopped by her side. "She's my partner, and a t'zil in the Moon Knights."

"Thanks, love." Dylori's arm was wrapped in a thick, cream-colored bandage, but it didn't seem to bother her. After giving Zora a quick pet, Dylori linked hands with Misti and kissed her temple. "Heard you tried to rescue Misti. Thanks for that. Tor was a sunbaked idiot."

Misti leaned into the woman's side. "Thankfully, he's not going to be a problem anymore." Misti's dual-colored eyes shimmered. "You were amazing, Zayla. Those vines? Remarkable."

"They're roots, actually. From my bitterroot offshoot. I just did what I had to do," Zayla replied. The humming within her quieted as she took a moment to look inward, searching for the worry she'd so gotten used to when thinking about her crafting, but that familiar worry never came. "Thank you for getting Oryn the care they needed. And getting me here, as well."

Misti looked at Dylori, her expression filled with nothing but love. "It was Dylori's companion animal, Dis, who got us here."

Dylori pointed to the snoring pile of fur. "He looks much more impressive when he's awake."

"Well, I'd like to thank Dis if I could then, too," Zayla said. Vagari and their animal companions were linked nearly as close as two souls could be.

While she knew she'd want to thank Dis, regardless, it would also be respectful of their culture. Thank the Vagari. Thank the companion animal. "When he's awake, of course."

Dylori's dark eyes glinted with mirth. "He should be awake right now, the lazy beast. And he wouldn't say no to those red spiny leaves you gave to Misti. He liked those."

She put her fingers to her lips and whistled, the sharp sound piercing the night air.

The mass of dark fur immediately stirred, lumbering to his feet. The creature stood taller than Zayla. Its stocky, bovine-like body bore thick fur and a thicker muzzle. Dis lumbered over, shaking himself a bit. His tiny black horns caught the daygem's light.

"A neades." Zayla breathed. These legendary beasts could break the ground with their roars.

Dis huffed, his large watery eyes locking on hers.

"Hello there, Dis." Zayla pulled out a tree seed from her pocket. She dipped into her crafting and created a few spindly crimson leaves in her palm. Now that she was in a more populated area, she'd had a messenger vulnix get a few more seeds from her mother's bryiuu offshoot. She offered the leaves to Dis. "Thank you for getting me here."

Dis nodded his large head and snorted, then licked the leaves off her palm. He munched on them happily, then lumbered back over to his sleeping spot and crunched on the stalks of white grain.

Orenda pushed herself off the paddock wall. "Before you absolutely destroyed Tor and his group, I heard you mention a goddess shard. Did you actually find one? I only ask because Aluriah led me to Ratnaa Grove specifically to get one. If you didn't find it, I'll need to start heading back to Ratnaa."

"I did." Zayla stuck her hand into her bag. She felt around for the chill that permeated the cloth. No one had realized what she had in her pocket when they left Ratnaa and during her recovery. After everything she'd done to find this shard, she'd kept it nearby always, kept it safe. Pulling it out, she unwrapped the layers of ripped tunic, piece by piece, until the shard lay on her palm. It gave off the same bright, azure light that it had in the underground ruins. Waves of cold air rippled from its surface.

Lips pressed into a thin line, Orenda moved closer and held out her hand. "May I?"

"Of course." Zayla handed the bundle to Orenda without a moment's hesitation. "I got it for you."

The woman's stoic demeanor fell away as she took the shard. A smile tugged at her lips. "This is a shard of Aluriah, my moon goddess." She looked at Zayla in awe. "I've been traveling to find this for a long time. Thank you."

"Will it help win the war against the sun goddess worshippers, Ren?" Misti peered around Orenda's shoulder.

Orenda nodded. Pulling out a long blue cloth that matched the shard's coloring, she reverently wrapped the shard, then placed it gently inside her rucksack. "Aluriah says there are only two more I have to find."

Misti knocked Orenda on the shoulder. "Two more, then you can save the world."

It sounded like teasing, but from the serious way Orenda nodded, Zayla suspected a hint of truth was threaded through. "What do you mean?"

"Zayla!" Another voice interrupted their conversation. "There you are!"

Tessero, the Seventh Circle of Ingo Grove, was moving swiftly up the path, followed close behind by a redheaded Divus in simple traveling clothes of grays and browns. The Divus carried a thick book and a black quill. *A scribe!* Scribes were the keepers of history, and only the highest rank carried a black quill. They knew the innermost secrets of the world. Zayla's stomach fluttered. *Perhaps I'll get to tell my story. She'd probably like to know what happened at Ratnaa Grove.*

Tessero's gray robe fluttered open as he moved closer, revealing the sagging gray skin around his belly and the baggy pants cinched tight around his thin waist. His sharp angled markings glinted in the daygem's light. He gave her a wide smile. "I've been meaning to meet with you. I didn't expect to see you so soon during your walk."

"Anoc-suna, Tessero." Zayla smiled at the elderly man, the Nemora greeting falling easily from her lips. "Thank you for taking us in."

"Always." Though Zayla had seen him just a season ago during her walk, Tessero's voice sounded even older, like wind whispering through a forest. His wispy silver hair drifted gently in the soft breeze.

"And who might you be?" Zayla shifted her attention to the redhead. The woman looked vaguely familiar, though Zayla couldn't quite place her.

"Adaris Kavari, wandering scribe!"

Zayla laughed. "I gathered that from the book and quill."

Adaris shrugged. "It's a pretty big tell."

"She's the Divus who healed me when we got to Ingo." Oryn smiled.

"Oh!" A wave of gratitude swept over Zayla. "Thank you."

"I was in the right place at the right time," Adaris replied easily, her gray eyes catching the daygem's light. "I'm just happy I could help."

Canting her head, Zayla blinked a few times. The way her eyes caught the light brought back a sudden memory. *Sunshine beat down on Zayla. A shadowy cave. A gang of sun goddess worshippers trudging up a hill. Someone was hiding in the cave, gray eyes catching the light, locking onto hers.* "Have we met before?"

Adaris' eyebrows rose. "I feel like I would've remembered you?" She tapped her book with the tip of her quill. "I have a pretty good memory."

"I know this might sound strange, but I...I think I've seen you before, hiding in a cave."

"A cave?" Misti glanced at Adaris.

"A cave," Adaris repeated. Her gray eyes raked over Zayla's body before her mouth dropped open. "Wait. You do look familiar! You were the one to warn me about the sun goddess worshippers." At Zayla's nod, Adaris grinned. "I can't wait to tell you what happened that day."

"Perhaps later. I have something I need to discuss with Zayla." Tessero leaned on the paddock wall, eyes only for Zayla. "Oryn's told me that you saved them and the others from Tor. Saved Ratnaa Grove. And that you used your crafting to do so, almost singlehandedly. You've grown so much. I'm impressed."

A burn flared to the tips of Zayla's ears. It was a great honor having a Seventh Circle—the leader of this Grove—say such things to her. "It wasn't all just me. Shadre, of the duskiron offshoot, helped."

The shimmer in Tessero's eyes vanished. "I know of whom you speak. Shadre is a thief and a murderer. You shouldn't give credit to her."

"She was set up." Zayla recalled Shadre's story. "Misled by the people she was with. And she's done good things since then. I would've died in the underground ruins of Alastra if it wasn't for her. And she saved Oryn's life. Ratnaa Grove only survived because she helped me."

"Is that so?" Tessero murmured.

"It's true," Oryn said, and both Misti and Orenda nodded their agreement.

"A story for another night." Tessero shook his head.

"A story I'd like to record," Adaris chimed in, waving her quill around. She pointed the dark feather to Zayla. "I'd like to hear your tale in Ratnaa as well."

"And so you shall, Adaris." Tessero turned his attention back to Zayla, hands slipping into the long sleeves of his robe. "I also heard you haven't yet completed your walk, young one."

Her walk. It had been ages since she'd thought of it. Walking the path hadn't mattered, not when Ratnaa Grove was in trouble or when her sibling and friends had been captured, but it could matter now. It was almost like a breath of fresh air to even consider it again. "There were more important things to deal with."

"As there always will be, but your needs are important, too." His gray eyes sparkled. "Would you like to complete your walk here?"

Zayla gasped. *I'm going to complete my walk!* She could finally go through her Choosing Ritual and stabilize her crafting. It seemed like ages ago when she'd first started her walk. A laugh suddenly bucked in her chest at her original motivation to complete her walk. She'd intended to never craft again. The thought seemed ludicrous now. Her crafting had healed her, protected her friends, saved her more than once. She didn't fear her crafting any longer, but she still respected its power. Curse every root and spore, she was powerful! Powerful enough to join the fight. "Yes, I'd like that very much."

Chapter Twenty-Eight

ZAYLA STOOD ON A platform made of silvery metal, behind Tessero in a daygem-lit courtyard. Her hands trembled with anticipation, so she pushed them into her pockets to stop anyone from noticing. Just a few nights ago she'd been fighting Tor. Since then, she'd given Orenda the goddess shard, discovered her bitterroot mushrooms could heal people, told her story to a black-quilled scribe for all to read in the history books, and now, she was finally beginning her Choosing Ritual. It all felt like a dream.

Metals of all colors—silvers, blues, golden hues, and even greens—twisted beautifully into rows of benches and covered gazebos. Blinking back tears, Zayla took in the crowd before her. Even now, during the busiest time of night, numerous Ingo Nemora had stopped working to witness her Choosing. Even those not from Ingo had joined. She noted a tall, impeccably dressed man with slicked back golden hair and golden eyes to match. Scars crisscrossed over his neck, marking him as another Divus. It was nice, these kind strangers joining her ceremony, but a strange ache started in the pit of her belly. If her bitterroot family still lived, they would be here, cheering her on. It was a silly thing to feel, since she hadn't really known her mothers. The only thing she remembered from her offshoot was the bitterroot plant itself. She searched the rows and rows of people, before finally landing on the familiar sky-blue eyes of her chosen sibling, her found family.

"You'll do great, Zayla," Oryn mouthed. They sat in the front row, straight backed and grinning.

Next to them, Misti smiled encouragingly, with Dylori on her other side. Orenda nodded along at Tessero's words. A young Ratnaa Nemora that Zayla remembered from Tor's prison gave her a little wave. Adaris sat in their little group as well, scribbling frantically with her black feathered pen.

Some of the metal structures were darker, warped, the signs of struggle clearly burned into them. Oryn had told her that the sun goddess worshippers had tried to take Ingo, but the Nemora had fought back. They'd won. That's why the healer's center she'd awoken in had been busy—so many Nemora had been injured defending their home.

Beyond the rows of people, the sacred Ingo tree still stood proudly in the center of the courtyard. Its cream-colored trunk and branches stretched far overhead, and its long, drooping, silver-blue leaves looked like strands of moonlight. A scorch mark blackened part of its trunk, as if it had been strafed by a flaming arrow, but most of the tree was whole and vibrant and alive.

Zayla's eyes burned at the sight, her memory tracing back to the ruined sacred tree of Ratnaa Grove. She couldn't help but wonder where the Ponuriah worshippers were now. What Nemora village were they attacking tonight? Would they come back to Ingo, to attack again? Of course they would. They wanted to take control of all the Groves. To do that, they'd have to overthrow this one, eventually. A thread of worry made her feel sick. She pushed that feeling down. This wasn't the time to think of such things.

Tessero's booming voice pulled her attention. "We are here, this night, to celebrate Zayla of the bitterroot offshoot and to witness her Choosing Ritual."

Soft music floated on the wind from far, far away. Zayla didn't recognize the happy melody, but she instantly knew who played it. *Shadre.* Zayla longed to see her in the crowd, but of course, Shadre wasn't allowed inside the Grove's limits.

"Zayla." Tessero's eyes brightened with Nemora crafting glow. He lifted his hand. The silvery metal beneath their feet arched upward like a water fountain and spread out to form a simple table before them. "Do you have proof of your walk?"

Zayla nodded. She pushed her hand into her bag and produced her offerings. She had to prove that she'd been to each Grove and passed the trial demonstrating her crafting ability to the Seventh Circle there, as was tradition. One by one, she set them on the table. The shards of blackstone from Hallr and patinaed metal from Ingo. A small vial of fresh water from Laidly. The rarest seed from Wyrtig. Purple bark from Dara, and a shriveled Myceli mushroom.

She didn't have any proof from Ratnaa since she hadn't technically done a trial there, but Tessero had assured her it would be okay.

She looked up to meet Tessero's eyes to discover him looking to the crowd. Suddenly worried there was a problem, she shifted her attention in that direction.

The small Ratnaa Nemora walked toward them, their mop of curly red hair bouncing with each step. They approached and set a stunning opalescent crystal upon the table. "For demonstrating not only your crafting, but your courage and willingness to set aside your own life to save Ratnaa Grove, we give you this. A starstone is the rarest gemstone we've found," they said. Canting their head, they gave her a soft private smile and whispered, "Minus the goddess shards, of course. You gave ours to the right person."

Tears pricked Zayla's eyes. The Grove had honored her with their words, and even more with their gift. It felt like a lifetime ago that she'd started her walk, ages ago that she'd decided to travel through the Cinder Forest to get to Ratnaa faster, just so she could complete her walk and never have to use her crafting, ever again. So much had happened—more than she'd ever imagined possible. Her fingers grew cold at the memory of the goddess shard. *Please let it turn the tide of this war.*

The Ratnaa Nemora turned to face the onlookers once more, widening their arms as if to embrace the nature around them. "Ratnaa Grove considers Zayla of the bitterroot offshoot's walk complete. She may proceed with the Choosing Ritual, using the sacred tree of Ingo Grove."

Tessero gestured Zayla toward the tree.

Straightening her shoulders, she took a deep breath and walked between the rows of kind strangers and her chosen family and friends. The sacred Ingo tree towered over everything, creating a peaceful shelter of light under the nighttime sky. She pressed a hand on its bark, the trunk smooth and soft against her palm. Sinking into her crafting, the familiar brown glaze pulled over her vision, and the tree glowed a deep golden hue in return.

A shimmering archway opened in the bark, just wide and tall enough for her to slip through. The vibrations in her body hummed in a soft, soothing kind of way, and the fluttering in her belly vanished. Taking one more deep breath, Zayla stepped into the tree. *It's time to choose who I'm going to be.*

Deep, gold light consumed her. She floated, weightless in its embrace. Opening her mind the best she could in this liminal space, Zayla welcomed nature in. Her senses spread outward. She could feel every root and spore, every water droplet, each pebble rattling on the ground, each berry and mineral ore. The raw power of nature pushed against her flesh and bones and prodded within her mind, seeking answers to an unspoken question.

I know who I am. She projected her thoughts outward, knowing she was not only talking to the sacred tree but also to all of nature around her. *I know what I am. The last remaining bitterroot Nemora. I want to honor that. I want to fight for that, defend the Nemora people. I want my crafting to settle, and I want to be female.*

It was all she had ever asked for. And from what she knew of the Choosing Ritual, nature would gift her that.

A vision slammed into her mind, the violence of it sending her spinning.

Green, glassy mushrooms sprouted on stubby, crimson trees with roots that she knew went deeper into the ground than the trunk's height promised. Feathered, purple leaves raged in a hot wind, and cracks in the bark oozed purple sap.

Her bitterroot offshoot.

Crackling flames erupted all around, setting the leaves on fire. The steady beat of wings filled the air, fanning the conflagration higher. The ground shuddered with the thump of a massive suncreature that landed across the thicket, folding its wings against its back. The creature was a firebird at its front half—shiny white beak, beady crimson eyes, and talons. Its back was an impuni—dappled fur, cloven hooves, and a long, swishing white tail. Twin white spiral horns curled like a crown across its head.

Suncreature or no, Zayla had never seen a griffon like that.

A high-pitched wail pierced the air. An infant, a noxling. Her chest and throat ached, and somehow, she knew who made that awful noise. *Me.*

Arms encircled her. For the first time, Zayla saw her parents.

Her mothers leaned over her. One, a redhead with Dara leaf markings decorating her forehead, and the other, a brown-haired woman with Myceli dots circling her neck. Though fear clearly shimmered in their warm gray and blue eyes, they both smiled down at her.

"We love you, Zayla." The words seemed to hang in space and time. "And we believe in you."

They lowered her into a crack in the bitterroot's trunk. Like a warm bath, Zayla sank into the thick purple sap, unharmed by the thick poisonous liquid. The sap covered her body, hiding her from view, and inched toward her face.

Muffled chanting reached her through the sap. Past the edge of the bitterroot bark, she could just see bitterroot Nemora standing around the griffon, hands raised.

Her Dara mother shoved a familiar azure crystal toward the suncreature.

A moon goddess shard.

Golden light poured from the bitterroot Nemora, filling their burning offshoot with blinding brilliance, the edges tinged with blue. The light spiraled into itself and formed a sphere. The orb floated to the moon goddess shard in Zayla's mother's hand and absorbed the shard completely, extinguishing the blue light. The orb shot forward and slammed into the griffin, disappearing into a blackened hole in the suncreature's chest.

The burning scent of feathers reached Zayla's nose.

The creature shrieked and let out a long stream of fire toward the Nemora. The Nemora disintegrated to ash without even time to scream. Her mothers burned away to cinders before Zayla's eyes. *No!* There was so much smoke and ash in the air, she couldn't even yell for them.

One burst of fire jetted toward Zayla. Her tiny limbs twitched, hindered by the sap. The bitterroot bark glowed a deep golden, and a shield of wood erupted over her, blocking the flames. A moment later, the bark fell away to ashes.

Flames crackled around her, and Zayla knew that the fire had consumed all the bitterroot Nemora. Her parents. The offshoot itself. Only the small pocket of sap remained, with her as an infant encased safely inside.

I didn't survive the attack by sheer luck or accident. My mothers saved me. The other bitterroot Nemora and nature itself helped me, too. The knowledge stunned her.

The suncreature shrieked in triumph, then launched into the air.

As it flew far away, vibrations started within her tiny body, her limbs still immobilized by the surrounding sap.

Despite her inability to move, her field of vision suddenly flew upward, traveling with the suncreature. Flying high above the clouds, the creature let out a caw, calling other griffon suncreatures to it. Two, four, no, a whole rush of griffons surrounded her. The rush flew for ages, dirt and stone and trees giving way to a wide, vast ocean. As if time passed in quick motion, the vision shimmered. Another land mass slowly came into focus. They dove, spiraling toward the broken, barren wasteland called the Sunglade.

The moment their talons touched the desiccated soil, the vision shattered like glass around her.

The golden light of the Ingo tree surrounded her once more. The tingles dancing across her skin pushed deeper, swordpoints instead of feather-light touches. Pain. Agony of her bones twisting, her tendons popping, her skin on fire. The golden light's buoyancy ended without warning. Her stomach lurched. Zayla plummeted down, down, down. She threw her arms out—

And landed on her hands and knees outside the tree.

She took a shuddering breath of air, a moment to assess. No pain in her palms, or scratches on her knees. She'd been falling from a great height. Now she simply wasn't.

The crowd's cheers rumbled like thunder.

Zayla blinked. Her mind reeled at everything she'd just seen.

Oryn's gentle hands helped her to her feet. Small but strong arms hugged her tight around the middle. "Fari-lunia, sibling." The Nemora word for congratulations. "You've chosen, Zayla. I'm so proud of you! Look, the tree finalized the ceremony."

"My gift?" Zayla glanced back at the sacred Ingo tree, coming back to herself and to the moment. She knew who she was. What she was. And so did the tree.

A staff that was taller than her leaned against the cream-colored trunk where the archway had been. Thicker on top and tapered to a blunt end at the bottom, the staff was made of gnarled, purple-green wood and speckled with tiny brown mushrooms. The precious gift was a nod to her Dara and Myceli crafting, as they intertwined to create the bitterroot offshoot. Since it was untreated wood and living mushrooms, she could easily use the staff as a source for her crafting. There was even a handful of tree seeds embedded in the wood, so she could grow full trees as well.

She hefted the staff, the weight lighter than she'd anticipated. Her gift from the tree meant her ceremony was officially over. Elation filled her heart. She glanced down at her soft, purple robe and the familiar rise of her chest, at her small, delicate hands decorated with the sharp markings of her craft.

I've chosen. It was what she'd wanted, and she'd finally done it. Her form had solidified; she would always be female now.

But vibrations still tingled within her. The sensation settled on her right shoulder, tugging eastward, and Zayla knew, without a shadow of a doubt, that the hum was pulling her toward the griffon suncreature from her vision. *But what am I supposed to do with the knowledge the sacred Ingo tree gave me?*

Chapter Twenty-Nine

CLUTCHING HER NEW STAFF, Zayla nodded gratefully to the tenth Nemora who congratulated her. A small crowd had formed after her ceremony, and she wanted to thank them all. Even Tessero caught her gaze and gave her a nod. Heat crept over Zayla's cheeks from all the attention, but she was grateful for all the people who stopped their usual tasks to watch her.

As the crowd dispersed, Misti, Dylori, Orenda, and Adaris slipped through.

"Congratulations." Misti gave Zayla a quick hug.

Surprised, Zayla hugged her in return, pleased to realize that, even though she didn't know Misti very well, the hug wasn't awkward at all. "Thank you," she murmured, pulling back.

Dylori gave her a wide grin. "It was a great ceremony."

"Yes, you did amazing." Orenda nodded.

"How do you feel now that it's over?" Adaris asked, black quill at the ready.

Zayla chose her words carefully, knowing they would be recorded in history. "I feel complete," she said.

"Complete." Adaris nodded, writing it down then tucking the quill behind her ear. "I haven't been to one before, so I'm glad I got to record yours."

Still by her side, Oryn leaned in. "Have I told you how proud I am, Zayla?"

Wrapping an arm around Oryn's shoulders, Zayla pulled them into a hug. Her heart felt so full it might burst. "You did. And thank you."

It was only her and her friends left in the courtyard, and Zayla's eyes kept drifting back to the sacred Ingo tree. It had shown her a vision, and she needed to figure out what it meant. "During my Choosing, the sacred tree showed me a vision," she confessed. "It showed me my bitterroot offshoot being destroyed."

"Oh, Zayla," Oryn murmured. They reached for Zayla's hand and squeezed. "That must've been awful."

"It was nice," Zayla said the words before she even had the chance to think about how Oryn might perceive them. She saw the shock on her sibling's face. "Not the destruction, of course, but I got to see my mothers. Hear their voices. I don't remember them, so it was kind of...nice to see them." A pang by her heart quieted her words, and a lump grew in her throat.

Swallowing past the lump, she continued, "In my vision, the bitterroot Nemora and my mothers did some kind of ritual. Using a moon goddess shard, they created an orb or something, I'm not quite sure. They shoved it into the suncreature. That's what the vibrations within my body are pointing to, the griffon suncreature who destroyed my home. I don't know why else the sacred tree would've shown me the vision, unless the orb was connected to the bitterroot offshoot."

"Was it a sporeseed?" Adaris flipped through her thick book, before stopping at a page and turning the book toward Zayla.

The crudely drawn image appeared to be light spiraling into an orb. Next to the drawing were a few hastily drawn notes in the Divus language, which Zayla couldn't read.

"Yes? I mean, it looks the same." Zayla tilted her head and squinted at the details.

Adaris nodded. "I learned about them at Myceli Grove, a few seasons back, where I met a Myceli Nemora called Thorn—nice kid, if a bit overenthusiastic. All 'did you know' this and 'did you know' that. She told me about them." The scribe ran her finger down the page, reviewing her notes. "Apparently, it's a really rare practice that the Nemora people can do with the help of a goddess shard. A sporeseed houses a single living seed within it. So if you can plant the sporeseed, the living seed you stored inside of it can grow. Any living seed. Theoretically, that means that you could regrow your bitterroot offshoot. Thorn mentioned that the ritual was a last-ditch attempt in the face of something horrible. Quite frankly, I think creating sporeseeds would be a good practice for every Nemora offshoot to do as a means of preservation. Especially now. It wouldn't bring back the Nemora people who cultivate that land, of course, but perhaps the sacred trees could do that. Link the next generation of Nemora noxlings to the new growth."

Zayla couldn't even speak. The sacred tree had tried to show her the path, but she hadn't understood until this black-quilled scribe translated the message.

Like a tree firmly taking root in her mind, Zayla knew what she was supposed to do.

"Thank you, Adaris." Zayla reached out and grabbed Adaris' shoulder, squeezing it briefly. "You just clarified a few very important details for me."

"You said this sporeseed seemed to absorb the goddess shard?" At Zayla's nod, Orenda leaned closer, green eyes bright with excitement. "Are you going to track down this suncreature from your vision?"

"I am," Zayla replied with determination.

"What?" Misti gasped, and leaned closer to Dylori, who slipped a protective arm over her shoulders.

Adaris' eyes grew wide. "Wait, really?"

Zayla nodded.

Oryn pulled their hand away, shock deepening the frown on their face. "Suncreatures are dangerous, Zayla," they said, words sharp with concern. "You can't track one down on your own!"

Zayla met her sibling's gaze. "I have to."

"Would you like some company?" Orenda patted a sword sheathed to her back. "I'm pretty good with the sword."

The offer warmed Zayla's heart. "I'd love some. We can leave tomorrow night."

Orenda nodded.

"You're going now?" Worry spiraled in Oryn's eyes.

Zayla shrugged. "Why wait?"

"There's a war happening, Zayla. I'm going to secure Hallr Grove, atop Hallr Mountain. You know our people will flock there if their Groves or offshoots fall."

Hallr Grove was the mountainous region in the center of the Nemora homeland, the Grove of stone and rock. Of course refugees would flee there. And it made sense that Oryn—the only Gale Nemora on the planet and the most powerful Nemora around—would defend it.

Twisting their fingers through the ends of their black hair, Oryn sighed. The look they gave Zayla nearly broke her heart. "I had hoped you'd come with me, sibling."

"I can't." Zayla shook her head, tears prickling behind her eyes. Parting from Oryn again would be painful, but she had to. "I have to find this suncreature. It has the bitterroot sporeseed and a moon goddess shard."

"I know but—"

Zayla grabbed hold of Oryn's arm. "Sibling, the sacred tree showed me this for a reason. Nature showed me this for a reason. This is how I can help win the war."

Oryn's gaze dropped to the ground, voice a mere whisper. "But it's not safe."

"Nowhere is safe." Zayla pulled Oryn in for a hug. They returned a tight embrace that said more than words and filled Zayla with warmth. When they let go, she gave her sibling a grin. "And I'm pretty good at taking care of myself now."

Oryn rolled their eyes, but their worried expression softened. "I know. Can you at least tell me where you're going?"

"The Sunglade." Zayla replied. The sacred tree had told her that much, but her gut clenched at the words. Not many people had been to the Sunglade and lived to tell the tale. The barren wasteland was home to the sun goddess worshippers and said to be full of deadly suncreatures. From what she knew, going there was basically a death sentence.

Oryn groaned. "Of course you are."

Misti stepped closer, a hard look in her eyes. "Can I come, too?"

Zayla arched an eyebrow at the woman. First Orenda, now Misti? A strange convergence was happening. "Really?"

"Yes. I'm looking for my sister. From what I've found out thus far, that's where she went." Misti took Dylori's hand. At her simple nod, Misti continued. "We'd like to come with you."

"I'm not half bad with the sword myself," Dylori added with a grin.

Adaris cleared her throat. "I can't believe I'm saying this, but if you need a guide, I've been there before."

"What?" Shocked, Zayla blinked. This was more than convergence. Zayla wasn't a religious person, but this was beginning to feel like Aluriah's intervention. Fate. "You've been to the Sunglade and back?"

Adaris tucked a strand of her long, red hair behind her ear. A curious, blue gemstone ring glowed on her finger. "It's a long story, but suffice to say; it's how I got my black quill. Before meeting you, I was actually traveling to Ratnaa Grove myself, looking for a particular gemstone that I need. I can be there and back again in a few nights, if you're willing to wait that long."

"You survived the Sunglade...and you'd be willing to go back. Why?"

A sly grin curled on Adaris' lips. Her gray eyes twinkled. "I'm always looking for a good story, and yours has officially captured my attention."

Zayla nodded, hardly daring to believe what was happening. She might not have Oryn, but she'd be traveling with more than enough help. She'd even have the knowledge of someone who had already set foot in the Sunglade. "Well, I'd love to have you along."

"I'm still not happy...but I'm grateful you're not going alone, Zayla." Oryn smiled weakly. They looked at the others. "Please take care of my sibling."

Dylori laughed. "After seeing her at Ratnaa Grove, I get the feeling she might be taking care of us."

"Actually." Zayla tilted her head, listening to the quiet melody still carried on the breeze. "There's one more person I need to talk to."

189

Chapter Thirty

THE QUIET MELODY FLOATING on the evening air drew Zayla to the outskirts of Ingo Grove. The song seeped into her, nudging away her worries about the Sunglade and the journey ahead. It had been too many nights since she'd seen Shadre, and Zayla was anxious to meet with her.

A steady wind cooled Zayla as she hiked up a small bluff, using her staff to test the stability of the rocky terrain. As she climbed, the music grew to a higher pitch and faster tempo. A joyful beat buoyed her to the top.

Shadre had camped next to a small cave. Her bedroll lay bunched inside. Pots and pans splayed out next to a small, flickering campfire where a hunk of meat sizzled, filling the air with a delicious, spiced aroma. A strange pang ached by Zayla's heart. She leaned on her new staff, taking in the scene. *Shadre has been out here, alone, while we were all celebrating.*

Shadre hadn't noticed her yet and continued playing on her burnt-orange metal flute with a gentle expression on her face, oblivious to her surroundings.

Shadre's shirt billowed slightly with the breeze, pulling the purple fabric away from her neck. The shirt dipped past where her shoulder wound would've been, but only smooth, silvery skin remained. Healed by a Divus no doubt. *Probably Adaris.* Shadre's soft, green slacks were muddied at the bottom, a visible reminder of just how long she had been alone outside the Grove.

As Shadre leaned away from the flames, still playing, she closed her eyes and relaxed onto the rock behind her. The melody slowed, settling into a peaceful rhythm.

Zayla moved silently toward Shadre as the musician held the final note for an entire breath, then set the flute down. Shadre lifted her head, appearing startled at the sight of Zayla standing a few paces away. Zayla couldn't quite read the emotions that flickered across Shadre's expression, but she watched Shadre's lips curve into a slow smile.

Zayla couldn't help but grin in return, heart thudding a frantic beat. She'd never heard Shadre play with such passion before. The way this woman made her feel was undeniable.

"That was stunning, Shadre."

"Not as stunning as you." Shadre's intense gaze warmed the back of Zayla's neck. "You were amazing back there against Tor and his guards. You saved Ratnaa Grove."

Propping her staff against a rock, Zayla moved closer and took a place next to the fire, hoping the warmth would cover her flush. "You helped."

"I…" A gust of wind fanned the crackling flames higher. Crimson sparks spiraled between them, snagging Shadre's attention for a moment.

"You, what?" Zayla pressed.

Shadre sucked in a shaky breath, gaze locking on Zayla's once more. "I could've done a lot more."

"What are you talking about? You did so much!" Was the woman sunsick, or just stubborn? "You helped save Ratnaa Grove, the Nemora. You saved Misti and Orenda and Dylori."

"I know, but it was because of me that you and Oryn were even in that dangerous place to begin with." Shadre shook her head. "I'm sor—"

"Stop apologizing. You helped when it mattered most. You saved Oryn's life and got the shackles off their wrists." Shadre's actions spoke volumes of who she actually was. Oryn's words came back. *I think deep down, she really is a good person.* Zayla turned the statement over in her mind. *But does Shadre believe that she's a good person herself?* "Quite frankly, we would've ended up there anyway! I was taking us straight to Ratnaa Grove, and who knows what could've happened once we reached there. We probably would've been captured anyway."

"Hells, I know, but I thought I owed them something for saving me, Zayla. I thought they were my family, but I was wrong." Shadre's voice cracked, but she pushed through, holding Zayla's gaze, unwaveringly. "I'm just disappointed that it was by my hand."

"Well, it was by your hand, and you'll have to live with that. Like you said when you found me underground, you'll make it up to me for the rest of your life." Zayla stood, hands closing into fists. "And you're doing good, now. You did good. You saved my sibling's life. You not only helped save Ratnaa, you saved *my* life." She jabbed a finger at herself, her voice getting louder and louder with each word, until she was actually shouting. Whether it was for Shadre, or for the rest of the world to hear, she didn't know. "You're a good person, Shadre. A good woman. And you're going to have to deal with that."

Shadre looked at Zayla as if she'd never seen her before in her life. A soft chuckle grew into a full-blown belly laugh that rang through the night.

"What?" Zayla asked, crossing her arms. "What's so funny?"

"I think you're—" Shadre dissolved into another fit of laughter. Tears leaked from her eyes before she wiped them away, and it took her a few moments before she could finally calm down enough to speak. "I think you're the first person to ever yell compliments at me."

Shoulders sagging, Zayla smiled weakly. "You're too stubborn to hear it otherwise."

"Well…" Shadre pushed a hand through her hair. "I might not believe it quite yet, but thank you for saying it anyway."

Sighing, Zayla moved around the fire and settled down next to Shadre. Close enough to feel comfortable, but not close enough to touch. "I'll keep saying it if you need me to."

Shadre nodded. "I appreciate you more than you know, Zayla. You're an amazing woman."

Zayla's entire body flushed from the kind words.

Feeling bold, she reached out and squeezed Shadre's hands, suddenly realizing the duskiron rings on her fingers were gone. The duskiron jewelry decorating Shadre's ears and nose had vanished, too.

"What happened to your earrings?" she asked.

"I had to use them to form weapons in the fight with Tor. I used everything I had against his guards," Shadre admitted. "It was such a scattered fight, and we left so quickly, that I didn't have the chance to pick up my stuff."

Shocked, Zayla glanced around. She didn't see Shadre's usual weapons or even her instruments, just the burnt-orange flute. Zayla had a sudden vision, recalling how ferociously Shadre had thrown her weapons during the battle with Tor and his guards. "You have nothing left?"

"I didn't say that," Shadre replied softly. "Some Ratnaa Nemora brought my weapons on their trek over to Ingo Grove." She pointed to the darkness of the small cave opening. "I just haven't reformed them into my instruments and jewelry yet." She straightened, as if suddenly remembering something. Pulling a scrap of paper out of her supplies, she offered it to Zayla. "Speaking of, the Ratnaa noxlings wanted me to give you this."

Vibrantly colored ink covered nearly the whole sheet. Slashes of purple-blue sky. Verdant grass. Deep brown stone. A break in coloring to show an opening, no…a cave. And in the cave, tiny people surrounded by creatures. Some were clearly suncreatures in white and crimson. The natural beasts were in white and black. They all sat together, enjoying each other's company.

"This is so thoughtful," Zayla murmured.

"Yeah, the noxlings were pretty adorable." Shadre scooted closer until their shoulders touched. She ran her finger over the painting. "These are called nadolyns."

"I've never heard of them." Zayla's skin tingled with awareness at Shadre's touch, and the tickle of firebugs circled in her stomach.

"The Ratnaa Nemora said they've lived with the nadolyns for ages, since before any of them could remember. They take care of the beasts—feed them, play with them, bond with them. Not how Vagari bond with animals, of course; the nadolyns are more like pets." Shadre tapped the suncreature image. "According to the Ratnaa Nemora, the suncreatures just arrived one night and started living with the natural beasts. It doesn't matter that some of them are suncreatures. After a short while living with the natural beasts, the suncreatures acted just like the natural ones. They appreciated the food, the company, everything. In return, the nadolyns protected the Ratnaa Nemora who explored the ruins of Alastra."

"So I was right," Zayla whispered. She'd suspected that the nadolyns protected her because she was a Nemora, even the suncreature nadolyns. It was unheard of, as far as she knew. Suncreatures only worked with the sun goddess worshippers. "I wonder if any other suncreatures are like those nadolyns. Ones that could get along with us, even though we don't worship Ponuriah?"

"Good question. Wish I knew the answer." Shadre gave Zayla a curious glance and leaned into her shoulder for a moment. "Fari-lunia on completing your Choosing Ritual, by the way. Your solidified markings look pretty."

Zayla's insides fluttered. Her gender would never be a question, ever again. "Thank you," Zayla replied softly, her attention drifting to her new staff, while her mind wandered back to the visions. Time for the real reason she'd set off without Oryn and the others to find Shadre. "The sacred Ingo tree gifted me that staff...and a vision."

At Shadre's eyebrow lift, Zayla told her about the vision, her plans to go to the Sunglade to find the griffon suncreature, and who she'd already gathered to go with her.

"I'd like it if you'd come with me, too."

Shadre blinked. "To the Sunglade."

"I know it's dangerous, but I have to go," Zayla explained. "I'm going to face a deadly suncreature, Shadre. I need all the help I can get, and you're—"

Zayla's words shuddered to a stop at Shadre's rust-orange gaze full of excitement and adventure and a clear desire. The slow smile creeping up

Shadre's lips looked almost predatory, but in a way that sent a kick through Zayla's stomach.

"I'm…?" Shadre urged her to continue.

Beautiful. Strong. Brave. Too many words to sum up with one.

"Fearless," Zayla said, honestly. "And I could use some of that bravery in the Sunglade."

Shadre laughed. "Fearless, eh? I like that." She ran her thumb across the back of Zayla's hand in slow, lazy circles.

Small shivers of delight raced through Zayla's veins.

"More than fearless," Zayla replied. "Wonderful. Someone I'd like to get to know better."

"And to get to know me better you're taking me to the Sunglade. The most dangerous continent around. One full of suncreatures and Ponuriah worshippers and who knows what else. Honestly, I think it's the worst location for a first date ever," Shadre teased, but then she squeezed Zayla's hand. Holding her gaze, Shadre ran her hand up Zayla's arm to Zayla's neck in a gentle hold.

The firebugs whirled in Zayla's stomach. She couldn't blame the flames for the heat creeping up her cheeks. Her instinct was to pull away, but the longing coiling inside her demanded something more. *Curse every root and spore, own your feelings!*

She leaned in closer to Shadre, then paused, searching Shadre's eyes to see if what she felt was true. If what she wanted was something Shadre desired as well.

Shadre immediately closed the distance, pressing her lips softly against Zayla's.

An explosion of desire seemed to consume Zayla from head to toe. Clasping the back of Shadre's neck, Zayla pulled her closer, deepening the kiss. Shadre tasted like smoke and salt and her own distinctly earthy flavor. Zayla couldn't get enough.

Shadre chuckled against her lips, curling her fingers through Zayla's hair. Then her mouth moved, gentle and passionate all at once, their breaths mingling as one.

Time seemed to still as they lingered in the kiss together.

After far too little time, Shadre broke the embrace, her cheeks flushing a dark brown Zayla found immensely attractive. "About that first date," Shadre murmured softly.

"Yes?" Zayla pulled back a little but kept contact with a hand on Shadre's arm. She never wanted to let go of this amazing woman.

Shadre smiled, determination in her eyes. "I'm in. I want to help you rebuild your home…then maybe you can help me face mine."

"I'd love that." A fresh sense of purpose curled within Zayla, and she added Shadre's request to her list. Find the griffon suncreature. Regrow her bitterroot offshoot. Help Orenda get the moon goddess shard to aid in the war. And now…help Shadre of the duskiron offshoot finally go home. And probably—no, definitely—kiss her again. "We'll leave in a few nights time."

Shifting closer to the fire, Shadre pulled the skewer off the spit and tested the meat. "Well, until then, let's share a meal. Maybe the Sunglade can be our second date." She winked.

Zayla laughed, leaning back against the rock. "I'd love that, too."

Pressing her fingers into the dirt, she opened her mind to nature—sensing the roots of the trees around her and the mycelium tucked under their boughs. The vibrations always within her body maintained a low, yet persistent hum. *Be patient,* she told her crafting. *I'll find the sporeseed soon.* The promise was to herself, to her bitterroot offshoot, to nature itself—a promise she was determined to fulfill. She had a new path to complete, but now she wouldn't be alone in her journey.

The End

About Kellie Doherty

Kellie Doherty is a queer science fiction and fantasy author who lives in Eagle River, Alaska. When she noticed that there wasn't much positive queer representation in the science fiction and fantasy realms, she decided to create her own! Kellie's work has been published in Image OutWrite 2019, Astral Waters Review, Life (as it) Happens, and Impact, among others. Her adult sci-fi debut novel—*Finding Hekate*—came out in April 2016 from Desert Palm Press and the sequel—*Losing Hold*—came out in April 2017. She's currently working on a five-book adult fantasy series. The first book *Sunkissed Feathers & Severed Ties* released in March 2019 from Desert Palm Press and won a 2019 Rainbow Award. The second book *Curling Vines & Crimson Trades* launched November 2020. An excerpt from *Curling Vines & Crimson Trades* won first place in an Alaska Writers Guild Fiction contest in 2020. In 2024, *Ink Stains & Ill-Fated Lies* was shorted listed for a Goldie in Fantasy.

Contact Kellie

Website https://kelliedoherty.com/

Editing Site https://editreviseperfect.weebly.com/

Twitter https://twitter.com/kellie_doherty

Facebook https://www.facebook.com/KellieDoherty89

Email kellie.f.doherty@gmail.com

Cover Design By : Rachel George
www.rachelgeorgeillustration.com

Note to Readers

Thank you for reading a book from Desert Palm Press. We appreciate you as a reader and want to ensure you enjoy the reading process. We would like you to consider posting a review on your preferred media sites and/or your blog or website.

For more information on upcoming releases, author interviews, contests, giveaways and more, please sign up for our newsletter and visit us at Desert Palm Press: www.desertpalmpress.com and "Like" us on Facebook: Desert Palm Press.

Bright Blessings